Harry Potter

CROCHET WIZARDRY

FROM THE FILMS OF

CROCHET WIZARDRY

THE OFFICIAL HARRY POTTER
CROCHET PATTERN BOOK

LEE SARTORI

PHOTOGRAPHY BY TED THOMAS

INSIGHT EDITIONS

SAN RAFAEL · LOS ANGELES · LONDON

CONTENTS

PROJECT SKILL LEVELS

⚡ BEGINNER

⚡⚡ INTERMEDIATE

⚡⚡⚡ ADVANCED

INTRODUCTION

For fans around the world, the Harry Potter films are a truly magical experience, immersing us in a spellbinding world of secret wizarding schools, mythical creatures, enchanted objects, heroes young and old, adventure, friendship, and love. While fans everywhere find joy in these delightful movies, something very special happens to crocheters when we watch the Harry Potter films. As the magic unfolds, amigurumi artists begin to imagine crocheting the amazing creatures one single crochet at a time. Garment crocheters take a closer peek at their favorite character's sweaters and costumes, carefully deducing how they're constructed. And every one of us has found inspiration for a blanket or two to stitch up.

This official book of crochet patterns is filled to the brim with just such projects, with inspiration taken straight from the films. Explore delightful and awe-inspiring amigurumi projects such as Fawkes (page 17), and The Sorting Hat (page 11). Conjure up amazing costume replicas, like Luna's Cropped Cardigan (page 83). Surround yourself with curios and keepsakes such as The Burrow Blanket (page 125) or the Potions Baskets (page 155).

Each section of the book features projects for crocheters at a variety of skill levels as well as a veritable cornucopia of techniques to try, from crochet colorwork to surface slip stitching to Tunisian crochet. Accompanying the detailed instructions, you'll find intriguing behind-the-scenes facts and insights, concept art, and film stills to help you learn more about the making of the epic films along the way.

Deciding which project to begin with is going to be a difficult task, whether it's The Dumbledore Hat (page 109) or Dobby (page 47). But whichever pattern you choose, be sure to get cozy in your favorite crochet spot with a warm drink and a Harry Potter movie marathon at the ready. With hook and yarn in hand, it's time to stitch up some crochet wizardry.

Accio Amigurumi!

"Less talking if you don't mind. I got a real treat for you today, a great lesson. Follow me!"

Rubeus Hagrid, *Harry Potter and the Prisoner of Azkaban*

THE SORTING HAT

Designed by **LEE SARTORI**

SKILL LEVEL ⚡⚡⚡

In the Harry Potter films, the Sorting Hat is a sentient piece of magical apparel that is responsible for sorting first-year students into their respective Hogwarts houses on their first night. The original plan for bringing the Sorting Hat to the screen was to use a puppet placed on top of the actors' heads. However, after testing the puppet in scenes, it was decided that digital animation would be a better solution to bring the hat to life. The hat we see in the films is a combination of the leather rendition designed by Judianna Makovsky and digital enhancement. When asked, "Where does it talk?" by visual effects supervisor Robert Legato, director Chris Columbus looked at Legato and said, "Well, she made the hat, you make it talk."

This crocheted Sorting Hat is a top-down pattern, worked in the round using a variety of crochet stitches. The hat bends and folds as the crochet work progresses, lending details to the Sorting Hat's defining features, including bold and expressive eyebrows, deep-set eyes, and a wide mouth that sits on top of a full brim. Add a final round of crochet around craft wire to keep the brim in shape, and get ready to be sorted into your Hogwarts house.

SIZE
One size

FINISHED MEASUREMENTS
Brim Circumference: 33 in. / 84 cm
Length (not including brim): 15½ in. / 39.5 cm

YARN
Worsted/aran weight (medium #4) yarn, shown in Lion Brand *Heartland* (100% acrylic; 251 yd. / 230 m per 5 oz. / 142 g skein): 3 skeins #126 Sequoia

HOOK
- US G-6 / 4 mm crochet hook or size needed to obtain gauge

NOTIONS
- Stitch markers
- Tapestry needle
- 1 roll of craft wire
- 4 in. / 10 cm wide burlap ribbon

GAUGE
18 sts and 20 rnds = 4 in. / 10 cm in sc
Make sure to check your gauge.

NOTES
- Hat is worked in continuous rounds unless otherwise indicated. Use a marker to mark rounds.
- When joining is indicated, slip stitch into top of first stitch of round.
- Hat is worked top down.

SPECIAL ABBREVIATIONS
fpsc (front post single crochet): Insert hook around indicated post from front to back to front, yo and draw up a loop, yo and draw through all loops.

MOUTH INSERT

Rnd 1: Ch 30, hdc in 2nd ch from hook and in each ch across to last ch, 3 hdc in last ch; rotate work to st into underside of foundation ch, hdc 28, 3 hdc in last ch underside, join—62 hdc.

Rnd 2: Ch 1, [hdc 30, 2 hdc in next hdc] twice, join—64 hdc.

Rnds 3–6: Ch 1, hdc around, join. Fasten off. Set insert aside.

HAT BODY

Rnd 1: Ch 2, 3 sc in 2nd ch from hook—3 sc.

Rnd 2: 2 sc in each sc around—6 sc.

Rnd 3: [2 sc in next sc, sc in next sc] 3 times—9 sc.

Rnd 4: [2 sc in next sc, sc in next 2 sc] 3 times—12 sc.

Rnd 5: [2 sc in next sc, sc in next 3 sc] 3 times—15 sc.

Rnd 6: [2 sc in next sc, sc in next 4 sc] 3 times—18 sc.

Rnds 7–13: Sc around.

Rnd 14: Fpsc around—18 fpsc.

Rnd 15: 2 sc in each fpsc around—36 sc.

FIRST WRINKLE

Rnd 16: Fphdc in each sc around—36 fphdc.

Fold upward toward the tip of the hat. Do not turn. Cont to create the first wrinkle.

Rnd 17: [Sc in next 4 fphdc, sc2tog over next 2 fphdc] around—30 sc.

Rnd 18: [Sc in next 3 sc, sc2tog over next 2 sc] around—24 sc.

Rnd 19: [2 hdc in next sc, hdc in next 3 sc] around—30 hdc.

Rnd 20: [2 hdc in next hdc, hdc in next 4 hdc] around—36 hdc.

Rnd 21: Hdc in each st around. Fold downward to finish first wrinkle.

Rnd 22: Sc around—36 sc.

SHORT ROWS

Pm in last st made.

Row 1 (RS): Sc in next 12 sc, turn—12 sc.

Rows 2–5: Ch 1, sc in next 12 sc, turn.

Row 6 (WS): Ch 1, sc in next 12 sc, do not turn (*WS facing*); working in row ends toward marked st, sc evenly down in each of next 5 row ends, sl st in marked st, turn—17 sc.

Rnd 23 (RS): Ch 1, sc in marked st (*RS facing*), mark as beg of rnd, sc up side of next 5 short row ends, sc in next 12 sc across top of short rows, sc down side of next 5 short row ends, sc in last 23 sts—46 sc.

Rnds 24–29: Sc around.

Rnd 30: 2 sc in first st, sc in each st around—47 sc.

Rnd 31: 2 sc in first st, sc in each st around—48 sc.

Rnd 32: Hdc in each st around—48 hdc.

Rnd 33: Sc in blo around—48 sc.

Rnds 34 and 35: Sc around.

Rnd 36: [2 sc in next sc, sc in next 7 sc] around—54 sc.

Rnd 37: [2 sc in next sc, sc in next 8 sc] around—60 sc.

Rnd 38: Hdc around—60 hdc.

Rnd 39: [Sc in next 8 hdc, sc2tog over next 2 hdc] around—54 sc.

Rnd 40: Sc around.

Rnd 41: Sc around; do not remove st marker.

EYEBROWS

Rnd 42: [2 fptr in next sc, fptr in next 8 sc] around, join—60 fptr.

Rnd 43: [2 sc in next fptr, sc in next 9 fptr] around—66 sc. Fasten off.

SHORT ROWS

Beginning in marked st from Rnd 41, count 15 sts to the right of the marked st, rm, and place beg-of-rnd st marker in line with the 12 sts of the previous set of short rows.

Row 1: Working in sts from Rnd 41, sc in next sc, sc in next 11 sc, turn—12 sc.

Rows 2–5: Ch 1, sc in next 12 sc, turn.

Row 6: Ch 1, sc in next 12 sc, do not turn (*WS facing*); working in row ends toward marked st, sc evenly down in each of next 5 row ends, sl st in marked st, turn—17 sc.

Rnd 44: Working in row ends and across top of short rows, sc 64 around—64 sc.

"HMM, DIFFICULT. VERY DIFFICULT. PLENTY OF COURAGE, I SEE. NOT A BAD MIND, EITHER. THERE'S TALENT, OH YES. AND A THIRST TO PROVE YOURSELF. BUT WHERE TO PUT YOU?"

The Sorting Hat, *Harry Potter and the Sorcerer's Stone*

EYES, NOSE, AND MOUTH

Rnd 45: Sc in first 35 sc, *dc in next sc, 2 tr in next sc, 3 tr in next sc, 2 tr in next sc, dc in next sc**, hdc in next 4 sc; rep from * to **, sc in last 15 sc—72 sts.

Rnd 46: Sc in first 35 sc, *tr in next dc, tr in next 7 tr, tr in next dc,** sc in next 4 hdc; rep from * to **, sc in last 15 sc—72 sts.

Rnd 47: [2 sc, in next st, sc in next 11 sts] 3 times, 2 sc in next st, sc in next 7 sts, hdc in next 4 sts, [2 sc in next st, sc in next 11 sts] twice

Rnd 48: Sc 48, hdc in next hdc, 2 hdc in next 2 hdc, hdc in next hdc, sc in last 26 sc—80 sts.

Rnd 49: Sc 48, hdc in next hdc, 2 hdc in next 4 hdc, hdc in next hdc, sc in last 26 sc—84 sts.

Rnd 50: Working in blo, [2 sc, sc 13] 3 times, 2 sc in next st, sc in next 5 st, hdc in next 10 hdc, 2 sc in next st, sc 13, 2 sc in next st, sc in last 11 sc—90 sts.

Push eyes inward to form recessed pockets.

Rnd 51: [2 sc in next st, sc in next 14 sts] around—96 sc.

Rnd 52: [2 sc in next st, sc in next 15 sts] around—102 sc.

Rnd 53: Sc around.

Rnd 54: [2 sc in next st, sc in next 16 sts] around—108 sc.

Rnd 55: Sc around.

Rnd 56: [2 sc in next st, sc in next 17 sts] around—114 sc.

Rnd 57: Sc in first 62 sc, fphdc in next 32 sc (*mouth top formed*), sc in last 20 sc—114 sts.

Place mouth insert parallel to 32 sts from mouth top. Using locking st markers, pin insert in place across mouth top.

Rnd 58: Sc in first 62 sc, hdc across bottom 32 sts of mouth insert, sk next 32 fphdc, sc in last 20 sc.

Using a scrap of yarn, and with WS facing, sl st rem 32 sts of mouth insert to unworked 32 sts of Rnd 57. Push mouth insert in to form a pocket.

Rnd 59: [2 sc in next st, sc in next 18 sts] around—120 sc.

Rnd 60: Sc around.

Rnd 61: [2 sc in next sc, sc in next 19 sc] around—126 sc.

Rnd 62: [2 sc in next sc, sc in next 20 sc] around—132 sc.

Rnd 63: [2 sc in next sc, sc in next 21 sc] around—138 sc.

Rnd 64: [2 sc in next sc, sc in next 22 sc] around—144 sc.

Rnd 65: [2 sc in next sc, sc in next 23 sc] around—150 sc.

SECOND WRINKLE

Rnd 66: [2 hdc in next sc, hdc in next 24 sc] around—156 hdc.

Rnd 67: [2 hdc in next hdc, hdc in next 25 hdc] around—162 hdc.

Rnd 68: [2 hdc in next hdc, hdc in next 26 hdc] around—168 hdc.

Rnd 69: [Sc in next 26 hdc, sc2tog over next 2 hdc] around—162 sc.

Rnd 70: [Sc in next 25 sc, sc2tog over next 2 sc] around—156 sc.

Rnd 71: [Sc in next 24 sc, sc2tog over next 2 sc] around—150 sc.

Fold hdc rounds down into a wrinkle.

Rnds 72 & 73: Sc around.

Rnd 74: Fpsc around.

Rnds 75–77: Rep Rnds 66–68.

Rnd 78: Sc blo around—168 sc.

BRIM

Note: Fan sts out by stretching and shaping the fabric as work progresses.

Rnd 79: [2 sc in next sc, sc in next 27 sc] around—174 sc.

Rnd 80: [2 sc in next sc, sc in next 28 sc] around—180 sc.

Rnd 81: [2 sc in next sc, sc in next 29 sc] around—186 sc.

Rnd 82: [Sc in next 15 sc, 2 sc in next sc, sc in next 15 sc] around—192 sc.

Rnd 83: [Sc in next 15 sc, 2 sc in next sc, sc in next 16 sc] around—198 sc.

Rnd 84: [2 sc in next sc, sc in next 32 sc] around—204 sc.

Rnd 85: [2 sc in next sc, sc in next 33 sc] around—210 sc.

Rnd 86: [Sc in next 15 sc, 2 sc in next sc, sc in next 19 sc] around—216 sc.

Rnd 87: [Sc in next 15 sc, 2 sc in next sc, sc in next 20 sc] around—222 sc.

Rnd 88: [2 sc in next sc, sc in next 36 sc] around—228 sc.

Rnd 89: [2 sc in next sc, sc in next 37 sc] around—234 sc.

Rnd 90: [Sc in next 15 sc, 2 sc in next sc, sc in next 23 sc] around—240 sc.

Rnd 91: [Sc in next 15 sc, 2 sc in next sc, sc in next 24 sc] around—246 sc.

Rnd 92: Hdc in each st around—246 hdc.

Rnd 93: Holding wire against work, hdc in each st around.

Rnd 94: Reverse sc around.

Fasten off.

FINISHING

Weave in ends.

With tapestry needle and yarn, sew a 10 in. / 25.5 cm long piece of burlap ribbon to inside left and inside right where the brim and hat body meet. Cut ribbon ends into V shape. Ribbon should dangle over ears, and strips should fall just past shoulders.

FAWKES

Designed by **EMMY SCANGA**

SKILL LEVEL ⚡⚡⚡

Fawkes is a phoenix, a magical creature who bursts into flames when it's time for him to die and is then reborn from the ashes. He is Professor Dumbledore's beloved companion and provides aid to both the headmaster and Harry at several dire moments in the films. Fawkes is able to heal wounds with his tears, and his feathers contain magical properties. In fact, it was known to Dumbledore that one of Fawkes's tail feathers formed the core of Harry Potter's wand, while another formed the core of Lord Voldemort's.

When designing Fawkes, concept artist Adam Brockbank drew his inspiration from depictions of the phoenix in classical mythology, combined with real-life observations of birds. "It was a given that Fawkes would be the color of fire," says Brockbank. "Fawkes's head is mainly burnt oranges and dark reds, while his underside is dominated by shades of gold."

This amigurumi version of Fawkes captures him in his early stages, when he is still growing. His luxurious crest of feathers offsets his deep, wise eyes. Fawkes features poseable wings and a beautiful, long set of tail feathers that trail out behind him. Add a few finishing touches of embroidery detail to his chest to bring this beloved companion to life.

SIZE
One size

FINISHED MEASUREMENTS
Height: 9 in. / 23 cm
Wingspan: 9 in. / 23 cm

YARN
Worsted weight (medium #4) yarn, shown in Cascade Yarns *220 Merino* (100% merino wool; 220 yds / 200 m per 3½ oz. / 100 g hank)
Color A: #09 True Red, 1 hank
Color B: #43 Daffodil, 1 hank
Color C: #34 Nutmeg, 1 hank
Color D: #38 Ganache, 1 hank
Color E: #04 Pureed Pumpkin, 1 hank

HOOK
- US D-3 / 3.25 mm crochet hook or size needed to obtain gauge

NOTIONS
- Tapestry needle
- Sewing pins
- ½ in. / 15 mm safety eyes
- Polyester stuffing

GAUGE
20 sts and 23 rows = 4 in. / 10 cm in sc
Gauge is not critical for a toy; just ensure the stitches are tight enough so the stuffing will not show through your finished project.

Continued on page 18

NOTES

- Some items are worked in the round and some are worked in rows. Items worked in the round are continuous rounds; do not join.
- Keep the feather sets organized for easier assembly.
- Use sewing pins to move and adjust the placement of pieces before sewing.
- Some pieces will require two yarns held together; use the same hook size throughout the pattern.
- The Fawkes shown here has wires in his wings and feet to make him poseable. If desired, add wire before sewing feet and wings closed.

SPECIAL ABBREVIATIONS

chbp (chain bump): Turn chain to back; work into yarn strand running down center of each chain.

MC: magic circle

BODY

Rnd 1: With A, MC 6 sc; do not join—6 sc.

Rnd 2: Inc in each sc around—12 sc.

Rnd 3: [Sc in next sc, inc in next sc] around—18 sc.

Rnd 4: [Sc in next sc, inc in next sc] around—27 sc.

Rnd 5: Sc around.

Rnd 6: [sc in next 2 sc, inc in next sc] around—36 sc.

Rnd 7: Sc around.

Rnd 8: [Sc in next 5 sc, inc in next sc] around—42 sc.

Rnd 9: Sc around.

Rnd 10: [Sc in next 6 sc, inc in next sc] around—48 sc.

Rnd 11: Sc in first 18 sc, ch 1, sk next sc, sc in next 10 sc, ch 1, sk next sc, sc in last 18 sc.

Rnd 12: Sc in first 18 sc, sc in ch-1 sp, sc in next 10 sc, sc in ch-1 sp, sc in last 18 sc.

Rnd 13: Sc around.

Rnd 14: [Sc in next 4 sc, dec over next 2 sc] around—40 sc.

Rnd 15: [Sc in next 8 sc, dec over next 2 sc] around—36 sc.

Place safety eyes in the ch-1 sp created in Rnd 11 before continuing.

Rnd 16: [Sc in next 4 sc, dec over next 2 sc] around—30 sc.

Rnds 17–20: Sc around.

Stuff the head firmly.

Rnd 21: [Sc in next 4 sc, inc in next sc] around—36 sc.

Rnd 22: Sc around.

Rnd 23: [Sc in next 5 sc, inc in next sc] around—42 sc.

Rnd 24: Sc around.

Rnd 25: [Sc in next 6 sc, inc in next sc] around—48 sc.

Rnds 26–30: Sc around.

Rnd 31: [Sc in next 10 sc, dec over next 2 sc] around—44 sc.

Rnd 32: Sc around.

Rnd 33: [Sc in next 9 sc, dec over next 2 sc] around—40 sc.

Rnds 34–39: Sc around.

Rnd 40: [Sc in next 6 sc, dec over next 2 sc] around—35 sc.

Rnds 41–43: Sc around.

Rnd 44: [Sc in next 3 sc, dec over next 2 sc] around—28 sc.

Rnd 45: [Sc in next 2 sc, dec over next 2 sc] around—21 sc.

Finish stuffing the body.

Rnd 46: [Sc in next sc, dec over next 2 sc] around—14 sc.

Rnd 47: Dec around—7 sc.

Fasten off, leaving a long tail for sewing. Sew closed.

BEAK

Rnd 1: With D, MC 5 sc; do not join—5 sc.

Rnd 2: Inc in first 2 sc, sc in next 3 sc—7 sc.

Rnd 3: Inc in first 2 sc, sc in next 4 sc, inc in last sc—10 sc.

Rnd 4: Inc in first sc, sc in next sc, inc in next sc, sc in last 7 sc—12 sc.

Rnd 5: Sc around.

Cut D.

Rnd 6: With C, inc in first 3 sc, sc in next 8 sc, inc in last sc—16 sc.

Rnd 7: Sc in first 9 sc, inc in next sc, sc in next sc, inc in next sc, sc in last 4 sc—18 sc.

Rnd 8: [Sc in next 2 sc, inc in next sc] around—24 sc.

Rnd 9: Sc in first st, sl st in next 7 sc, sk next 2 sc, sc in next 12 sc, sk last 2 sc.

Sl st in what would be the first st of the next rnd. Fasten off, leaving a long tail for sewing beak onto the body.

EYE DETAIL
(MAKE 2)

With C, ch 8. Fasten off. Tie tail ends together to create a loop.

BEHIND THE MAGIC

While Fawkes was created digitally for some scenes in the films,
in others he was played by a full-size animatronic puppet that
could perform a variety of actions. The puppet was so believable
that actor Richard Harris, who played Professor Dumbledore in
the first two films, initially believed it was a live, trained bird.

TOP: Concept sketch of Fawkes by Adam Brockbank. ABOVE: Harry meets Fawkes the phoenix in *Harry Potter and the Chamber of Secrets*.

WINGS (MAKE 2)

Rnd 1: With A, MC 6 sc; do not join—6 sc.

Rnd 2: Inc in each sc around—12 sc.

Rnd 3: [Sc in next sc, inc in next sc] around—18 sc.

Rnd 4: Sc around.

Rnd 5: [Sc in next 2 sc, inc in next sc] around—24 sc.

Rnd 6: [Sc in next 3 sc, inc in next sc] around—30 sc.

Rnd 7: Sc around.

Rnd 8: [Sc in next 4 sc, inc in next sc] around—36 sc.

Rnd 9: [Sc in next 5 sc, inc in next sc] around—42 sc.

Rnds 10–13: Sc around.

Note: Now you will create feathers by chaining and working in the chbp; do not skip the first chbp from the hook. You may need to make a looser last ch in order to comfortably fit your hook.

Rnd 14: [Flo sc, ch 11, turn, hdc in next 11 chbp, flo sc in next st of the rnd] 3 times, [flo sc, ch 9, turn, hdc in next 9 chbp, flo sc in next st of the rnd] 3 times, flo sc, ch 7, turn, hdc in next 7 chbp, flo 2 sc of the rnd, ch 5, turn, hdc in next 5 chbp, flo sc, sc, 3 hdc, 2 dc, 3 hdc, sc, flo sc, ch 5, turn, hdc in next 5 chbp, 2 flo sc, ch 7, turn, hdc in next 7 chbp, flo sc, [flo sc, ch 9, turn, hdc in next 9 chbp, flo sc in next st of the rnd] 3 times, [flo sc, ch 11, turn, hdc in next 11 chbp, flo sc in next st of the rnd] 3 times— 16 feathers.

Fasten off, leaving a tail for sewing. Fold in half so the tail of the yarn is on one side and the feathers are on top of each other. Lay flat and, using the yarn tail, sew the unused back loops together, stopping at the 10 regular sts (sc, 3 hdc, 2 dc, 3 hdc, sc) for attaching to the body. Tie to secure and leave tail for later assembly. Lightly stuff if desired.

LEGS (MAKE 2)

Rnd 1: With A, MC 12 sc; do not join—12 sc.

Rnd 2: [Sc in next 2 sc, inc in next sc] around—16 sc.

Rnds 3 and 4: Sc around.

Rnd 5: [Sc in next 3 sc, inc in next sc] around—20 sc.

Rnd 6: [Sc in next 4 sc, inc in next sc] around—24 sc.

Rnd 7: [Sc in next 5 sc, inc in next sc] around—28 sc.

Rnd 8: Sc around.

Fasten off, leaving a long tail for sewing to the body.

FEET (MAKE 2)

Rnd 1: With C, MC 4 sc; do not join—4 sc.

Rnds 2–6: Sc around.

Rnd 7: Inc in each sc around—8 sc.

Rnd 8: [Sc in next 3 sc, inc in next sc] around—10 sc.

Rnd 9: [Sc in next 4 sc, inc in next sc] around—12 sc.

Rnds 10 and 11: Sc around.

Rnd 12: Sc in first sc, sk next 4 sc, sc in next 2 sc, sk next 4 sc, sc in last sc—4 sc.

Rnds 13–17 (center toe): Sc around.

Fasten off. Sew toe closed.

Note: Stuffing feet is optional. Stuff foot here if desired.

For other two toes, attach 4 sc to the skipped sts of Rnd 12 on either side of the completed center toe. Rep Rnds 13–17. Fasten off and sew each toe closed. Hide tail in the foot.

CHEST CHEVRON

Note: There is no ch-1 turning st; work directly in first st from hook for each row.

With B, ch 19.

Row 1: Working in each chbp across (do not sk first chbp), sc in next 9 chbp, (3 sc) in next chbp, sc in last 9 chbp, turn—21 sc.

Row 2: Dec over first 2 sc, sc in next 8 sc, (3 sc) in next sc, sc in next 8 sc, dec over last 2 sc, turn.

Rows 3–11: Rep Row 2.

Row 12: Dec over first 2 sc, sc in next 8 sc, inc in next sc, sc in next 8 sc, dec over last 2 sc—20 sc.

Fasten off, leaving a long tail to sew onto the body.

HEAD FEATHERS

Note: Each row is one feather.

Feathers A (Make 1 each with B, E, and A)

Row 1: Ch 5, turn, hdc in first 3 chbp, sc in last 2 chbp.

Row 2: Ch 7, turn, hdc in first 5 chbp, sc in last 2 chbp.

Rows 3 and 4: Rep Row 2.

Row 5: Rep Row 1.

Fasten off, leaving a long tail for sewing onto the head.

FEATHERS B
(MAKE 1 WITH A)

Row 1: Ch 11, turn, sc in first chbp, dc in next 7 chbp, hdc in last 3 chbp.

Row 2: Ch 7, turn, sc in first chbp, dc in next 4 chbp, hdc in last 2 chbp.

Rows 3–5: Rep Row 2.

Row 6: Rep Row 1.

Fasten off, leaving a long tail for sewing onto the head.

FEATHERS C
(MAKE 1 WITH A)

Row 1: Ch 9, turn, sc in first chbp, dc in last 8 chbp.

Rows 2–5: Rep Row 1.

Fasten off, leaving a long tail for sewing onto the head.

FEATHERS D
(MAKE 1 WITH A)

Row 1: Ch 18, turn, sc in first chbp, hdc in next chbp, dc in next 12 chbp, hdc in last 4 chbp.

Rows 2–4: Rep Row 1.

Fasten off, leaving a long tail for sewing onto the head.

FEATHERS E
(MAKE 1 WITH A AND D HELD TOGETHER)

Row 1: Ch 18, turn, sc in first chbp, dc in next 12 chbp, hdc in next 3 chbp, sc in last 2 chbp.

Rows 2 and 3: Rep Row 1.

Fasten off, leaving a long tail for sewing onto the head.

FEATHERS F
(MAKE 2 IN B)

Row 1: Ch 2, turn, hdc in first chbp, sc in last chbp.

Row 2: Ch 3, turn, hdc in first chbp, sc in last 2 chbp.

Row 3: Rep Row 1.

Fasten off, leaving a long tail for sewing around the eye detail.

WING FEATHERS

Note: Each row is one feather.

FEATHERS G
(MAKE 2 WITH B)

Row 1: Ch 11, turn, sc in first chbp, hdc in next 10 chbp.

Row 2: Rep Row 1.

Row 3: Ch 7, turn, sc in first chbp, hdc in last 6 chbp.

Row 4: Ch 5, turn, hdc in each chbp.

Fasten off, leaving a long tail for sewing onto the underside of the wings.

TAIL FEATHERS

FEATHERS H
(MAKE 1 WITH A)

Row 1: Ch 13, turn, sc in first chbp, dc in next 11 chbp, hdc in last chbp.

Rows 2 and 3: Rep Row 1.

Row 4: Ch 20, turn, sc in first chbp, dc in next 18 chbp, hdc in last chbp.

Rows 5–7: Rep Row 4.

Rows 8–10: Rep Row 1.

Fasten off, leaving a long tail for sewing onto the body.

FEATHERS I
(MAKE 1 WITH E)

Row 1: Ch 30, turn, sc in first chbp, dc in next 28 chbp, hdc in last chbp.

Rows 2–6: Rep Row 1.

Fasten off, leaving a long tail for sewing onto the body.

FEATHERS J
(MAKE 1 WITH E AND D HELD TOGETHER)

Row 1: Ch 30, turn, sc in first 3 chbp, dc in next 26 chbp, hdc in last chbp.

Rows 2–4: Rep Row 1.

Fasten off, leaving a long tail for sewing onto the body.

FEATHERS K
(MAKE 1 WITH B AND D HELD TOGETHER)

Row 1: Ch 38, turn, sc in first 3 chbp, dc in last 35 chbp.

Row 2: Rep Row 1.

Fasten off, leaving a long tail for sewing onto the body.

ASSEMBLY

EYE DETAIL

Place the tied end of the loop on the inner corner of the eye. Using the tail, sew every other chbp to the edge of the eye. Rep on the second eye.

BEAK

Place beak between eyes and sew the first 6 sts after the sl st directly along Rnd 14 of the head. Sew the upper portion of the beak in an upside down U-shape between the eyes. Stuff before closing completely.

LEGS

Align the tails of yarn from the legs to the last rnd of the body. Pin in place. The outer opposite edge of the leg will land about 9 rnds up the body. This will create a V shape in both the front and back of the body to help align tail feathers and chest piece. Attach legs to the bottom of the body, stuffing legs before completely closing.

FEET

Once the legs are attached, they will point outward. Place feet directly under the legs so the phoenix stands on its own. Use pins to help keep feet aligned. Using C, sew feet to the legs.

CHEST CHEVRON

Line the bottom pointed end between the legs using the V created from attaching the legs. Align the top points to the sides of the body. Using the tail, attach chevron to the stomach.

Note: Before continuing assembly, it's highly suggested to block all remaining pieces (all feathers and wings) to keep feathers from curling too much.

WINGS

Using the remaining tail of yarn from sewing the wing closed, attach the remaining 10 sts to the body between Rnd 20 and Rnd 23, just above the points of the chest chevron.

WING FEATHERS

Attach Feathers G to the underside of the wing. The longer feathers of G will align to the outer edge, while the shorter feather of G will be closer to the body. Use the tail of the Feather Set G to sew the base of the feathers. Tack the centers of each feather of the set. Tie ends and hide in the wing.

EYE FEATHERS

Align Feathers F to the outer half of the eye, next to the eye detail. Don't cover the eye detail. Attach to each eye using the tail. Tie ends and hide in the body.

HEAD FEATHERS

All feathers will be sewn to the body at the base of each set of feathers; do not sew every part of the feather down. Attach Feathers A in color B directly onto the top of the beak between the eyes. All other head feathers will be placed behind this first set of feathers. Use sewing pins to plan out placement before sewing into place. The order of feathers on the head starting from Feathers A in Color B to the back of the head are as follows:

Feathers A (Color B attached to beak with 5 feathers)
Feathers A (Color E with 5 feathers)
Feathers A (Color A with 5 feathers)
Feathers B (Color A with 6 feathers)
Feathers C (Color A with 5 feathers)
Feathers D (Color A with 4 feathers)
Feathers E (Colors A and D with 3 feathers)
Use the tail of each feather set to sew the base of the feathers down. Tie ends and hide in the body.

TAIL FEATHERS

All feathers will be sewn to the back of the body at the base of each set of feathers; do not sew every part of the feather down. Attach the Feathers K directly onto the top of the V made from the leg assembly on the back. All other tail feathers will be placed on top of this first set of feathers. Use sewing pins to plan out placement before sewing into place. The order of feathers on the tail starting from Feathers K on the bottommost next to the legs to the topmost feathers seen on back of the body are as follows:

Feathers K (Colors B and D with 2 feathers, attached to the center between the legs)
Feathers J (Colors E and D with 4 feathers, above Set K)
Feathers I (Color E with 6 feathers, above Set J)
Feathers H (Color A with 10 feathers, topmost set)
Use the tail of each feather set to sew the base of the feathers down. Tie ends and hide in the body.

EXTRA DETAILS

Using different colors of yarn, embroider more feathers. This includes around the beak in B, around the chest chevron in B and E held together, and around the eye feathers in A.

PROFESSOR McGONAGALL'S ANIMAGUS

Designed by **MARANATHA ENOIU**

SKILL LEVEL ⚡⚡

On the first day of Transfiguration class in *Harry Potter and the Sorcerer's Stone*, Harry, Ron, and their classmates are stunned to meet Professor McGonagall in her Animagus form: a gorgeous gray tabby cat. This is not the only time Professor McGonagall makes an entrance in this form, though. Earlier in the film, her Animagus is seen watching the Dursley family home on Privet Drive for some time before Professor Dumbledore arrives with the infant Harry. When not in her Animagus form, Professor McGonagall can usually be spotted wearing her tall witch's hat and a beautiful green tartan. Stern but fair, she is an exceptionally gifted witch and extremely capable of keeping her students well in hand.

This whimsical take on Professor McGonagall's Animagus features beautiful tapestry crochet to bring out the markings on the cat's fur. Sitting in a watchful position, the cat waits at attention, ready to spot any trouble. Top this adorable cat with a witch's hat as a nod to Professor McGonagall, and set her to keep a watchful eye in your house, too.

SIZE
One size

FINAL MEASUREMENTS
Height: 13½ in. / 34.5 cm

YARN
Worsted weight (medium #4) yarn, shown in Berroco *Ultra Wool* (100% superwash wool; 219 yd. / 200 m per 3½ oz. / 100 g ball)
Color A: #33170 Granite, 2 balls
Color B: #33113 Black Pepper, 1 ball
Color C: #33108 Frost, 1 ball

Worsted weight (medium #4) yarn, shown in Lion Brand *Pound of Love* (100% acrylic; 1,020 yd. / 918 m per 16 oz. / 448 g ball)
Color D: #153 Black, 1 ball

HOOK
- US G-6 / 4 mm crochet hook or size needed to obtain gauge

NOTIONS
- Stitch marker
- Tapestry needle
- ½ in. / 15 mm green safety cat eyes
- Polyester stuffing
- Black crochet thread
- 4 in. / 10 cm wide oval doll glasses

GAUGE
20 sts and 20 rnds = 4 in. / 10 cm in sc
Gauge is not critical for a toy; just ensure the stitches are tight enough so the stuffing will not show through your finished project.

Continued on page 26

─── ─☆─ ───

"HONESTLY, HOW OFTEN DO YOU GET TO WALK AROUND AS A WIZARD WITH GREAT CLOTHES?"

Dame Maggie Smith, on playing Professor McGonagall

─── ☀ ───

RIGHT: Dame Maggie Smith as Professor McGonagall in *Harry Potter and the Order of the Phoenix*.

CAT

Starting at the neck:

With A, ch 40. Join into the rnd with a sl st in first ch, making sure ch is not twisted.

Rnd 1: Sc in each ch around.—40 sc.

Rnd 2: With B, sc in first 3 sc; with A, sc in next 2 sc; with B, sc in next 9 sc; with A, sc in next 19 sc; with B, sc in last 7 sc.

Rnd 3: With B, sc in first 4 sc; with A sc in next sc; with B, sc in next 10 sc; with A, sc in next 17 sc; with B, sc in last 8 sc.

Rnd 4: With B, sc in first 18 sc; with A, sc in next 11 sc; with B, sc in last 11 sc.

Rnd 5: With B, sc in first 23 sc; with A, sc in next 3 sc; with B, sc in last 14 sc.

Rnd 6: With B, sc in first 4 sc; with A, sc in next 3 sc, inc in next sc, sc in next 4 sc; with B, sc in next 3 sc, inc in next sc, with A, [sc in next 7 sc, inc in next sc] 3 times—45 sc.

Rnd 7: With B, inc in first sc, sc in next 3 sc; with A, inc in next sc, sc in next 3 sc, inc in next sc, sc in next sc; with B, sc in next 11 sc; with A, sc in next 16 sc, [inc in next sc, sc in next 3 sc] twice—50 sc.

Rnd 8: With B, sc in first 2 sc, inc in next 3 sc; with A, inc in next 7 sc, sc in last 38 sc—60 sc.

Rnd 9: With B, sc in first 8 sc; with A, sc in last 52 sc.

Rnds 10 and 11: With B, sc in first 8 sc; with A, sc in last 52 sc.

Rnd 12: With B, sc in first 8 sc; with A, sc in next sc, inc in next sc, sc in next 3 sc; with B, sc in next 6 sc, inc in next sc, sc in next 9 sc, inc in next sc, sc in next 6 sc; with A, sc in next 3 sc, inc in next sc, sc in next 7 sc; with B, sc in next 2 sc, inc in next sc, sc in next 9 sc, inc in last sc—66 sc.

Rnd 13: With B, sc in first 8 sc; with A, sc in next 2 sc, inc in next sc, sc in next 3 sc; with B, sc in next 7 sc, inc in next sc, sc in next 10 sc, inc in next sc, sc in next 6 sc; with A, sc in next 4 sc, inc in next sc, sc in next 7 sc; with B, sc in next 3 sc, inc in next sc, sc in next 10 sc, inc in last sc—72 sc.

Rnd 14: With B, sc in first 4 sc; with A, sc in next 7 sc, inc in next sc, sc in next 3 sc; with B, sc in next 8 sc, inc in next sc, sc in next 11 sc, inc in next sc, sc in next 10 sc; with A, sc in next sc, inc in next sc, sc in next 7 sc; with B, sc in next 4 sc, inc in next sc, sc in next 11 sc, inc in last sc—78 sc.

Rnd 15: With B, sc in first 3 sc; with A, sc in next 9 sc, inc in next sc, sc in next sc; with B, sc in next 5 sc; with A, sc in next 6 sc, inc in next sc; with B, sc in next 3 sc; with A, sc in next 5 sc; with B, sc in next 4 sc, inc in next sc, [sc in next 12 sc, inc in next sc] 3 times—84 sts.

Rnd 16: With B, sc in first 2 sc; with A, sc in next 11 sc, inc in next sc, sc in next 2 sc; with B, sc in next 4 sc; with A, sc in next 7 sc, inc in next sc; with B, sc in next 3 sc; with A, sc in next 5 sc; with B, sc in next 5 sc, inc in next sc, [sc in next 13 sc, inc in next sc] 3 times—90 sts.

Rnd 17: With A, sc in first 9 sc; with B, sc in next sc; with A, sc in next 4 sc, inc in next sc, sc in next 2 sc; with B, sc in next 4 sc; with A, sc in next 8 sc, inc in next sc; with B, sc in next 3 sc; with A, sc in next 11 sc, inc in next sc, sc in next 6 sc; with B, sc in next sc; with A, sc in next 7 sc, inc in next sc, [sc in next 14 sc, inc in next sc] 2 times—96 sts.

Rnd 18: With A, sc in first 8 sc; with B, sc in next 3 sc; with A, sc in next 7 sc; with B, sc in next 4 sc; with A, sc in next 10 sc; with B, sc in next 3 sc; with A, sc in next 18 sc; with B, sc in next 2 sc; with A, sc in last 41 sc.

Rnd 19: With A, sc in first 8 sc; with B, sc in next 3 sc; with A, sc in next 8 sc; with B, sc in next 4 sc; with A, sc in next 9 sc; with B, sc in next 3 sc; with A, sc in next 17 sc; with B, sc in next 2 sc; with A, sc in last 42 sc.

Rnd 20: With A, sc in first 7 sc; with B, sc in next 5 sc; with A, sc in next 9 sc; with B, sc in next 4 sc; with A, sc in next 7 sc; with B, sc in next 3 sc; with A, sc in next 16 sc; with B, sc in next 2 sc; with A, sc in last 43 sc.

Rnd 21: With A, sc in first 7 sc; with B, sc in next 5 sc; with A, sc in next 9 sc; with B, sc in next 4 sc; with A, sc in next 7 sc; with B, sc in next 3 sc; with A, sc in next 15 sc; with B, sc in next 2 sc; with A, sc in next 40 sc, with B, sc in last 4 sc.

Rnd 22: With A, sc in first 6 sc; with B, sc in next 6 sc; with A, sc in next 9 sc; with B, sc in next 4 sc; with A, sc in next 7 sc; with B, sc in next 3 sc; with A, sc in next 14 sc; with B, sc in next 2 sc; with A, sc in next 41 sc; with B, sc in last 4 sc.

Rnd 23: With A, sc in first 6 sc; with B, sc in next 6 sc; with A, sc in next 9 sc; with B, sc in next 4 sc; with A, sc in next 7 sc; with B, sc in next 3 sc; with A, sc in next 13 sc; with B, sc in next 2 sc; with A, sc in next 42 sc; with B, sc in last 4 sc.

Rnd 24: With A, sc in first 6 sc; with B, sc in next 6 sc; with A, sc in next 3 sc, inc in next sc, sc in next 5 sc; with B, sc in next 4 sc; with A, sc in next 6 sc,

inc in next sc; with B, sc in next 3 sc; with A, sc in next 12 sc; with B, inc in next sc; with A, [15 sc, inc] 2 times, sc in next 12 sc; with B, sc in next 3 sc, inc in last sc—102 sts.

Rnd 25: With A, sc in first 6 sc; with B, sc in next 7 sc; with A, sc in next 3 sc, inc in next sc, sc in next 6 sc; with B, sc in next 2 sc; with A, sc in next 8 sc, inc in next sc; with B, sc in next 3 sc; with A, sc in next 12 sc; with B, sc in next sc, inc in next sc, sc in next 13 sc; with A, sc in next 3 sc, inc in next sc, sc in next 16 sc, inc in next sc; with B, sc in next 16 sc, inc in last sc—108 sts.

Rnd 26: With A, sc in first 6 sc; with B, sc in next 7 sc; with A, sc in next 4 sc, inc in next sc, sc in next 6 sc; with B, sc in next 2 sc; with A, sc in next 9 sc, inc in next sc; with B, sc in next 3 sc; with A, sc in next 12 sc; with B, sc in next 2 sc, inc in next sc, sc in next 14 sc; with A, sc in next 3 sc, inc in next sc, sc in next 17 sc, inc in next sc; with B, sc in next 17 sc, inc in last sc—114 sts.

Rnd 27: With A, sc in first 6 sc; with B, sc in next 7 sc; with A, sc in next 12 sc; with B, sc in next 2 sc; with A, sc in next 11 sc; with B, sc in next 3 sc; with A, sc in next 66 sc; with B, sc in last 7 sc.

SEPARATE FOR THE LEGS

Rnd 28: With A, sc in first 6 sc; with B, sc in next 7 sc; with A, sc in next 12 sc; with B, sc in next 2 sc; with A, sc in next 11 sc; with B, sc in next 3 sc; with A, sc in next 15 sc, pm, sc in next 20 sc, ch 10; join into the marker st with a sl st.

FIRST FRONT LEG

Rnd 1: With A, sc in each sc and in all 10 ch—30 sc.

Rnds 2 and 3: With B, sc around—30 sc.

Rnd 4: With A, [sc in next 4 sc, dec over next 2 sc] 5 times—25 sc.

Rnd 5: [Sc in next 3 sc, dec over next 2 sc] 5 times—20 sc.

Rnd 6: Sc around.

Rnds 7–10: With B, sc around.

Rnds 11–16: With A, sc around.

Rnd 17: With B, sc around.

If you are not on the back of the leg at this point, sc until you are.

Rnd 18: With A, sc in first 8 sc, puff st in next 4 sc, sc in last 8 sc.

Rnd 19: [Dec over next 2 sc] around—10 sc.

Rnd 20: [Dec over next 2 sc] around—5 sc.

Stuff the leg.

SECOND FRONT LEG

With A, join yarn with sl st into next unworked st of Rnd 28, sc into the same st as sl st, dec over next 2 sc, (sc in next sc, dec over next 2 sc) 2 times, pm, sc in next 20 sc, ch 10, join into the marked st with a sl st.

Rep Rnds 1–20 of first front leg. Stuff the second leg.

CONTINUING BODY

Note: Stuff body as you stitch.

Join yarn in the marked st that indicates the beg of the rnd, pm.

Rnd 1: With A, sc in first 6 sc; with B, sc in next 7 sc; with A, sc in next 12 sc; with B, sc in next 2 sc; with A, sc in next 11 sc; with B, sc in next 3 sc; with A, sc in next 14 sc, 1 sc in corner worked st from Rnd 28, work 1 sc into back of each ch, 1 sc in corner worked st from Rnd 28, sc in next 5 sc, 1 sc in corner worked st from Rnd 28, work 1 sc into back of each ch, 1 sc in corner worked st from Rnd 28, sc in next 2 sc, with B, sc in next 7 sc—93 sc.

Rnd 2: With A, sc in first 6 sc; with B, sc in next 7 sc; with A, sc in next 12 sc; with B, sc in next 2 sc; with A, sc in next 11 sc; with B, sc in next 3 sc; with A, sc in next 45 sc; with B, sc in last 7 sc.

Rnd 3: With A, sc in first 6 sc; with B, sc in next 7 sc; with A, sc in next 12 sc; with B, sc in next 2 sc; with A, sc in next 11 sc; with B, sc in next 3 sc; with A, sc in next 25 sc, [dec over next 2 sc, sc in next sc] 2 times, dec over next 2 sc, sc in next 12 sc; with B, sc in last 7 sc—90 sc.

Rnd 4: With A, sc in first 6 sc; with B, sc in next 7 sc; with A, sc in next 12 sc; with B, sc in next 2 sc; with A, sc in next 11 sc; with B, sc in next 3 sc; with A, sc in next 24 sc, dec over next 2 sc, sc in next sc, dec over next 2 sc, sc in next sc, dec over next 2 sc, sc in next 10 sc; with B, sc in next 7 sc—87 sc.

Rnd 5: With A, sc in first 6 sc; with B, sc in next 7 sc; with A, sc in next 12 sc; with B, sc in next 2 sc; with A, sc in next 11 sc; with B, sc in next 3 sc; with A, sc in next 38 sc; with B, sc in next 3 sc; with A, sc in next 3 sc; with B, sc in last 2 sc.

Rnd 6: With B, sc in first 2 sc; with A, sc in next 6 sc; with B, sc in next 4 sc; with A, sc in next 13 sc; with B, sc in next 6 sc; with A, sc in next 6 sc; with B, sc in next 11 sc; with A, sc in next 31 sc; with B, sc in next 3 sc; with A, sc in next 3 sc; with B, sc in next 2 sc.

Rnd 7: With B, sc in first 2 sc, with A, sc in next 6 sc; with B, sc in next 4 sc; with A, sc in next 5 sc, inc in next sc, sc in next 6 sc, inc in next sc; with B, sc in next 6 sc; with A, inc in next sc, sc in next 5 sc; with B, sc in next 11 sc; with A, sc in next 31 sc; with B, sc in next 3 sc; with A, sc in next 3 sc; with B, sc in last 2 sc—90 sc.

Rnd 8: With B, sc in first 4 sc; with A, sc in next 2 sc; with B, sc in next 6 sc; with A, sc in next 2 sc, inc in next sc, sc in next 12 sc; with B, sc in next 2 sc, inc in next sc, sc in next 3 sc; with A, sc in next 7 sc; with B, sc in next 4 sc, inc in next sc, sc in next 6 sc; with A, sc in next 8 sc, inc in next sc, sc in next 14 sc, inc in next sc, sc in next 7 sc; with B, sc in next 3 sc; with A, sc in next 3 sc; with B, sc in next sc, inc in last sc—96 sc.

Rnd 9: With B, sc in first 4 sc; with A, sc in next 2 sc; with B, sc in next 6 sc; with A, sc in next 16 sc; with B, sc in next 7 sc; with A, sc in next 7 sc; with B, sc in next 12 sc; with A, sc in next 33 sc; with B, sc in next 3 sc; with A, sc in next 3 sc; with B, sc in last 3 sc.

Rnd 10: With B, sc in first 4 sc; with A, sc in next 2 sc; with B, sc in next 6 sc; with A, sc in next 3 sc, inc in next sc, sc in next 12 sc; with B, sc in next 3 sc, inc in next sc, sc in next 3 sc; with A, sc in next 7 sc; with B, sc in next 5 sc, inc in next sc, sc in next 6 sc; with A, sc in next 9 sc, inc in next sc, sc in next 15 sc, inc in next sc, sc in next 7 sc; with B, sc in next 3 sc; with A, sc in next 3 sc; with B, sc in next 2 sc, inc in last sc—102 sc.

Rnd 11: With B, sc in first 4 sc; with A, sc in next 2 sc; with B, sc in next 6 sc; with A, sc in next 17 sc; with B, sc in

next 8 sc; with A, sc in next 7 sc; with B, sc in next 13 sc; with A, sc in next 35 sc; with B, sc in next 3 sc; with A, sc in next 3 sc; with B, sc in last 4 sc.

Rnd 12: With B, sc in first 4 sc; with A, sc in next 2 sc; with B, sc in next 6 sc; with A, sc in next 7 sc, inc in next sc, sc in next 9 sc; with B, sc in next sc, inc in next sc, sc in next 6 sc; with A, sc in next 4 sc, inc in next sc, sc in next 2 sc; with B, sc in next 13 sc; with A, sc in next 35 sc; with B, sc in next 3 sc; with A, sc in next 3 sc; with B, sc in last 4 sc—105 sc.

Rnd 13: With B, sc in first 4 sc; with A, sc in next 2 sc; with B, sc in next 6 sc; with A, sc in next 18 sc; with B, sc in next 9 sc; with A, sc in next 8 sc; with B, sc in next 13 sc; with A, sc in next 35 sc; with B, sc in next 3 sc; with A, sc in next 3 sc; with B, sc in next 4 sc.

Rnd 14: With B, sc in first 4 sc; with A, sc in next 2 sc; with B, sc in next 6 sc; with A, sc in next 9 sc, inc in next sc, sc in next 5 sc, inc in next sc, sc in next 2 sc; with B, sc in next 7 sc, inc in next sc, sc in next sc; with A, sc in next 3 sc, inc in next sc, sc in next 4 sc; with B, sc in next 13 sc; with A, sc in next 35 sc; with B, sc in next 3 sc; with A, sc in next 3 sc; with B, sc in last 4 sc—109 sc.

Rnd 15: With B, sc in first 4 sc; with A, sc in next 2 sc; with B, sc in next 6 sc; with A, sc in next 20 sc; with B, sc in next 10 sc; with A, sc in next 9 sc; with B, sc in next 13 sc; with A, sc in next 35 sc; with B, sc in next 3 sc; with A, sc in next 3 sc; with B, sc in last 4 sc.

Rnd 16: With B, sc in first 4 sc; with A, sc in next 2 sc; with B, sc in next 6 sc; with A, sc in next 13 sc, inc in next sc, sc in next 5 sc, inc in next sc; with B, sc in next 5 sc, inc in next sc, sc in next 4 sc; with A, sc in next 9 sc; with B, sc in next 13 sc; with A, sc in next 35 sc; with B, sc in next 3 sc; with A, sc in next 3 sc; with B, sc in last 4 sc—112 sc.

Rnds 17 and 18: With B, sc in first 6 sc; with A, sc in next 28 sc; with B, sc in next 11 sc; with A, sc in next 9 sc; with B, sc in next 4 sc; with A, sc in last 54 sc.

Rnd 19: With B, sc in first 6 sc, dec over next 2 sc, sc in next 4 sc; with A, sc in next 2 sc, dec over next 2 sc, [sc in next 6 sc, dec over next 2 sc] 2 times, sc in next 2 sc; with B, sc in next 4 sc, dec over next 2 sc, sc in next 5 sc; with A, sc in next sc, dec over next 2 sc, [sc in next 6 sc, dec over next 2 sc] 8 times—98 sc.

Rnd 20: With B, sc in first 11 sc; with A, sc in next 19 sc; with B, sc in next 10 sc; with A, sc in next 7 sc; with B, sc in next 4 sc; with A, sc in next 39 sc; with B, sc in last 8 sc.

Rnd 21: With B, sc in first 5 sc, dec over next 2 sc, sc in next 4 sc; with A, sc in next sc, dec over next 2 sc, [sc in next 5 sc, dec over next 2 sc] 2 times, sc in next 2 sc; with B, sc in next 3 sc, dec over next 2 sc, sc in next 5 sc, dec over next 2 sc; with A, sc in next 5 sc, dec over next 2 sc; with B, sc in next 3 sc; with A, sc in next 2 sc, dec over next 2 sc, [sc in next 5 sc, dec over next 2 sc] 5 times; with B, sc in next 5 sc, dec over last 2 sc—84 sc.

Rnd 22: With B, sc in first 10 sc; with A, sc in next 16 sc; with B, sc in next 10 sc; with A, sc in next 6 sc; with B, sc in next 3 sc; with A, sc in next 33 sc; with B, sc in last 6 sc.

Rnd 23: With B, [sc in next 4 sc, dec over next 2 sc] 2 times; with A, [sc in next 4 sc, dec over next 2 sc] 2 times, sc in next 2 sc; with B, sc in next 2 sc, dec over next 2 sc, sc in next 4 sc, dec over next 2 sc; with A, sc in next 4 sc, dec over next 2 sc; with B, sc in next 3 sc; with A, sc in next sc, dec over next 2 sc, [sc in next 4 sc, dec over next 2 sc] 5 times; with B, sc in next 4 sc, dec in last sc—70 sc.

Rnd 24: With B, sc in first 10 sc; with A, sc in next 12 sc; with B, sc in next 8 sc; with A, sc in next 5 sc; with B, sc in next 3 sc; with A, sc in next 27 sc; with B, sc in last 5 sc.

Rnd 25: With B, [sc in next 3 sc, dec over next 2 sc] 2 times; with A, [sc in next 3 sc, dec over next 2 sc] 2 times, sc in next 2 sc; with B, sc in next sc, dec over next 2 sc, sc in next 3 sc, dec over next 2 sc; with A, sc in next 3 sc, dec over next 2 sc; with B, sc in next 3 sc, dec over next 2 sc; with A, [sc in next 3 sc, dec over next 2 sc] 5 times; with B, sc in next 3 sc, dec over last 2 sc—56 sc.

Rnd 26: With B, sc in next 8 sc; with A, sc in next 10 sc; with B, sc in next 6 sc; with A, sc in next 4 sc; with B, sc in next 4 sc; with A, sc in next 20 sc; with B, sc in last 4 sc.

Rnd 27: With B, [sc in next 2 sc, dec over next 2 sc] 2 times; with A, [sc in next 2 sc, dec over next 2 sc] 2 times, sc in next 2 sc; with B, dec over next 2 sc, sc in next 2 sc, dec over next 2 sc; with A, sc in next 2 sc, dec over next 2 sc; with B, sc in next 2 sc, dec over next 2 sc; with A, [sc in next 2 sc, dec over next 2 sc] 5 times; with B, sc in next 2 sc, dec over last 2 sc—42 sc.

Rnd 28: With B, [sc in next sc, dec over next 2 sc] 14 times—28 sc.

Rnd 29: [Sc in next 2 sc, dec over next 2 sc] 7 times—21 sc.

Rnd 30: [Sc in next sc, dec over next 2 sc] 7 times—14 sc.

Rnd 31: [Dec over next 2 sc] around—7 sc. Fasten off.

HEAD

With B, make magic ring.

Rnd 1: 6 sc into magic ring—6 sc.

Rnd 2: Inc in each sc around—12 sc.

Rnd 3: (Sc in next sc, inc in next sc) 6 times—18 sc.

Rnd 4: With B, sc in first 2 sc, inc in next sc; with A, sc in next 2 sc, inc in next sc; with B, [sc in next 2 sc, inc in next sc] 2 times; with A, sc in next 2 sc, inc in next sc; with B, sc in next 2 sc, inc in last sc—24 sc.

Rnd 5: With B, sc in first 2 sc; with A, sc in next sc, inc in next sc, sc in next 3 sc, inc in next sc, sc in next 2 sc; with B, sc in next sc; with A, inc in next sc; with B, sc in next 3 sc; with A, inc in next sc; with B, sc in next sc; with A, sc in next 2 sc, inc in next sc, sc in next 3 sc, inc in last sc—30 sc.

Rnd 6: With B, sc in first 2 sc; with A, sc in next 2 sc, inc in next sc, sc in next 4 sc, inc in next sc, sc in next 2 sc; with B, sc in next sc; with A, sc in next sc, inc in next sc; with B, sc in next 3 sc; with A, sc in next sc, inc in next sc; with B, sc in next sc; with A, sc in next 3 sc, inc in next sc, sc in next 4 sc, inc in last sc—36 sc.

Rnd 7: With B, sc in first 2 sc; with A, sc in next 3 sc, inc in next sc, sc in next 5 sc, inc in next sc, sc in next 3 sc; with B, sc in next sc; with A, sc in next sc, inc in next sc; with B, sc in next 2 sc; with A, sc in next 3 sc, inc in next sc; with B, sc in next sc; with A, sc in next 4 sc, inc in next sc, sc in next 5 sc, inc in last sc—42 sc.

Rnd 8: With B, sc in first 2 sc; with A, sc in next 4 sc, inc in next sc, sc in next 6 sc, inc in next sc, sc in next 3 sc; with B, sc in next sc; with A, sc in next 2 sc, inc in next sc, sc in next sc; with B, sc in next sc; with A, sc in next 4 sc; with B, inc in next sc; with A, [sc in next 6 sc, inc in next sc] 2 times—48 sc.

Rnd 9: With B, sc in first 2 sc; with A, sc in next 5 sc, inc in next sc, sc in next 7 sc, inc in next sc, sc in next 3 sc; with B, sc in next sc; with A, sc in next 3 sc, inc in next sc, sc in next sc; with B, sc in next sc; with A, sc in next 5 sc; with B, inc in next sc; with A, [sc in next 7 sc, inc in next sc] 2 times—54 sc.

Rnd 10: With B, sc in first 2 sc; with A, sc in next 6 sc, inc in next sc, sc in next 8 sc, inc in next sc, sc in next 3 sc; with B, sc in next sc; with A, sc in next 4 sc, inc in next sc, sc in next sc; with B, sc in next sc; with A, sc in next 6 sc; with B, inc in next sc; with A, [sc in next 8 sc, inc in next sc] 2 times—60 sc.

Rnd 11: With B, sc in first 2 sc; with A, sc in next 21 sc; with B, sc in next sc; with A, sc in next 7 sc; with B, sc in next sc; with A, sc in next 6 sc; with B, sc in next 2 sc; with A, sc in last 20 sc.

Rnd 12: With B, sc in first 2 sc; with A, sc in next 21 sc; with B, sc in next sc; with A, sc in next 7 sc; with B, sc in next sc; with A, sc in next 6 sc; with B, sc in next 2 sc; with A, sc in last 20 sc.

Rnd 13: With B, sc in next 2 sc; with A, sc in next 21 sc; with B, sc in next sc; with A, sc in next 7 sc; with B, sc in next sc; with A, sc in next 6 sc; with B, sc in next 2 sc; with A, sc in last 20 sc.

Rnd 14: With B, sc in next 2 sc; with A, sc in next 2 sc; with B, sc in next sc; with A, sc in next 18 sc; with B, sc in next sc; with A, sc in next 14 sc; with B, sc in next sc; with A, sc in next 16 sc; with B, sc in next sc; with A, sc in last 4 sc—60 sc.

Rnd 15: With B, sc in first 2 sc; with A, sc in next 2 sc; with B, sc in next sc; with A, sc in next 18 sc; with B, sc in next sc; with A, sc in next 3 sc, (3 sc) in each of next 2 sc, sc in next 5 sc, (3 sc) in each of next 2 sc, sc in next 2 sc; with B, sc in next sc; with A, sc in next 16 sc; with B, sc in next sc; with A, sc in last 4 sc—68 sc.

Rnd 16: With B, sc in first 2 sc; with A, sc in next 2 sc; with B, sc in next sc; with A, sc in next 18 sc; with B, sc in next sc; with A, sc in next 8 sc, inc in next sc, sc in next 5 sc, inc in next sc, sc in next 7 sc; with B, sc in next sc; with A, sc in next 16 sc; with B, sc in next sc; with A, sc in last 4 sc—70 sc.

RIGHT: Professor McGonagall in her Animagus form presiding over her first years' Transfiguration class in *Harry Potter and the Sorcerer's Stone*.

Rnd 17: With B, sc in first 2 sc; with A, sc in next 2 sc; with B, sc in next sc; with A, sc in next 22 sc, [dec over next 2 sc] 3 times, inc in next sc, sc in next 5 sc, inc in next sc, [dec over next 2 sc] 3 times, sc in next 2 sc; with B, sc in next sc; with A, sc in next 16 sc; with B, sc in next sc; with A, sc in last 4 sc—66 sc.

Rnd 18: With B, sc in first 2 sc; with A, sc in next 2 sc; with B, sc in next sc; with A, sc in next 18 sc; with B, sc in next 6 sc; with A, [dec over next 2 sc] 2 times, inc in next sc, sc in next 2 sc, inc in next sc, [dec over next 2 sc] 2 times, sc in next sc; with B, sc in next 5 sc; with A, sc in next 14 sc; with B, sc in next sc; with A, sc in last 4 sc—64 sc.

Rnd 19: With B, sc in first 2 sc; with A, sc in next 2 sc; with B, sc in next sc; with A, sc in next 15 sc; with B, sc in next 5 sc; with A, sc in next 3 sc, dec over next 2 sc, sc in next 9 sc, dec over next 2 sc, sc in next sc; with B, sc in next 5 sc; with A, sc in next 12 sc; with B, sc in last 5 sc—62 sc.

Rnd 20: With B, sc in first sc; with A, sc in next 3 sc; with B, sc in next sc; with A, sc in next 14 sc; with B, sc in next 4 sc; with A, sc in next 5 sc, dec over next 2 sc, sc in next 6 sc, dec over next 2 sc, sc in next 5 sc; with B, sc in next 4 sc; with A, sc in next 10 sc; with B, sc in last 5 sc—60 sc.

Attach eyes between Rnds 17 and 18.

Rnd 21: With A, sc in first 4 sc; with B, sc in next sc; with A, sc in next 32 sc; with B, sc in next sc; with A, sc in next 17 sc; with B, sc in last 5 sc.

Rnd 22: With A, sc in first 4 sc; with B, sc in next sc; with A, sc in next 19 sc; with B, sc in next 2 sc; with A, sc in next 11 sc; with B, sc in next sc; with A, sc in next 17 sc; with B, sc in next 4 sc; with A, sc in last sc.

Rnd 23: With A, sc in first 4 sc; with B, sc in next sc; with A, sc in next 14 sc; with B, sc in next 7 sc; with A, sc in next 12 sc; with B, sc in next sc; with A, sc in next 16 sc; with B, sc in last 5 sc.

Rnd 24: With B, sc in first sc; with A, sc in next 3 sc; with B, sc in next sc; with A, sc in next 33 sc; with B, sc in next sc; with A, sc in next 16 sc; with B, sc in last 5 sc.

Rnd 25: With B, sc in first 2 sc; with A, sc in next 2 sc; with B, sc in next sc; with A, sc in next 34 sc; with B, sc in next 2 sc; with A, sc in next 14 sc; with B, sc in last 5 sc.

Rnd 26: With B, sc in first 3 sc; with A, sc in next sc; with B, sc in next sc; with A, sc in next 36 sc; with B, sc in next 2 sc; with A, sc in next 12 sc; with B, sc in last 5 sc.

Rnd 27: With B, sc in next 3 sc; with A, sc in next 38 sc; with B, sc in next 6 sc; with A, sc in next 8 sc; with B, sc in last 5 sc.

Rnd 28: With A, sc in first 4 sc; with B, sc in next sc; with A, sc in next 5 sc, dec over next 2 sc, [sc in next 10 sc, dec over next 2 sc] 3 times, sc in next 8 sc; with B, sc in next 2 sc, dec over last 2 sc—55 sc.

Rnd 29: With A, sc in first 5 sc; with B, sc in next sc; with A, sc in next 3 sc, dec over next 2 sc, [sc in next 9 sc, dec over next 2 sc] 3 times, sc in next 4 sc; with B, sc in next sc; with A, sc in next 3 sc; with B, sc in next sc; dec over last 2 sc—50 sc.

Rnd 30: With A, [sc in next 8 sc, dec over next 2 sc] 4 times; sc in next 3 sc; with B, sc in next 3 sc; with A, sc in next 2 sc; with B, dec over last 2 sc—45 sc.

Rnd 31: With A, [sc in next 7 sc, dec over next 2 sc] 4 times, sc in next 2 sc; with B, sc in next 5 sc, dec over last 2 sc—40 sc.

Stuff head firmly.

Rnd 32: With A, [sc in next 6 sc, dec over next 2 sc] 4 times, sc in next 2 sc; with B, sc in next 4 sc, dec over last 2 sc—35 sc.

Rnd 33: With A, [sc in next 5 sc, dec over next 2 sc] 4 times, sc in next 2 sc; with B, sc in next 3 sc, dec over last 2 sc—30 sc.

Rnd 34: With A, [sc in next 4 sc, dec over next 2 sc] 4 times, sc in next 2 sc; with B, sc in next 2 sc, dec over last 2 sc—25 sc.

Rnd 35: With A, [sc in next 3 sc, dec over next 2 sc] 4 times, sc in next 2 sc; with B, sc in next sc, dec over last 2 sc—20 sc.

Rnd 36: With A, [dec over next 2 sc] around—10 sc.

Rnd 37: [Dec over next 2 sc] around—5 sc.

Fasten off.

EARS (MAKE 2)

With A, make a magic ring.

Rnd 1: 6 sc into magic ring—6 sc.

Rnd 2: Sc around.

Rnd 3: [Sc in next sc, inc in next sc] 3 times—9 sc.

Rnd 4: Sc evenly around.

Rnd 5: [Sc in next 2 sc, inc in next sc] 3 times—12 sc.

Rnd 6: Sc around.

Rnd 7: [Sc in next 2 sc, inc in next sc] 4 times—16 sc.

Rnd 8: Sc around.

Rnd 9: [Sc in next 3 sc, inc in next sc] 4 times—20 sc.

Rnd 10: Sc around.

Rnd 11: [Sc in next 4 sc, inc in next sc] 4 times—24 sc.

Rnd 12: Sc around.

Rnd 13: [Sc in next 5 sc, inc in next sc] 4 times—28 sc.

Fasten off, leaving a long tail for sewing. Do not stuff. Flatten ears.

TAIL

With B, make magic ring.

Rnd 1: 8 sc in magic ring.

Rnd 2: Inc in each sc around—16 sc.

Rnds 3–10: Sc around.

Rnds 11-14: With A, sc around.

Rnds 15–17: With B, sc around.

Rnds 18–25: With A, sc around.

Rnds 26 and 27: With B, sc around.

Rnds 28–40: With A, sc around.

Stuff tip of tail. Fasten off, leaving a long tail for sewing.

BACK FEET (MAKE 2)

With A, ch 11.

Rnd 1: Sc in 2nd ch from hook and in each of next 9 ch, inc in end of ch, work 1 sc into the back of each ch, inc in sk ch—24 sc.

Rnd 2: [Sc in next sc, inc in next sc] 12 times—36 sc.

Rnd 3: Sc in first 16 sc, inc in each of next 4 sc, sc in last 16 sc—40 sc.

Rnd 4: Sc in first 18 sc, puff st in next 4 sc, sc in last 18 sc.

Rnd 5: [Dec over next 2 sc] around—20 sc.

Rnd 6: Sc around.

Rnd 7: Sc in first 8 sc, [dec over next 2 sc] 2 times, sc in last 8 sc—18 sc.

Rnd 8: Sc in first 5 sc, [dec over next 2 sc] 4 times, sc in last 5 sc—14 sc.

Rnd 9: [Dec over next 2 sc] around—7 sc.

Stuff the front of the foot by toes and leave the back flat. Fasten off, leaving a long tail for sewing.

MUZZLE

With C, make a magic ring.

Rnd 1: 10 sc into the magic ring—10 sc.

Rnd 2: [Sc in first sc, inc] 3 times; with A, [sc in next sc, inc in next sc] 2 times—15 sc.

Rnd 3: With C, [sc in first 2 sc, inc in next sc] 3 times; with A, [sc in first 2 sc, inc in next sc] 2 times—20 sc.

Rnd 4: With C, [sc in first 3 sc, inc in next sc] 3 times; with A, [sc in first 3 sc, inc in next sc] 2 times—25 sc.

Rnd 5: With C, [sc in first 4 sc, inc in next sc] 3 times; with A, [sc in first 4 sc, inc in next sc] 2 times—30 sc.

Rnd 6: With C, [sc in first 5 sc, inc in next sc] 3 times; with A, [sc in first 5 sc, inc in next sc] 2 times—35 sc.

Rnd 7-8: With C, sc in first 21 sc; with A, sc in last 14 sc—35 sc.

Fasten off, leaving a long tail for sewing.

HAT

With D, make a magic ring.

Rnd 1: 4 sc into magic ring—4 sc.

Rnd 2-4: Sc around.

Rnd 5: Inc in each sc around—8 sc.

Rnd 6 and 7: Sc around.

Rnd 8: [Sc in next 3 sc, inc in next sc] 2 times—10 sc.

Rnd 9-11: Sc around.

Rnd 12: Sc in BLO around—10 sc.

Rnd 13: Sc around.

Rnd 14: [Sc in next 4 sc, inc in next sc] 2 times—12 sc.

Rnd 15: Sc around.

Rnd 16: [Sc in next 3 sc, inc in next sc] 3 times—15 sc.

Rnd 17-20: Sc around.

Rnd 21: [Sc in next 4 sc, inc in next sc] 3 times—18 sc.

Rnd 22: Sc around.

Rnd 23: [Sc in next 5 sc, inc in next sc] 3 times—21 sc.

Rnd 24: [Sc in next 6 sc, inc in next sc] 3 times—24 sc.

Rnd 25 and 26: Sc around.

Rnd 27: [Sc in next 7 sc, inc in next sc] 3 times—27 sc.

Rnd 28: [Sc in next 8 sc, inc in next sc] 3 times—30 sc.

Rnd 29: Sc around.

Rnd 30: [Sc in next 9 sc, inc in next sc] 3 times—33 sc.

Rnd 31: [Sc in next 10 sc, inc in next sc] 3 times—36 sc.

Rnd 32: Sc around.

Rnd 33: [Sc in next 11 sc, inc in next sc] 3 times—39 sc.

Rnd 34: [Sc in next 12 sc, inc in next sc] 3 times—42 sc.

Rnd 35: Sc around.

Rnd 36: [Sc in next 13 sc, inc in next sc] 3 times—45 sc.

Rnd 37: [Sc in next 14 sc, inc in next sc] 3 times—48 sc.

Rnd 38: Sc around.

Rnd 39: [Sc in next 3 sc, inc in next sc] 12 times—60 sc.

Rnd 40: [Sc in next 4 sc, inc in next sc] 12 times—72 sc.

Rnd 41: [Sc in next 5 sc, inc in next sc] 12 times—84 sc.

Rnd 42: [Sc in next 6 sc, inc in next sc] 12 times—96 sc.

Rnd 43: [Sc in next 7 sc, inc in next sc] 12 times—108 sc.

Rnd 44: Sc around.

Fasten off. To create a curved tip, fold hat together at across Rnd 12 and sew across.

ASSEMBLY

Weave in ends.

Using tapestry needle and long straight sts, embroider around eyes with black crochet thread. Stuff neck of body. Sew head onto body.

Sew ears on top of head, then sew tail onto the back of the body. Sew the back feet to the body.

Sew muzzle on head. On the bottom half of muzzle, embroider the nose with black crochet thread. To create whiskers, cut four 4 in. / 10 cm lengths of black crochet thread. Wrap each length of thread around a st, then knot on the outside. Stitch a straight line of black crochet thread from bottom point of nose to bottom of muzzle.

Place glasses and hat on cat's head.

MANDRAKE

Designed by **JILLIAN HEWITT**

SKILL LEVEL ⚡⚡

In *Harry Potter and the Chamber of Secrets*, the second-year students participate in a Herbology lesson where they learn all about the Mandrake root. This magical plant has a leafy top and a root that, when uncovered, resembles a wriggling, disgruntled infant. The students have to take great care when uncovering Mandrakes because their cries are deadly to humans!

Although the Mandrakes seen in *Harry Potter and the Chamber of Secrets* look, essentially, like infants, "they had to have an element to them that wasn't too lovable," says creature effects designer Nick Dudman. "They couldn't be cuddly teddy bears, because you know they're going to eventually be destroyed to make a potion, so we made them screeching, scrawling things." Ultimately, the creature and makeup effects teams created over fifty animatronic Mandrake puppets that sat in the top halves of the flowerpots, operated manually from underneath the tables.

Be sure to cover your ears upon completing this amigurumi Mandrake! Easy crochet stitches work up this magical creature, but the details really bring it to life. Worked in two pieces and then seamed together, the Mandrake looks like it's ready to start crying at any second.

SIZE
One size

FINISHED MEASUREMENTS
Height: 11 in. / 28 cm
Width: 9 in. / 23 cm

YARN
DK weight (light #3) yarn, shown in Patons *Astra* (100% acrylic; 133 yd. / 122 m per 1¾ oz. / 50 g ball)
Color A: Medium Tan, 1 ball
Worsted weight (medium #4) yarn, shown in Patons *Canadiana* (100% acrylic; 205 yd. / 187 m per 3½ oz. / 100 g ball)
Color B: Dark Green Tea, small amounts
Color C: Medium Green Tea, small amounts
Color D: Cherished Green, small amounts

HOOK
- C-2 / 2.75 mm crochet hook or size needed to obtain gauge

NOTIONS
- Black crochet thread
- Polyester stuffing
- Tapestry needle

GAUGE
12 sts and 13 rows = 2 in. / 5 cm in sc with Color A
Gauge is not critical for a toy; just ensure the stitches are tight enough so the stuffing will not show through your finished project.

Continued on page 36

NOTES

- The amigurumi is worked in flat panels from the bottom up.
- Each leg is assembled first by holding both panels together and single crocheting around the edges. The roots are worked during assembly. The piece is then stuffed.
- The arms and body are worked as one panel. The body is assembled by holding both panels together and single crocheting around the edges. The roots are worked during assembly. The legs are stitched into the panels during assembly. The piece is then stuffed.
- When working on the front panel, yarn tails should remain on the back. When working on the back panel, yarn tails should be on the front, so that all yarn tails are facing inside when the panels are lined up and joined.
- The chain 1 at end of each row does not count as a stitch.

LEFT LEG

*With A, ch 3.

Row 1: Sc in 2nd ch from hook and in last ch, turn—2 sc.

Row 2: Sc in each sc across.

Fasten off. Rep from *, but do not fasten off. Ch 1, turn, cont to Row 3. Crochet across both pieces to join:

Row 3: Sc in first sc, inc in next sc, working into second piece sc in next 2 sc, ch 1, turn—5 sc across two segments.

Row 4: Dec over first 2 sc, sc in next sc, dec over next 2 sc, ch 1, turn—3 sc.

Rows 5-10: Sc in each sc across, ch 1, turn.

Row 11: Inc in first sc, sc in next 2 sc, ch 1, turn—4 sc.

Row 12: Dec over first 2 sc, inc in each of last 2 sc, ch 1, turn—5 sc.

Row 13: Inc in first sc, sc in next 4 sc, ch 1, turn—6 sc.

Row 14: Sc in first 5 sc, inc in next sc, ch 1, turn—7 sc.

Row 15: Sc in first 6 sc, inc in next sc, ch 1, turn—8 sc.

Row 16: Dec over first 2 sc, sc in next 5 sc, inc in next sc, ch 1, turn.

Row 17: Sc in first 4 sc, [dec] twice across last 4 sc, ch 1, turn—6 sc.

Row 18: Dec over first 2 sc, sc in next 4 sc, ch 1, turn—5 sc.

Row 19: Sc in first 3 sc, dec over next 2 sc, ch 1, turn—4 sc.

Row 20: Dec over first 2 sc, sc in next 2 sc, ch 1, turn—3 sc.

Row 21: Sc in first sc, dec over last 2 sc, ch 1, turn—2 sc.

Row 22: Dec—1 st.

Fasten off. Rep Rows 1-22 for second leg panel, place panels together with all edges lined up, so that the curve of the outer leg is on the right when the front is facing you. Insert hook through both panels into any st at the top left side of the leg. Sc along the edge of both panels to join until you reach the bottom corner of the first leg segment, then work the following:

Row 1: Ch 10, turn, sl st in 2nd ch from hook and in each ch across, sl st to next st at bottom of leg—9 sl sts.

Row 2: Ch 13 to create main root, turn, sl st in 2nd ch from hook and in next 6 ch along main root, ch 7 to create secondary root, sl st in 2nd ch from hook and in each ch along secondary root, sl st in next 5 ch along main root, sl st to bottom of leg to join—18 sl sts.

Cont joining the panels until you reach the bottom of the second leg segment, then work the following:

Row 1: Ch 10 to create main root, sl st in 2nd ch from hook and in next 6 ch, ch 8 to create secondary root, sl st in 2nd ch from hook and in next 6 ch along secondary root, sl st in next 2 ch along main root, sl st to bottom of leg to join—16 sl sts.

Row 2: Ch 15, sl st in 2nd ch from hook and in each ch across, sl st to bottom of leg to join—14 sl sts.

Row 3: Ch 10, sl st in 2nd ch from hook and in each ch across, sl st to bottom of leg to join—9 sl sts.

Begin stuffing leg. Cont to fill as you join, stopping after every 3 or 4 sts. Sl st to beginning st to close. Weave in ends.

Rep the above for the right leg. When joining the panels on the right leg, the curve of the hip should be on the left when front is facing you; this will ensure the legs are inverses of each other.

LEFT ARM
(MAKE 2 PANELS)

SEGMENT 1

With A, ch 2.

Row 1: Sc in 2nd ch from hook, ch 1, turn—1 sc.

Row 2: Inc in first sc, ch 1, turn—2 sc.

Row 3: Dec over first 2 sc, insert hook into last st where dec was worked, sc in st, ch 1, turn.

ABOVE: Professor Sprout demonstrates how to repot a Mandrake during a Herbology lesson in *Harry Potter and the Chamber of Secrets.*

Row 4: Sc in next 2 sc, ch 1, turn.
Row 5: Dec, insert hook into last st where dec was worked, sc in st. Fasten off. Put aside.

SEGMENT 2

With A, ch 3.
Row 1: Sc in 2nd ch from hook and in last ch, ch 1, turn—2 sc.
Row 2: Sc in first sc, insert hook into same st and work a dec, ch 1, turn.
Row 3: Dec over first 2 sc, insert hook into last st where dec was worked, sc in st, ch 1, turn.
Rows 4–5: Rep Rows 2 and 3.
Row 6: Dec over first 2 sc, insert hook into last st where dec was worked, sc in st, ch 1, turn.
Rows 7–9: Rep Rows 2 and 3, ending with a Row 2.
Position pieces so that segment 1 is on the left with yarn tail on the right and segment 2 is positioned to the right of segment 1, also with yarn

tails on the right. Crochet across segment 1 and segment 2 in Row 10 to join:
Row 10: Sc in first 2 sc, working into second piece sc in next 2 sc, ch 1, turn—4 sc across two segments.
Row 11: Dec over first 2 sc, sc in last 2 sc, ch 1, turn—3 sc.
Row 12: Inc in first sc, dec over last 2 sc, ch 1, turn.
Row 13: Sc in first 2 sc, inc in next sc, ch 1, turn—4 sc.
Row 14: Inc in first sc, sc in next sc, dec over last 2 sc, ch 1, turn.
Row 15: Sc in first 3 sc, inc in next sc, ch 1, turn—5 sc.
Row 16: Inc in first sc, sc in next 4 sc, ch 1, turn—6 sc.
Row 17: Dec over first 2 sc, sc in last 4 sc, ch 1, turn—5 sc.
Row 18: Inc in first sc, sc in last 4 sc—6 sc.
Fasten off.

RIGHT ARM
(MAKE 2 PANELS)

With A, ch 2.
Row 1: Sc in 2nd ch from hook, ch 1, turn—1 sc.
Row 2: Inc in sc, ch 1, turn—2 sc.
Row 3: Inc in first sc, sc in last sc, ch 1, turn—3 sc.
Row 4: Dec over first 2 sc, inc in next sc, ch 1, turn.
Row 5: Sc in each sc across, ch 1, turn.
Row 6: Dec over first 2 sc, inc in last sc, ch 1, turn.
Row 7: Sc in each sc across, ch 1, turn.
Row 8: Inc in first sc, sc in next 2 sc, ch 1, turn—4 sc.
Row 9: Inc in first sc, sc in next 3 sc, ch 1, turn—5 sc.
Row 10: Sc in each sc across, ch 1, turn.
Row 11: Inc in first sc, sc in next 2 sc, dec over last 2 sc, ch 1, turn.
Row 12: [Dec over next 2 sc] twice, sc in last sc—3 sc.
Fasten off. Set aside.

BELLY
(MAKE 2 PANELS)

With A, ch 8.

Row 1: Sc in 2nd ch from hook and in each ch across, ch 1, turn—7 sc.

Row 2: Inc in first 2 sc, sc in next 3 sc, inc in last 2 sc, ch 1, turn—11 sc.

Row 3: Inc in first sc, sc in next 9 sc, inc in last sc, ch 1, turn—13 sc.

Row 4: Inc in first sc, sc in next 11 sc, inc in last sc, ch 1, turn—15 sc.

Row 5: Inc in first sc, sc in next 13 sc, inc in last sc, ch 1, turn—17 sc.

Row 6: Inc in first sc, sc in next 15 sc, inc in last sc, ch 1, turn—19 sc.

Row 7: Sc in each sc across, ch 1, turn.

Row 8: Inc in first sc, sc in next 17 sc, inc in last sc, ch 1, turn—21 sc.

Rows 9 and 10: Sc in each sc across, ch 1, turn.

Row 11: Dec over first 2 sc, sc in next 17 sc, dec over last 2 sc, ch 1, turn—19 sc.

Row 12: Sc in each sc across.

Fasten off.

BODY
(MAKE 2 PANELS)

Line body pieces up as follows: right arm with outer curve of the arm on the outside left, belly, then left arm with Segment 1 on the right and Segment 2 on the left. Cont to join all three pieces tog in the next row:

Row 1: Dec over first 2 sc of left arm, sc in next 3 sc, inc in next sc, sc over next 19 sc of belly, inc in first sc of right arm, dec over last 2 sc, ch 1, turn—28 sc across right arm, belly, and left arm.

Row 2: Sc in first 26 sc, dec over last 2 sc, ch 1, turn—27 sc.

Row 3: Dec over first 2 sc, sc over next 23 sc, dec over last 2 sc, ch 1, turn—25 sc.

Row 4: Sc in first 21 sc, [dec over next 2 sc] twice, ch 1, turn—23 sc.

Row 5: Dec over first 2 sc, sc in next 19 sc, dec over last 2 sc, ch 1, turn—21 sc.

Row 6: Dec over first 2 sc, sc in next 17 sc, dec over last 2 sc, ch 1, turn—19 sc.

Row 7: Dec over first 2 sc, sc in next 15 sc, dec over last 2 sc, ch 1, turn—17 sc.

Row 8: [Dec] twice over next 4 sc, sc in next 11 sc, dec over last 2 sc, ch 1, turn—14 sc.

Row 9: [Dec] twice over next 4 sc, sc in next 6 sc, [dec] twice over next 4 sc, ch 1, turn—10 sc.

Row 10: Inc in first sc, sc in next 8 sc, inc in last sc, ch 1, turn—12 sc.

Row 11: Sc in each sc across, ch 1, turn.

Row 12: Inc in first sc, sc in next 10 sc, inc in last sc, ch 1, turn—14 sc.

Row 13: Sc in each sc across, ch 1, turn.

Row 14: Dec over first 2 sc, sc in next 10 sc, dec over last 2 sc, ch 1, turn—12 sc.

Row 15: Dec over first 2 sc, sc in next 8 sc, dec over last 2 sc, ch 1, turn—10 sc.

Row 16: Dec over first 2 sc, sc in next 6 sc, dec over last 2 sc, ch 1, turn—8 sc.

Rows 17 and 18: Sc in each sc across, ch 1, turn.

Row 19: Dec over first 2 sc, sc in next 4 sc, dec over last 2 sc, ch 1, turn—6 sc.

Row 20: [Sc3tog] twice, ch 1, turn—2 sc.

Row 21: Sc in each sc across, ch 1, turn.

Row 22: [Inc in next sc] twice, ch 1, turn—4 sc.

Start first head branch:

Row 23: Inc in first sc, leave rem sts unworked, ch 1, turn—2 sc.

Row 24: Sc in each sc across, ch 1, turn.

Row 25: Sc in first sc, leave rem st unworked, ch 1, turn—1 sc.

Row 26: Inc in sc, ch 1, turn—2 sc.

Row 27: Sc in first sc, leave rem st unworked, ch 1, turn—1 sc.

Rows 28 and 29: Sc in sc, ch 1, turn.

Fasten off.

Turn work so that the first completed head branch is on the left. Insert hook into unworked st of Row 22 and rep Rows 23–29 for second head branch.

Fasten off.

LEAF
(MAKE 1 WITH B; MAKE 2 EACH WITH C AND D)

Row 1: Ch 5, sl st in 2nd ch from hook, sc in next 2 ch, 6 hdc in last ch, working on opposite side of ch, sc in next 2 ch, sl st in next ch, ch 1, sl st to beg sl st to join—13 sts.

Fasten off. Weave in ends.

ASSEMBLY

FACE

Using black crochet thread, st two sideways Vs between Rows 13 and 15 of the body section.

Using black crochet thread, make several running sts across 3 sts in Rows 11 and 12 to create the mouth.

Using A, surface sl st in a *V* shape above the eyes to create a ridge. Fasten off.

BODY AND LEGS

Cut two lengths of A yarn about 12 in. / 30.5 cm long each and set aside for later.

Place the two body panels together, lining up all sides. The front of the amigurumi should be facing you as you crochet around the outside to join.

Starting on the left side, at the top of the head, below the head branches, begin attaching the panels together by inserting your hook through a st on the edge of the panels. Single crochet along the edge, through both panels, to join them until you reach the end of the right arm, then work the following:

Row 1: Ch 9, sl st in 2nd ch from hook and in each ch across, sl st to bottom of arm to join—8 sl sts.

Row 2: Ch 10, sl st in 2nd ch from hook and in each ch across, sl st to arm to join—9 sl sts.

Row 3: Ch 7, sl st in 2nd ch from hook and in each ch across, sl st to arm to join—6 sl sts.

Cont crocheting around the arm, joining the panels. Stuff the arm.

Insert the right leg between the two body panels. Using a length of A that was set aside earlier, st the leg in place between the panels by stitching through all three pieces (front body panel, leg, and back body panel). Tie a knot to secure. Hide the yarn tails between the panels.

Cont crocheting down the body. At the leg, crochet in the sts of the front panel only, since this section is already sewn shut. Cont crocheting both panels together as usual, stopping at the bottom center of the belly. Using the second length of yarn that was set aside earlier, insert the left leg and secure in place the same way as the right leg.

Cont crocheting around the panels until you reach the bottom of the first branch of the left arm, then work the following:

Row 1: Ch 12, sl st in 2nd ch from hook and in next 6 chs to create main root, ch 9 to create secondary root, sl st in 2nd ch from hook and in next 7 ch along secondary root, sl st in next 4 ch along main root, sl st to first branch to join—19 sl sts.

Row 2: Ch 8, sl st in 2nd ch from hook and in each ch across, sl st to first branch to join—7 sl sts.

Cont crocheting up the other side of the first branch of the left arm. Stuff.

At the bottom of the second branch of the left arm, work the following:

Row 1: Ch 7, sl st in 2nd ch from hook and in each ch across, sl st to second branch to join—6 sl sts.

Row 2: Ch 9, sl st in 2nd ch from hook, sl st in each ch across, sl st to second branch to join—8 sl sts.

Cont to crochet up the arm. Stuff.

Crochet up the body and head, and around the head branches, topping up stuffing as you go. Stuff firmly.

When you are satisfied with the stuffing, close with a sl st to first st. Fasten off. With tapestry needle, poke the yarn tail back inside the piece.

FINISHING TOUCHES

St the leaves to the head branches. Weave in ends.

Using a long length of A, create dimples in various places on the belly and legs as follows:

With tapestry needle, weave A through a st on the front of the amigurumi and out a st on the back, leaving a long tail on the front. Weave the yarn tail on the front through a st next to the first st on the front of the amigurumi and out through the same st on the back of the amigurumi as the first one. Pull the yarn tails on the back firmly to create a dimple. Tie a knot to secure, hiding knot inside. Rep for as many dimples as you prefer. Weave in ends.

RIGHT: Concept art of the Mandrake by Dermot Power for *Harry Potter and the Chamber of Secrets.*

HEDWIG

Designed by **EMMY SCANGA**

SKILL LEVEL ⚡⚡⚡

Hedwig is Harry Potter's pet and companion, and she was purchased from Eeylops Owl Emporium by Hagrid as a birthday present for Harry. Her snowy white feathers and amber eyes give her a soft and wise personality. While staying with Harry at Hogwarts, Hedwig delivers mail, visits Harry in his dormitory, and also spends time in the Hogwarts Owlery with the other school owls. When designing the set for the Hogwarts Owlery, production designer Stuart Craig took inspiration from a rock ridge in Inverness. He took great care to ensure that owls of all shapes could live comfortably in the setting. "The owls are of varying sizes," explains Craig, "but we measured and designed perches with the optimum shape for them to grip onto," although in the films half of the perches are either empty or occupied by faux owls.

Crocheted in the round, this amigurumi Hedwig is an adorable replica of Harry's beloved friend. Parts of her body are brushed out to give her a bit of softness and to mimic piles of feathers. Finally, small details are embroidered on Hedwig to put the finishing touches on this special toy.

SIZE
One size

FINISHED MEASUREMENTS
Height: 9 in. / 23 cm
Wingspan: 10 in. / 25.5 cm

YARN
Worsted weight (medium #4) yarn, shown in Sugar Bush *Bold* (100% extra fine superwash merino; 190 yd. / 176 m per 3½ oz. / 100 g ball)
Color A: Fresh Snow, 2 balls
Color B: Rockies, 1 ball
Color C: Prairie Gold, 1 ball
Color D: Georgian Grey, 1 ball

HOOK
- US D-3 / 3.25 mm crochet hook or size needed to obtain gauge

NOTIONS
- Sewing pins
- Tapestry needle
- ½ in. / 15 mm black safety eyes
- Polyester stuffing
- Pet brush or bristle brush

GAUGE
22 sts and 23 rows = 4 in. / 10 cm in sc
Gauge is not critical for a toy; just ensure the stitches are tight enough so the stuffing will not show through your finished project.

SPECIAL ABBREVIATIONS
chbp (chain bump): Turn chain to back; work into yarn strand running down center of each chain.

Continued on page 42

EYE DISCS
(MAKE 2)

Rnd 1: With A, MC 12 sc (*do not pull the circle completely closed; the safety eye will need to fit inside*); do not join—12 sc.

Rnd 2: Inc in each sc around—24 sc.

Rnd 3: Sc around.

Rnd 4: [Hdc in next sc, hdc inc in next sc] around; slip st in first hdc to join—36 hdc.

Fasten off, leaving long tail for sewing. Using a pet brush, brush out the entire circumference of the disc. Set aside.

BODY

Rnd 1: With A, MC 8 sc; do not join—8 sc.

Rnd 2: Inc around—16 sc.

Rnd 3: [Sc in next sc, inc in next sc] around—24 sc.

Rnd 4: [Sc in next 2 sc, inc in next sc] around—32 sc.

Rnd 5: Sc around.

Rnd 6: [Sc in next 3 sc, inc in next sc] around—40 sc.

Rnd 7: Sc around.

Rnd 8: [Sc in next 4 sc, inc in next sc] around—48 sc.

Rnds 9–12: Sc around.

Rnd 13: Sc in first 18 sc, ch 1, sk 1 sc, sc in next 10 sc, ch 1, sk 1 sc, sc in last 18 sc.

Rnd 14: Sc in first 18 sc, sc in ch-1 sp, sc in next 10 sc, sc in ch-1 sp, sc in last 18 sc.

Rnds 15–18: Sc around.

Rnd 19: [Sc in next 14 sc, dec over next 2 sc] around—45 sc.

Rnds 20–22: Sc around.

Place a safety eye in the center of each eye disc, then place the safety eye with the disc into the ch-1 sps created in Rnd 13. Secure with the washers included with the safety eyes. Be sure the tails of the eye discs are to the sides of the head parallel to Rnd 13. Cont working body.

Rnd 23: [Sc in next 4 sc, inc in next sc] around—54 sc.

Stuff the head firmly.

Rnds 24–28: Sc around.

Rnd 29: [Sc in next 5 sc, inc in next sc] around—63 sc.

Rnds 30–33: Sc around.

Rnd 34: [Sc in next 7 sc, dec over next 2 sc] around—56 sc.

Rnds 35–46: Sc around.

Rnd 47: [Sc in next 2 sc, dec over next 2 sc] around—42 sc.

Rnd 48: Sc around.

Rnd 49: [Sc in next sc, dec over next 2 sc] around—28 sc.

Rnd 50: [Sc in next 2 sc, dec over next 2 sc] around—21 sc.

Finish stuffing the body.

Rnd 51: [Sc in next sc, dec over next 2 sc] around—14 sc.

Rnd 52: Dec around—7 sc.

Fasten off, leaving a long tail for sewing. Sew closed.

ABOVE: Harry Potter and Hedwig in *Harry Potter and the Sorcerer's Stone*.

EYE DETAIL
(MAKE 2)

With C, ch 5. Fasten off, leaving a long tail for sewing.

LEGS (MAKE 2)

Rnd 1: With A, MC 12 sc; do not join—12 sc.

Rnd 2: [Sc in next 2 sc, inc in next sc] around—16 sc.

Rnd 3: [Sc in next sc, inc in next sc] around—24 sc.

Rnd 4: Sc around.

Rnd 5: [Sc in next sc, inc in next sc] around—36 sc.

Rnds 6–8: Sc around.

Fasten off, leaving a long tail for sewing to the body.

FEET (MAKE 2)

Rnd 1: With D, MC 8 sc; do not join—8 sc.

Rnds 2–6: Sc around.

Rnd 7: [Sc in next sc, inc in next sc] around—12 sc.

Rnd 8: [Sc in next 2 sc, inc in next sc] around—16 sc.

Rnd 9: [Sc in next 3 sc, inc in next sc] around—20 sc.

Rnds 10 and 11: Sc around.

Rnd 12: Sc in first 5 sc, sk 10 sc, sc in last 5 sc—10 sc.

Rnds 13–17: Sc around.

Rnd 18: Dec around—5 sc.

Fasten off. Sew toe closed.

Note: Stuffing feet is optional. Stuff foot here if desired.

For the other toe, attach 10 sc to the skipped sts of Rnd 12. Rep Rnds 13–17. Stuffing the feet is optional but not required. Fasten off and sew each toe closed. Hide tail in the foot, then brush out the entire foot.

WING 1

Rnd 1: With 2 strands of A held together, MC 6 sc; do not join—6 sc.

Rnd 2: Inc around—12 sc.

Rnd 3: [Sc in next sc, inc in next sc] around—18 sc.

Rnd 4: Sc around.

Rnd 5: [Sc in next 2 sc, inc in next sc] around—24 sc.

Rnd 6: [Sc in next 3 sc, inc in next sc] around—30 sc.

Rnd 7: Sc around.

Rnd 8: [Sc in next 4 sc, inc in next sc] around—36 sc.

Rnd 9: [Sc in next 5 sc, inc in next sc] around—42 sc.

Rnds 10 and 11: Sc around.

Note: Now you will create feathers by chaining and working in the chbp; do not skip the first chbp from the hook. You may need to make a looser last ch in order to comfortably fit your hook.

Rnd 12: [Sc in next sc, ch 9, turn, sc in first chbp, dc in next 7 chbp, hdc in next chbp, sc in next sc of the rnd] 4 times, [sc, ch 7, turn, sc in first chbp, dc in next 5 chbp, hdc in next chbp, sc in next sc of the rnd] twice, [sc, ch 5, turn, sc in first chbp, hdc in next 4 chbp, sc in next st of the rnd] twice, sc in last 26 sc of the rnd.

Fasten off, leaving a long tail for sewing. Fold in half so the yarn tail from creating the wing is next to the first largest feather. Lay flat and, using the yarn tail, sew the last 18 sts of Rnd 12 to the feathers, stopping at the edge of the last smallest feather. Leave the rem 8 sts to attach to the body later in the assembly process. Lightly stuff if desired.

WING 2

Rep Rnds 1–11 of Wing 1.

Rnd 12: Sc in first 26 sc, [sc in next sc, ch 5, turn, sc in first chbp, hdc in next 4 chbp, sc in next st of the rnd] twice, [sc, ch 7, turn, sc in first chbp, dc in next 5 chbp, hdc in next chbp, sc in next st of the rnd] twice, [sc, ch 9, turn, sc in first chbp, dc in next 7 chbp, hdc in next chbp, sc in next st of the rnd] 4 times.

Fasten off, leaving a long tail for sewing. Fold in half so the yarn tail from creating the wing is next to the first largest feather. Lay flat and, using the yarn tail, sew the first 18 sts

of Rnd 12 to the feathers, stopping at the edge of the last smallest feather. Leave the remaining 8 sts to attach to the body later in the assembly process. Lightly stuff if desired.

TAIL FEATHERS A (MAKE 2)

Note: Turning ch at end of each row does not count as a st.

With 2 strands of A held together, ch 14.

Row 1: Hdc in each chbp, ch 1, turn—14 hdc.

Row 2: Hdc in first 11 hdc, hdc inc in next hdc, ch 1, turn (sk last 2 hdc)—13 hdc.

Row 3: Hdc in first 12 hdc, hdc inc in next hdc, ch 1, turn—14 hdc.

Rows 4–7: Rep Rows 2 and 3.

Fasten off, leaving a long tail for sewing to the body.

Mirror the tails, creating a V shape and slightly overlapping one row. Tack the two pieces together where the two inner tails overlap. Leave long tails for sewing.

TAIL FEATHERS B (MAKE 2)

Note: Turning ch at end of each row does not count as a st.

With a strand of A and D held together, ch 14.

Row 1: Working in chbps, hdc in each chbp, ch 1, turn—14 hdc.

Row 2: Hdc in first 11 hdc, hdc inc in next hdc, ch 1, turn (sk last 2 hdc)—13 hdc.

Row 3: Hdc in first 12 hdc, hdc inc in next hdc, ch 1, turn—14 hdc.

Rows 4 and 5: Rep Rows 2 and 3.

Fasten off, leaving a long tail for sewing to the body.

ASSEMBLY

LEGS

Align the tails of yarn from the legs to the last rnd of the body. Pin in place. The outer opposite edge of the leg will land about 9 rnds up the body. This will create a V shape in both the front and back of the body. Attach legs to the bottom of the body, stuffing legs before completely closing.

BODY BRUSHING

Thoroughly brush out the head (move eye discs around to protect the safety eyes from scratches), chest, and the bottom of the owl (both legs and lower stomach where the legs attach). These should be as fluffy as you can make them. Make sure the areas around and behind the eye discs are also brushed.

FEET

Place feet directly under the legs with the two toes in front so the owl stands on her own. Use pins to help keep feet aligned. Sew feet to the legs using a length of D or A.

Note: Before continuing assembly, it's highly suggested to block the wings and tail feathers to keep feathers from curling too much.

WINGS

Using the rem tail of yarn from sewing the wing closed, attach the rem 8 sts to the body between Rnds 20 and 23.

EYE DISCS

Using the tail of the eye disc at Rnd 13, sew 10 sts of the last rnd from the side of the head to below the eye. The bottom outer corner of each eye disc is the only edge sewn down;

the rest of the sewing will be along Rnd 3 of the eye disc. Pinch the inner portions of the discs together in the center of the face with WSs together. Sew these two discs together with 3–4 sts to create the bridge of the owl's nose. With the remainder of the yarn, tack the top of the eye disc above the eye. Secure and hide ends.

EYE DETAIL

Place the eye detail on the outer corner of the eye. Using the tail, sew every other chbp to the edge of the eye. Rep on the second eye.

TAIL FEATHERS

Mirror Tail Feathers B, placing them side by side. Sew Tail Feathers B on the back of the body about 3–4 rows above the topmost seam of the legs. Bring Tail Feathers B to meet about halfway down and tack them together, slightly overlapping one row. Sew Tail Feathers A about 3–4 rows above Tail Feathers B.

BEAK

Using B, create a skinny triangle starting underneath the eye discs between the eyes extending 4 rnds down. The bottom of the beak should be approximately in line with the bottom of the eye discs.

Extra Details: Using D for the chest and B for the wings, embroider more feathers. Touch up any brushing from sewing pieces on the legs or face. Embroider B and D around the eyes for more detail.

"I CAN'T LET YOU OUT, HEDWIG! I'M NOT ALLOWED TO USE MAGIC OUTSIDE OF SCHOOL."

Harry Potter, *Harry Potter and the Chamber of Secrets*

DOBBY

Designed by **LEE SARTORI**

SKILL LEVEL ⚡⚡

Dobby is a house-elf who serves the Malfoys, a Dark wizarding family. Going against his masters, Dobby finds, warns, and befriends Harry Potter in *Harry Potter and the Chamber of Secrets*, becoming a loyal and trustworthy ally to Harry throughout the films. Dobby's servitude to the Malfoys ends abruptly when he is accidentally given a sock by Lucius Malfoy, which sets him free, according to wizarding law. With his freedom, Dobby sets out to live a happy life and help his friends in any situation he can.

In the films, Dobby was brought to life digitally as well as by using dummies in order to integrate the CG model with the live-action elements of the scenes. "People had to relate to Dobby, to empathize with him when he died," says visual effects supervisor Tim Burke. "If Dobby didn't look like he had a soul, we would have lost any sadness at the end of the film. Toby Jones gave us a brilliant performance to reference, and then the excellent animators at Framestore rendered a highly emotional moment just beautifully."

Our Dobby is worked in a variety of pieces that are then assembled. Each piece is worked in continuous rounds with simple shaping to emphasize Dobby's features. A gentle rag robe wraps Dobby up, while bright green craft eyes bring him to life.

SIZE
One size

FINISHED MEASUREMENTS
Height: 21 in. / 53.5 cm

YARN
DK weight (light #3), shown in Berroco *Arno* (57% cotton, 43% merino wool; 159 yd. / 145 m per 1¾ oz. / 50 g ball)
Color A: #5003 Biscotti, 4 balls
Color B: #5002 Cream, 3 balls

HOOK
- US C-2 / 2.75 mm crochet hook or size needed to obtain gauge

NOTIONS
- Tapestry needle
- Stitch marker
- Polyester stuffing
- 1 in. / 25 mm green safety eyes
- Pipe cleaner
- ¼ in. / 6 mm diameter wooden dowel, 6 in. / 15 cm long

GAUGE
10 sts and 12 rows = 2 in. / 5 cm in sc
Gauge is not critical for a toy; just ensure the stitches are tight enough so the stuffing will not show through your finished project.

NOTES
- Pieces are worked in continuous rounds; do not join.

HEAD

With A, make a magic ring.

Rnd 1: 6 sc in ring—6 sc.

Rnd 2: 2 sc in each st around—12 sc.

Rnd 3: [2 sc in next sc, sc in next sc] around—18 sc.

Rnd 4: [2 sc in next sc, sc in next 2 sc] around—24 sc.

Rnd 5: [2 sc in next sc, sc in next 3 sc] around—30 sc.

Rnd 6: [2 sc in next sc, sc in next 4 sc] around—36 sc.

Rnd 7: [2 sc in next sc, sc in next 5 sc] around—42 sc.

Rnd 8: [2 sc in next sc, sc in next 6 sc] around—48 sc.

Rnd 9: [2 sc in next sc, sc in next 7 sc] around—54 sc.

Rnd 10: [2 sc in next sc, sc in next 8 sc] around—60 sc.

Rnd 11: [2 sc in next sc, sc in next 9 sc] around—66 sc.

Rnd 12: [2 sc in next sc, sc in next 10 sc] around—72 sc.

Rnd 13: [2 sc in next sc, sc in next 11 sc] around—78 sc.

Rnd 14: [2 sc in next sc, sc in next 12 sc] around—84 sc.

Rnd 15: [2 sc in next sc, sc in next 13 sc] around—90 sc.

Rnds 16–34: Sc in each sc around—90 sc.

Rnd 35: [Sc in next 13 sc, sc2tog over next 2 sc] around—84 sc.

Rnd 36: [Sc in next 12 sc, sc2tog over next 2 sc] around—78 sc.

Rnd 37: [Sc in next 11 sc, sc2tog over next 2 sc] around—72 sc.

Rnd 38: [Sc in next 10 sc, sc2tog over next 2 sc] around—66 sc.

Rnd 39: [Sc in next 9 sc, sc2tog over next 2 sc] around—60 sc.

Rnd 40: [Sc in next 8 sc, sc2tog over next 2 sc] around—54 sc.

Rnd 41: [Sc in next 7 sc, sc2tog over next 2 sc] around—48 sc.

Rnd 42: [Sc in next 6 sc, sc2tog over next 2 sc] around—42 sc.

Using pipe cleaner, insert from inside head through Rnd 23, and back inside head. Sk approx 14 sts of Rnd 23, pull end of pipe cleaner out and back inside again. Twist ends of pipe cleaner to cinch eyes and create dents. Stuff head lightly.

Rnd 43: [Sc in next 5 sc, sc2tog over next 2 sc] around—36 sc.

Rnd 44: [Sc in next 4 sc, sc2tog over next 2 sc] around—30 sc.

Rnd 45: [Sc in next 3 sc, sc2tog over next 2 sc] around—24 sc.

Rnd 46: [Sc in next 2 sc, sc2tog over next 2 sc] around—18 sc.

Rnd 47: [Sc in next sc, sc2tog over next 2 sc] around—12 sc.

Rnd 48: [Sc2tog] around—6 sc.

Fasten off.

EYES (MAKE 2)

With B, ch 2.

Rnd 1: 6 sc in 2nd ch from hook—6 sc.

Rnd 2: 2 sc in each sc around—12 sc.

Rnd 3: [2 sc in next sc, sc in next sc] around—18 sc.

Rnd 4: [2 sc in next sc, sc in next 2 sc] around—24 sc.

Rnd 5: [Sc in next 2 sc, sc2tog over next 2 sc] around—18 sc.

Fasten off, leaving a long tail for sewing. Insert eye in center of Rnd 1.

With A, join to any st around.

Rnd 6: Ch 1 (*does not count as a st*), [fpsc in next 2 sc, fphdc in next 5 sc, fpsc in next 2 sc] twice.

Rnd 7: 2 fphdc in each st around—36 fphdc.

Rnd 8: Hdc in each fphdc around—36 hdc.

Fasten off. Weave in ends. Fold Rnds 6–8 upward toward eye.

Attach eyes to indented sockets, leaving Rnds 6–8 of eyes upturned. Pinch approx 10 rnds of the fabric above each eye to form eyebrows and sew the folds with A to secure.

MOUTH

With A, ch 10.

Rnd 1: Sc in 2nd ch from hook and in next 7 ch, 3 sc in next ch, rotate work to sc in next 8 ch, 3 sc in last ch—22 sc.

Rnd 2: Sc in first 9 sc, 3 sc in next sc, sc in next 10 sc, 3 sc in next sc, sc in last sc—26 sc.

Rnd 3: Sc around.

Rnd 4: Sc in first 10 sc, 3 sc in next sc, sc in next 12 sc, 3 sc in next sc, sc in last 2 sc—30 sc.

Rnd 5: Sc around.

Rnd 6: Sc in first 11 sc, 3 sc in next sc, sc in next 14 sc, 3 sc in next sc, sc in last 3 sc—34 sc.

Rnd 7: Sc around.

Rnd 8: Sc in first 12 sc, 2 sc in next sc, sc in next 16 sc, 2 sc in next sc, sc in last 4 sc—36 sc.

Rnd 9: [2 hdc in next sc, hdc in next 5 sc] around—42 hdc.

Fasten off, leaving a long tail for sewing. Stuff lightly.

NOSE

With A, ch 2.

Rnd 1: 3 sc in 2nd ch from hook—3 sc.

Rnd 2: 2 sc in first sc, sc in last 2 sc—4 sc.

Rnd 3: 2 sc in first sc, sc in last 3 sc—5 sc.

Rnd 4: 2 sc in first sc, sc in last 4 sc—6 sc.

Rnd 5: [2 sc in next sc, sc in next sc] around—9 sc.

Rnd 6: [2 sc in next sc, sc in next 2 sc] around—12 sc.

Rnd 7: [2 sc in next sc, sc in next sc] around—18 sc.

Rnds 8–13: Sc around.

Rnd 14: Sc in first 6 sc, leave rem 12 sts unworked—6 sc.

Rnd 15: Sc around (*nostril made*).

Fasten off, leaving a tail for sewing.

Rnd 16: Working on skipped sts of Rnd 14, sk 3 sts, sc in next 6 sc, leave 3 sts unworked—6 sc.

Rnd 17: Sc around (*nostril made*).

Fasten off, leaving a long tail for sewing.

Row 18: Working on skipped sts from Rnd 14, join in same st as nostril, sc in join, sc in 3 skipped sts, sc in same st as opposite nostril, turn—5 sc.

Rows 19–32: Ch 1, sc across, turn—5 sc.

Fasten off, leave a long tail for sewing. Sew each nostril shut. Stuff nose lightly.

"Harry Potter must not go back to Hogwarts School of Witchcraft and Wizardry this year!"

Dobby, *Harry Potter and the Chamber of Secrets*

LEFT: Dobby tries to prevent Harry from going back to Hogwarts in *Harry Potter and the Chamber of Secrets*.

OUTER EAR (MAKE 2)

With **A**, ch 2.

Rnd 1: 3 sc in 2nd ch from hook—3 sc.

Rnd 2: 2 sc in first sc, sc in last 2 sc—4 sc.

Rnd 3: 2 sc in first sc, sc in last 3 sc—5 sc.

Rnd 4: 2 sc in first sc, sc in last 4 sc—6 sc.

Rnds 5–21: Sc around.

Rnd 22: 2 sc in each sc around—12 sc.

Rnd 23: [2 sc in next sc, sc in next sc] around—18 sc.

Rnd 24: [2 sc in next sc, sc in next 2 sc] around—24 sc.

Rnd 25: [2 sc in next sc, sc in next 3 sc] around—30 sc.

Fasten off, leaving a long tail for sewing.

INNER EAR (MAKE 2)

With **A**, ch 2.

Rnd 1: 6 sc in 2nd ch from hook—6 sc.

Rnd 2: 2 sc in each st around—12 sc.

Rnd 3: [2 sc in next sc, sc in next sc] around—18 sc.

Rnd 4: [2 sc in next sc, sc in next 2 sc] around—24 sc.

Rnd 5: [2 sc in next sc, sc in next 3 sc] around—30 sc.

Rnd 6: 2 sc in first sc, sc in next 8 sc, 2 sc in next sc, sc in next 5 sc, hdc in next 5 sc, ch 1, hdc in next 5 sc, sc in last 5 sc—22 sc, 10 hdc, 1 ch-1 sp.

Rnd 7: 2 sc in first sc, sc in next 10 sc, 2 sc in next sc, sc in next 5 sc, hdc in next 5 hdc, (hdc, ch 1, hdc) in ch-1 sp, hdc in next 5 hdc, sc in last 5 sc—24 sc, 12 hdc, 1 ch-1 sp.

Rnd 8: 2 sc in first sc, sc in next 12 sc, 2 sc in next sc, sc in next 5 sc, hdc in next 6 hdc, (hdc, ch 1, hdc) in ch-1 sp, hdc in next 6 hdc, sc in last 5 sc—26 sc, 14 hdc, 1 ch-1 sp.

Fasten off, leaving a long tail for sewing.

EAR DETAIL (MAKE 2)

Row 1: With **A**, and leaving a long tail, ch 20. Fasten off. Sew ear detail to inner ear, forming a U shape around Rnd 4 of inner ear.

BODY

With B, make a magic ring.

Rnd 1: 6 sc in ring—6 sc.

Rnd 2: 2 sc in each st around—12 sc.

Rnd 3: [2 sc in next sc, sc in next sc] around—18 sc.

Rnd 4: [2 sc in next sc, sc in next 2 sc] around—24 sc.

Rnd 5: [2 sc in next sc, sc in next 3 sc] around—30 sc.

Rnd 6: [2 sc in next sc, sc in next 4 sc] around—36 sc.

Rnd 7: [2 sc in next sc, sc in next 5 sc] around—42 sc.

Rnd 8: [2 sc in next sc, sc in next 6 sc] around—48 sc.

Rnd 9: [2 sc in next sc, sc in next 7 sc] around—54 sc.

Rnd 10: [2 sc in next sc, sc in next 8 sc] around—60 sc.

Rnds 11–32: Sc around.

Change to A.

Rnds 33–35: Sc around.

Rnd 36: [Sc in next 8 sc, sc2tog over next 2 sc] around—54 sc.

Rnd 37: [Sc in next 7 sc, sc2tog over next 2 sc] around—48 sc.

Rnd 38: [Sc in next 6 sc, sc2tog over next 2 sc] around—42 sc.

Rnd 39: [Sc in next 5 sc, sc2tog over next 2 sc] around—36 sc.

Rnd 40: [Sc in next 4 sc, sc2tog over next 2 sc] around—30 sc.

Stuff body firmly.

Rnd 41: [Sc in next 3 sc, sc2tog over next 2 sc] around—24 sc.

Rnd 42: [Sc in next 2 sc, sc2tog over next 2 sc] around—18 sc.

Rnds 43-46: Sc around.

Fasten off, leave a long tail for sewing. Stuff body firmly. Insert wooden dowel in neck, and up into head for neck support. Insert approximately 2 rnds of head into body, then sew body to head.

ROBE (MAKE 2)

With B, ch 61.

Row 1: Hdc in 2nd ch from hook and in each ch across, turn—60 hdc.

Row 2: Ch 1 (*does not count as a st*), hdc in next 40 sts, leaving rem 20 left unworked (*tie made*), turn—40 hdc.

Rows 3-22: Ch 1, hdc across, turn.

Fasten off, weave in ends.

After completing the second robe panel, match ties together at the top of each panel, then seam the sides starting at the bottom of either side. Sl st through both panels in the first 25 sts, sl st on back panel for 10 sts

(*armhole made*), sl st through both panels in last 5 sts. Fasten off. Tie the ties together in a bow. Place robe on body with the tie on the right shoulder.

UPPER ARMS AND LEGS (MAKE 4)

With A, make a magic ring.

Rnd 1: 6 sc in ring—6 sc.

Rnd 2: 2 sc in each st around—12 sc.

Rnd 3: [2 sc in next sc, sc in next sc] around—18 sc.

Rnds 4-20: Sc around.

Fasten off, leaving a long tail for sewing. Stuff firmly.

FEET (MAKE 2)

With A, make a magic ring.

Rnd 1: 6 sc in ring—6 sc.

Rnd 2: 2 sc in each st around—12 sc.

Rnd 3: [2 sc in next sc, sc in next sc] around—18 sc.

Rnd 4: [2 sc in next sc, sc in next 2 sc] around—24 sc.

Rnd 5: [2 sc in next sc, sc in next 3 sc] around—30 sc.

Rnd 6: [2 sc in next sc, sc in next 4 sc] around—36 sc.

Rnd 7: Sc around.

Rnd 8: [Sc2tog over next 2 sc, sc in next 16 sc] twice—34 sc.

Rnd 9: [Sc2tog over next 2 sc, sc in next 15 sc] twice—32 sc.

Rnd 10: [Sc2tog over next 2 sc, sc in next 14 sc] twice—30 sc.

Rnd 11: [Sc2tog over next 2 sc, sc in next 13 sc] twice—28 sc.

Rnd 12: [Sc2tog over next 2 sc, sc in next 12 sc] twice—26 sc.

Rnd 13: [Sc2tog over next 2 sc, sc in next 11 sc] twice—24 sc.

Rnds 14-18: Sc around.

Rnd 19: Sc in first 3 sc, ch 6, sk 6 sts, sc in last 15 sc—18 sc, 6 ch.

Rnd 20: Sc in each sc and ch around—24 sc.

Rnd 21: Sc around.

Rnd 22: [Sc in next 2 sc, sc2tog over next 2 sc] around—18 sts.

Rnd 23: [Sc in next sc, sc2tog over next 2 sc] around—12 sts.

Rnd 24: [Sc2tog] around—6 sts.

Fasten off. Stuff lightly. Sew rem sts closed.

LOWER LEG (MAKE 2)

Join yarn to first skipped sc from Rnd 19 at top of foot.

Rnd 25: Sc in 6 skipped sc, sc in next 6 sc; join into the rnd—12 sc.

Rnds 26-42: Sc around.

Fasten off, leaving a long tail for sewing. Stuff firmly.

BIG TOE (MAKE 2)

With A, make a magic ring.

Rnd 1: 6 sc in ring.

Rnd 2: 2 sc in each st around—12 sc.

Rnds 3-6: Sc around.

Fasten off, leaving a long tail for sewing.

MIDDLE TOES (MAKE 6)

With A, make a magic ring.
Rnd 1: 6 sc in ring.
Rnd 2: [2 sc in next sc, sc in next sc] around—9 sc.
Rnd 3: Sc around.
Fasten off, leaving a long tail for sewing.

BABY TOE (MAKE 2)

With A, make a magic ring.
Rnd 1: 6 sc in ring—6 sc.
Rnd 2: Sc around.
Fasten off, leaving a long tail for sewing.

HAND AND LOWER ARM (MAKE 2)

With A, make a magic ring.
Rnd 1: 6 sc in ring.
Rnd 2: 2 sc in each sc around—12 sc.
Rnd 3: [2 sc in next sc, sc in next sc] around—18 sc.
Rnd 4: [2 sc in next sc, sc in next 2 sc] around—24 sc.
Rnd 5: [2 sc in next sc, sc in next 3 sc] around—30 sc.
Rnd 6: Sc around.
Rnd 7: [Sc2tog over next 2 sc, sc in next 13 sc] twice—28 sc.
Rnd 8: Sc around.
Rnd 9: [Sc2tog over next 2 sc, sc in next 12 sc] twice—26 sc.
Rnd 10: Sc around.
Rnd 11: [Sc2tog over next 2 sc, sc in next 11 sc] twice—24 sc.
Stuff hand lightly.
Rnds 12–28: Sc around.
Stuff lower arm firmly.
Fasten off, leaving a long tail for sewing.

PINKY FINGER (MAKE 2)

With A, make a magic ring.
Rnd 1: 6 sc in ring.
Rnds 2–5: Sc around.
Fasten off, leaving a long tail for sewing.

CENTER FINGERS (MAKE 6)

With A, make a magic ring.
Rnd 1: 6 sc in ring.
Rnds 2–7: Sc around.
Fasten off, leaving a long tail for sewing.

THUMB (MAKE 2)

With A, make a magic ring.
Rnd 1: 6 sc in ring.
Rnd 2: [2 sc in next sc, sc in next sc] around—9 sc.
Rnds 3–6: Sc around.
Fasten off, leaving a long tail for sewing.

ASSEMBLY

Sew outer ears to side of head just above eyebrows. Sew inner ear to outer ear and attach to side of face. Bottom of inner ear should fold in slightly. Sew 1 arm to each side of body at shoulders. Sew legs to bottom of body. Sew lower leg to upper leg at an angle, pointing down. Sew big toe to top inside edge of foot. Sew middle toes 3 toes to top middle of each foot. Sew baby toe to top outside edge of foot. Sew the lower arm to the upper arm at a right angle to elbow. Using a length of A approximately 8 in. / 10.5 cm long, tie around wrist to cinch wrist tightly at Rnd 12. Sew fingers and thumb inline at top edge of hand. Sew mouth piece to lower face. Sew nose in place between eyes and above mouth.
Weave in ends.

PATRONUS

Designed by **JILLIAN HEWITT**

SKILL LEVEL ⚡⚡

Expecto Patronum is one of the most famous and powerful defensive spells in the wizarding world, usually used to repel Dementors. When the charm is cast, a Patronus erupts from the user's wand, taking on the form of a creature or animal with which the witch or wizard shares a deep affinity. Harry learns to cast a Patronus with the help of Professor Lupin in *Harry Potter and the Prisoner of Azkaban*. Later, Harry learns that his mother's Patronus was a doe, as is Professor Snape's, who casts it as a result of his lifelong love for her. It is Snape's Patronus that leads Harry to the sword of Gryffindor in *Harry Potter and the Deathly Hallows – Part 1*, one of the many instances of Snape coming to Harry's aid, unbeknownst to the young wizard.

The design of this Patronus doe is made in a shimmery blue yarn to capture the ethereal qualities of the Patronuses in the Harry Potter films. After you've crocheted its easy shapes and seamed them together, add a safety eye as the finishing touch to complete this elegant amigurumi.

SIZE
One size

FINISHED MEASUREMENTS
Height: 7½ in. / 19 cm (excluding antlers)
Width: 5 in. / 12.5 cm

YARN
DK weight (light #3) yarn, shown in Lion Brand *Truboo* (100% rayon from bamboo; 241 yd. / 220 m per 3½ oz. / 100 g skein)
Color A: #105 Light Blue, 1 skein
Color B: #149 Silver, small amount

HOOK
- US B-1 / 2.25 mm crochet hook or size needed to obtain gauge

NOTIONS
- ¼ in. / 6 mm black safety eye
- Polyester stuffing
- Stitch marker
- Tapestry needle

GAUGE
9 sts and 9 rows = 1 in. / 2.5 cm in sc
Gauge is not critical for a toy; just ensure the stitches are tight enough so the stuffing will not show through your finished project.

Continued on page 54

- The amigurumi is worked in flat panels from the bottom up.
- Three of the four legs are assembled first by crocheting two panels, then holding both panels together and single crocheting around the edges. The legs are numbered L1 through L4 from left to right.
- The fourth leg and the body are worked as one panel. The body is assembled by holding both panels together and single crocheting around the edges. The ear, tail and remaining legs are stitched into the panels during assembly. The piece is then stuffed. Optional antlers are stitched on at the end.
- When working on the front panel, yarn tails should remain on the back. When working on the back panel, yarn tails should be on the front, so that all yarn tails are facing inside when the panels are lined up and joined.
- The chain 1 at the end of each row does not count as a stitch.
- To change colors, work the last stitch before color change as follows: Insert hook into stitch, yarn over and pull up a loop; with new color, yarn over and pull up a loop. Continue to work first stitch of new color as usual.

FIRST LEG (L1)

With A, ch 4.
Row 1: Sc in 2nd ch from hook and in each ch across, ch 1, turn—3 sc.
Rows 2–8: Sc in each sc, ch 1, turn.
Row 9: Sc in first 2 sc, inc in last sc, ch 1, turn—4 sc.
Row 10: Sc in each sc across, ch 1, turn.
Row 11: Dec over first 2 sc, sc in last 2 sc, ch 1, turn—3 sc.
Rows 12–16: Sc in each sc across, ch 1, turn.
Row 17: Sc in first 2 sc, inc in last sc, ch 1, turn—4 sc.
Rows 18 and 19: Sc in each sc across, ch 1, turn.
Row 20: Inc in first sc, sc in last 3 sc, ch 1, turn—5 sc.
Row 21: Sc in each sc across, ch 1, turn.
Row 22: Sc in first 3 sc, dec over last 2 sc, ch 1, turn—4 sc.
Row 23: [Dec] twice over first 4 sc, work a sc into last st of the last dec, ch 1, turn—3 sc.
Row 24: Inc in first sc, dec over last 2 sc, ch 1, turn.
Row 25: Sc3tog—1 sc.
Fasten off.
Rep Rows 1–25 for second L1 panel. Place panels together with all edges lined up, ensuring the starting yarn tails are on the left. Insert hook into any st at the top left side of the leg through both panels. Sc along the edge of both panels to join, stopping at the bottom of the panel (the hoof), then work the following into each corner:
Corner: (Sc, ch 1, sc) in same st.
Cont crocheting up the opposite side and across the top to join the panels, stuffing after every 3 or 4 sts. Top up stuffing. Sl st to beg st to close. Fasten off. Set aside for later.

SECOND LEG (L2)

With A, ch 4.
Row 1: Sc in 2nd ch from hook and in each ch across, ch 1, turn—3 sc.
Rows 2–8: Sc in each sc, ch 1, turn.
Row 9: Inc in first sc, sc in last 2 sc, ch 1, turn—4 sc.
Row 10: Sc in each sc across, ch 1, turn.
Row 11: Sc in first 2 sc, dec over last 2 sc, ch 1, turn—3 sc.
Rows 12–14: Sc in each st across, ch 1, turn.
Row 15: Inc in first sc, sc in next 2 sc, ch 1, turn—4 sc.
Row 16: Dec over first 2 sc, sc in last 2 sc, ch 1, turn—3 sc.
Row 17: Sc in each sc across, ch 1, turn.
Row 18: Sc in first 2 sc, inc in last sc, ch 1, turn—4 sc.
Rows 19 and 20: Sc in each sc across, ch 1, turn.
Row 21: Sc in first 3 sc, inc in last sc, ch 1, turn—5 sc.
Rows 22 and 23: Sc in each sc across, ch 1, turn.
Row 24: Inc in first sc, sc in next 3 sc, inc in last sc, ch 1, turn—7 sc.
Row 25: Sc in each sc across, ch 1, turn.
Row 26: Inc in first sc, sc in last 6 sc, ch 1, turn—8 sc.
Row 27: Sc in first 7 sc, inc in last sc, ch 1, turn—9 sc.
Row 28: Sc in first 8 sc, inc in last sc, ch 1, turn—10 sc.
Rows 29 and 30: Sc in each sc across.
Row 31: Sc in first 9 sc, inc in last sc, ch 1, turn—11 sc.
Row 32: Sc in first 9 sc, dec over last 2 sc, ch 1, turn—10 sc.
Row 33: Sc in each sc across.
Fasten off.
Rep Rows 1–33 for second L2 panel. Place panels together with all edges lined up, ensuring the starting yarn tails are on the left. Insert hook into any st at the top left side of the leg through both panels. Sc along the edge of both panels to join, stopping at the bottom of the panel (the

ABOVE: Luna Lovegood practices her Patronus Charm during a meeting of Dumbledore's Army in *Harry Potter and the Order of the Phoenix.*

hoof), then work the following into each corner:

Corner: (Sc, ch 1, sc) in same st.

Cont crocheting up the opposite side and across the top to join the panels, stuffing after every 3 or 4 sts. Top up stuffing. Sl st to beg st to close. Fasten off. Set aside for later.

THIRD LEG (L3)

With A, ch 4.

Row 1: Sc in 2nd ch from hook and in each ch across, ch 1, turn—3 sc.

Row 2: Dec over first 2 sc, inc in last sc, ch 1, turn.

Row 3: Sc in first sc, dec over last 2 sc, ch 1, turn—2 sc.

Row 4: Sc in each sc, ch 1, turn.

Row 5: Sc, insert hook into same st and work a dec across current and next sc, ch 1, turn.

Row 6: Sc in each sc, ch 1, turn.

Rows 7–9: Rep Rows 5 and 6, then rep Row 5 again.

Row 10: Sc in first sc, inc in last sc, ch 1, turn—3 sc.

Row 11: Sc in first sc, dec over last 2 sc, ch 1, turn—2 sc.

Row 12: Sc in first sc, inc in last sc, ch 1, turn—3 sc.

Row 13: Sc in each sc across, ch 1, turn.

Row 14: Sc in first 2 sc, inc in last sc, ch 1, turn—4 sc.

Row 15: Inc in first sc, sc in last 3 sc, ch 1, turn—5 sc.

Row 16: Sc in each sc across, ch 1, turn.

Row 17: Sc in first 4 sc, inc in last sc, ch 1, turn—6 sc.

Row 18: Inc in first sc, sc in next 3 sc, dec over last 2 sc, ch 1, turn.

Row 19: Dec over first 2 sc, sc in next 2 sc, inc in each of last 2 sc, ch 1, turn—7 sc.

Row 20: Inc in first sc, sc in last 6 sc, ch 1, turn—8 sc.

Row 21: Dec over first 2 sc, sc in last 6 sc—7 sc.

Fasten off.

Rep Rows 1–21 for second L3 panel. Place panels together with all edges lined up, ensuring the starting yarn tails are on the left. Insert hook into any st at the top left side of the leg through both panels. Sc along the edge of both panels to join, stopping at the bottom of the panel (the hoof), then work the following into each corner:

Corner: (Sc, ch 1, sc) in same st.

Cont crocheting up the opposite side and across the top to join the panels, stuffing after every 3 or 4 sts. Top up stuffing. Sl st to beg st to close. Fasten off. Set aside for later.

TAIL

With A, ch 2.

Row 1: Sc in 2nd ch from hook, ch 1, turn—1 sc.

Row 2: (3 sc) in same st, ch 1, turn—3 sc.

Rows 3–5: Sc in each sc across, ch 1, turn.

Row 6: Sc in each sc across.

Fasten off.

Rep Rows 1–6 for second tail panel. Place panels together with all edges lined up, ensuring the starting yarn tails are on the left. Insert hook into any st at the top left side of the tail through both panels. Sc along the edge of both panels to join, stopping at the tip of the tail, then work the following into the tip:

Tip of tail: (Sc, ch 2, sc) in same st.

Cont crocheting around the opposite side and across the wide end of the tail to join the panels. Stuff. Sl st to beg st to close. Fasten off. Set aside for later.

EAR

With A, ch 7.

Row 1: Sc in 2nd ch from hook and in each ch across, ch 1, turn—6 sc.

Row 2: Dec over first 2 sc, sc in last 4 sc, ch 1, turn—5 sc.

Row 3: Sc in each sc across, ch 1, turn.

Row 4: Dec over first 2 sc, sc in last 3 sc, ch 1, turn—4 sc.

Row 5: Sc in first 2 sc, dec over last 2 sc, ch 1, turn—3 sc.

Row 6: Dec over first 2 sc, sc in last sc, ch 1, turn—2 sc.

Row 7: Sc in first sc, leave rem st unworked—1 sc.

Fasten off.

Rep Rows 1–7 for second ear panel. Place panels together with all edges lined up, ensuring the starting yarn tails are on the left. Insert hook into any st at the top left side of the ear through both panels. Sc along the edge of both panels to join, stopping at the bottom of the panel, then work the following into each corner:

Corner: (Sc, ch 1, sc) in same st.

Cont crocheting up the opposite side to join the panels, stuffing after every 3 or 4 sts. When you reach the tip of the ear, work the following:

Tip of ear: (Sc, ch 2, sc) in same st.

Top up stuffing. Sl st to beg st to close. Fasten off. Set aside for later.

BODY

HEAD

With A, ch 4.

Row 1: Sc in 2nd ch from hook and in each ch across, ch 9, turn—3 sc, 9 chs.

Row 2: Sc in 2nd ch from hook and in each ch, sc in next 2 sc, inc in last sc, ch 1, turn—12 sc.

Row 3: Sc in first 11 sc, inc in last sc, ch 1, turn—13 sc.

Row 4: Inc in first sc, sc in next 10 sc, dec over last 2 sc, ch 1, turn.

Row 5: Dec over first 2 sc, sc in next 10 sc, inc in last sc, ch 1, turn.

Rows 6 and 7: Sc in each sc across.

Row 8: Dec over first 2 sc, sc in next 9 sc, dec across last 2 sc—11 sc.

Fasten off. Set aside.

FOURTH LEG (L4)

With A, ch 5.

Row 1: Sc in 2nd ch from hook and in each ch across, ch 1, turn—4 sc.

Row 2: Sc in each sc across, ch 1, turn.

Row 3: Dec over first 2 sc, sc in last 2 sc, ch 1, turn—3 sc.

Row 4: Sc in each sc across, ch 1, turn.

Row 5: Dec over first 2 sc, sc in last sc, ch 1, turn—2 sc.

Row 6: Sc, insert hook into same st and work a dec across current and last sc, ch 1, turn.

Row 7: Sc in each sc across, ch 1, turn.

Row 8: Sc, insert hook into same st and work a dec across current and last sc, ch 1, turn.

Rows 9–11: Sc in each sc across, ch 1, turn.

Row 12: Inc in first sc, sc in last sc, ch 1, turn—3 sc.

Rows 13–15: Sc in each sc across, ch 1, turn.

Row 16: Inc in first sc, dec over last 2 sc, ch 1, turn.

Row 17: Sc in each sc across, ch 1, turn.

Row 18: Inc in first sc, dec over last 2 sc, ch 1, turn.

Row 19: Sc in first 2 sc, inc in last sc, ch 1, turn—4 sc.

Row 20: Inc in first sc, sc in last 3 sc, ch 1, turn—5 sc.

Row 21: Sc in each sc across, ch 1, turn.

Row 22: Sc in first 3 sc, dec over last 2 sc, ch 1, turn—4 sc.

Row 23: Sc in each sc across, ch 1, turn.

Row 24: Sc in each sc across.

Fasten off. Set aside.

BELLY

With A, ch 17.

Row 1: Sc in 2nd ch from hook and in each ch across, ch 1, turn—16 sc.

Row 2: Inc in each of the first 2 sc, sc in next 12 sc, inc in each of the last 2 sc, ch 1, turn—20 sc.

Row 3: Inc in first sc, sc in next 18 sc, inc in last sc, ch 1, turn—22 sc.

Position L4 panel to the left of the belly panel with the finishing yarn tail of L4 on the left. Join L4 to the belly by crocheting across both pieces in the next row.

Row 4: Inc in first 2 sc of belly, sc in next 19 sc, inc in last sc of belly, sc in next 3 sc across L4 to join, inc in last sc of L4, ch 1, turn—30 sc.

Row 5: Sc in first 29 sc, inc in last sc, ch 1, turn—31 sc.

Row 6: Sc in first 30 sc, inc in last sc, ch 1, turn—32 sc.

Row 7: Sc in first 31 sc, inc in last sc, ch 1, turn—33 sc.

Row 8: Inc in first sc, sc in last 32 sc, ch 1, turn—34 sc.

Row 9: Sc in each sc across, ch 1, turn.

Row 10: Inc in first sc, sc in next 32 sc, inc in last sc, ch 1, turn—36 sc.

Row 11: Sc in first 35 sc, inc in last sc, ch 1, turn—37 sc.

Row 12: Sc in each sc across, ch 1, turn.

Row 13: Sc in first 36 sc, inc in last sc, ch 1, turn—38 sc.

Row 14: Sc in each sc across, ch 1, turn.

Row 15: Dec over first 2 sc, sc in next 35 sc, inc in last sc, ch 1, turn.

Row 16: Sc in each sc across, ch 1, turn.

Row 17: Dec over first 2 sc, sc in last 36 sc, ch 1, turn—37 sc.

Row 18: Inc in first sc, sc in next 34 sc, dec over last 2 sc, ch 1, turn.

Row 19: Dec over first 2 sc, place st marker in previous st worked, sc in last 35 sc, ch 1, turn—36 sc.

Row 20: Sc in first 18 sc, leave rem sts unworked, ch 1, turn—18 sc.

Row 21: Dec over first 2 sc, sc in last 16 sc, ch 1, turn—17 sc.

Row 22: Sc in first 12 sc, dec over next 2 sc, leave rem sts unworked, ch 1, turn—13 sc.

Row 23: Dec over first 2 sc, sc in last 11 sc, ch 1, turn—12 sc.

Row 24: Inc in first sc, sc in next 7 sc, [dec] twice over last 4 sc, ch 1, turn—11 sc.

Row 25: Sc in each sc across, ch 1, turn.

Row 26: Sc in first 9 sc, dec over last 2 sc, ch 1, turn—10 sc.

Rows 27–30: Sc in each sc across, ch 1, turn.

Row 31: Dec over first 2 sc, sc in last 8 sc, ch 1, turn—9 sc.

Row 32: Sc in first sc, insert a st marker into previous sc, sc in next 6 sc, dec over last 2 sc, ch 1, turn—8 sc.

Row 33: Sc in first 6 sc, dec over last 2 sc, ch 1, turn—7 sc.

Row 34: Sc in first 5 sc, dec over last 2 sc, ch 1, turn—6 sc.

Row 35: Dec over first 2 sc, sc in next 2 sc, dec over last 2 sc, ch 1, turn—4 sc.

Position head panel to the left of the body panel with the finishing yarn tail of the head on the left. Join head to body by crocheting across both pieces in the next row.

Row 36: Sc in first 4 sc across body, sc in next 11 sc across head to join, ch 1, turn—15 sc.

Row 37: Dec over first 2 sc, sc in next 11 sc, dec over last 2 sc; with B ch 4, turn—13 sc, 4 chs

Row 38: With B sc in 2nd ch from hook and in next 2 ch; with A sc in last 13 sc, ch 1, turn—16 sc.

Row 39: With A dec over first 2 sc, sc in next 11 sc; with B sc in next sc, inc in last 2 sc, ch 1, turn—17 sc.

Row 40: With B inc in first sc, sc in next 4 sc; with A sc in next 8 sc, [dec] twice over last 4 sc—16 sc.

Fasten off.

With the head on the right and the front facing you, insert hook into 8th st from the right and rejoin yarn.

Row 41: With A sc in first 4 sc; with B sc in last 5 sc, ch 1, turn—9 sc.

Row 42: With B inc in first sc, sc in next 4 sc; with A sc in next 2 sc, dec over last 2 sc, ch 1, turn.

Row 43: With A dec over first 2 sc, sc in next 2 sc; with B sc in last 5 sc, ch 1, turn—8 sc.

Row 44: With A sc in first sc; with B sc in next 3 sc; with A sc in next 2 sc, dec over last 2 sc, ch 1, turn—7 sc.

Row 45: With A, [dec] twice over first 4 sc, sc in last 3 sc—5 sc.

Fasten off.

With the head on the left, remove the st marker from Row 19. Insert hook into same st and work the following to complete the body panel and add a curve to the back:

Row 1: [Dec] twice over first 4 sts, sc in next 6 sc, dec over last 2 sc—9 sc.

Fasten off. Weave in ends to the back of the panel.

Rep all of the instructions in the body section to complete the second back body panel, working the entire section in A and omitting Color B. Weave in ends to the front of the back panel so that all ends are facing the inside when the panels are matched up.

ANTLERS (OPTIONAL)

With A, ch 3.

Row 1: Sc in 2nd ch from hook and in next ch, ch 1, turn—2 sc.

Rows 2–7: Sc in each sc, ch 1, turn.

Row 8: Dec over first 2 sc, insert hook into same st, sc in st, ch 1, turn.

Row 9: Sc in first sc, insert hook into same st and work a dec over current and next sc, ch 1, turn.

Row 10: Rep Row 8.

Row 11: Inc in first sc, sc in last sc, ch 1, turn—3 sc.

Row 12: Dec over first 2 sc, inc in last sc, ch 1, turn.

Row 13: Inc in first sc, dec over last 2 sc.

Fasten off. Turn piece so that it is horizontal, with the starting ch on the bottom right. Insert hook into panel between Row 7 and 8 and work the following:

Rows 1 and 2: Sc in each sc, ch 1, turn—2 sc.

Row 3: Dec over first 2 sc, insert hook into same st and work sc, ch 1, turn.

Row 4: Sc in first sc, insert hook into same st and work a dec over current and next sc.

Fasten off. Weave in ends.

Rep instructions in the antler section for second antler panel. Place both panels together. Insert hook through both panels and sc around the edges of the panels to join them. Sl st to beg st to close. Stuffing is not necessary.

Rep for second antler.

ASSEMBLY

Insert a ¼ in. / 6 mm safety eye into the front panel between Rows 6 and 7 of the head and between sts 6 and 7 counting from the left.

Cut four lengths of A yarn about 12 in. / 30 cm long each and set aside for later.

Place the two body panels together, lining up all sides. The front of the amigurumi (the side with Color B) should be facing you as you crochet around the outside to join.

JOINING BODY AND LEGS

Remove the st marker at Row 32 of both the front and back body panels. Insert hook into the same st on both panels. With A, sc along the edge of both panels to join them together. Crochet down the neck until you reach the bottom curve of the neck/belly about 7 rows up from the bottom of the belly.

Insert L1 between the two body panels. Using a length of A that was set aside earlier, stitch L1 in place between the panels by stitching through all three pieces: the front body panel, L1, and the back body panel. Tie a knot to secure. Hide the yarn tails between the panels.

Cont crocheting across the bottom of the belly. At L1, crochet in the sts of the front panel only, since this section is already sewn shut. Cont crocheting both panels together as usual until you reach about halfway across the bottom of the belly.

Using the second length of yarn that was set aside earlier, insert L3 between the panels and secure in place the same way as L1.

Cont crocheting around the panels by crocheting down L4 until you reach the bottom corners of L4 (the hoof), then work the following:

CORNER

(Sc, ch 1, sc) in same st.
Cont to crochet up the opposite side of L4, stuffing after every 3 or 4 sts, until you reach the top right corner of the body.

TAIL

Insert the tail between the panels and stitch in place using a length of yarn set aside earlier.
Cont crocheting across the back, crocheting loosely to ensure smooth lines. Stuff body firmly.

Cont crocheting up the neck, stuffing firmly after every 3 or 4 sts. Crochet around the bottom and side of the head until you reach the top right corner of the head. Stuff head firmly.

EAR

Insert the ear into the top of the head and stitch in place using a length of yarn set aside earlier.

Cont crocheting around the top of the head and the other ear, stuffing after every 3 or 4 sts.

At the tip of the ear work the following:

TIP OF EAR

(Sc, ch 2, sc) all into same st.

Cont down the ear, changing to B when you reach the B section of the ear. There will now be a small opening under the ear. Finish stuffing. Change back to A and cont crocheting around. When satisfied with the stuffing, close with a sl st to first st. Fasten off. With your tapestry needle, poke the yarn tail back inside the piece.

LEG (L2)

Stitch L2 onto the front of the piece about 5 rows down from the top of the body (so that the bottom of the legs all line up in length). Tack L1 and L2 together at hooves if desired.

Stitch on antlers, one behind each ear, if desired.

BEHIND THE MAGIC

When Harry first learns to cast a Patronus, he is only able to conjure a misty, insubstantial shield. The visual effects team tried out many different looks for the shield version of the Patronus, including tests they referred to as blow torch, Silly String, magic smoke, and liquid metal before settling on the final look.

ABOVE: A concept sketch of the doe Patronus by Adam Brockbank.

CONJURING COSTUMES

RON WEASLEY: "MUM SENT ME A DRESS!"

HARRY POTTER: "WELL, IT DOES MATCH YOUR EYES.
IS THERE A BONNET? AHA!"

Harry Potter and the Goblet of Fire

THE HOGWARTS HOUSE SCARVES

Designed by **KAELYN GUERIN**

SKILL LEVEL ⚡

Each of the houses at Hogwarts has its own animal, motto, and house colors. For the students, displaying their house colors is an important show of house pride. These colors become a defining feature in identifying their friends and expressing themselves, and are reflected in what they wear. During Quidditch matches, Gryffindors show their support for their team by wearing reds and golds, Slytherins wear silvers and greens, Hufflepuffs wear yellows and blacks, and Ravenclaws wear blues and grays. Among the most popular garments for displaying your house colors are the famous house scarves.

This crochet pattern is worked using a Tunisian crochet hook, a hook with an elongated or corded handle. Tunisian crochet is a mixture of crocheting and knitting and can give the look of a knit fabric with the ease of crochet stitches. This beginner-friendly Tunisian design is perfect for first-time Tunisian crocheters who want to show off their Hogwarts house pride.

SIZE
One size

FINISHED MEASUREMENTS
Width: 6¼ in. / 16 cm
Length: 72 in. / 183 cm

YARN
Aran weight (medium #4) yarn, shown in Cascade 220 Superwash Aran (100% superwash merino wool; 150 yd. / 137.5 m per 3½ oz. / 100 g hank), Main Color (MC), 1 hank; Contrast Color (CC), 1 hank

Colorways:

Gryffindor: #809 Really Red (MC) and #241 Sunflower (CC**)**

Hufflepuff: #821 Daffodil (MC) and #815 Black (CC)

Ravenclaw: #813 Blue Velvet (MC) and #875 Feather Grey (CC)

Slytherin: #801 Army Green (MC) and #875 Feather Grey (CC)

HOOK
• US H-8 / 5 mm Tunisian crochet hook or size needed to obtain gauge

NOTIONS
• Tapestry needle

GAUGE
16 sts and 21 rows = 4 in. / 10 cm in Tunisian knit st
Make sure to check your gauge.

Continued on page 64

NOTES

- The loop already on the hook at the beginning of the forward pass counts as the first stitch. Do not work into the first chain from the hook, but instead work into the second. This first loop also counts as the first stitch for rows after the foundation row. Insert hook into the second vertical bar to complete Tks.

- All color changes begin on the last stitch of the forward pass. Yarn over with new color and pull through last 2 loops. Complete return pass with new color. Cut yarn after color changes, leaving a tail long enough to weave in ends.

SPECIAL ABBREVIATIONS

BO (bind off): Insert your hook under the next vertical bar, yo and pull through both the vertical bar and the loop on the hook (similar to a slip stitch); rep across until 1 loop rem. Cut yarn, leaving a tail to weave through, and pull loop through to fasten off.

RetP (return pass): Yo, pull yarn through 1 loop, *yo, pull through 2 loops; rep from * until 1 loop remains on the needle.

Tks (Tunisian knit stitch): Beginning in the 2nd vertical bar, insert hook from front to back between the front and back vertical bars and draw up a loop. Rep this in each pair of vertical bars across, working under both bars on the last st.

SPECIAL TECHNIQUES
TUNISIAN CROCHET

Tunisian crochet is a technique that is worked using a Tunisian crochet hook (also called an afghan hook), a crochet hook with an elongated handle or cord. Tunisian crochet consists of two rows: the forward row and the reverse or return pass (RetP). Tunisian knit stitch results in stitches that look like knit stitches. Each ridge on the wrong side of the pattern consists of both the forward and return pass, and the work is never turned.

Tunisian crochet begins with foundations rows:

Chain desired number of stitches.

Row 1 (foundation row, forward pass): Pull up a loop in the back bump of the 2nd chain from the hook and each remaining chain, leaving loops on the hook; repeat across, do not turn.

Row 1 (foundation row, RetP): Yarn over, pull yarn through 1 loop, *yarn over, pull yarn through 2 loops; rep from * until 1 loop remains on the needle.

After foundation rows are completed, begin working in rows. Each row has a forward pass and a return pass. To work a forward pass, work Tunisian knit stitch across the row as follows:

Tks (Tunisian knit stitch): Beginning in the 2nd vertical bar, insert hook from front to back between the front and back vertical bars and draw up a loop. Repeat this in each pair of vertical bars across, working under both bars on the last stitch.

Then work a return pass as follows:

RetP (return pass): Yarn over, pull yarn through 1 loop, *yarn over, pull through 2 loops; repeat from * until 1 loop remains on the needle.

To bind off stitches when work is complete, insert your hook under the next vertical bar, yarn over, and pull through both the vertical bar and the loop on the hook (similar to a slip stitch); repeat across until 1 loop remains. Cut yarn, leaving a tail to weave through, and pull loop through to fasten off.

ABOVE: Cedric Diggory and Cho Chang in their Hufflepuff and Ravenclaw scarfs in *Harry Potter and the Goblet of Fire*.

SCARF

With MC, ch 25.

Row 1 (foundation row, Forward Pass): Pull up a loop in the back bump of the 2nd ch from the hook and each remaining ch, leaving loops on the hook; rep across, do not turn.

Row 1 (foundation row, RetP): Yo, pull yarn through 1 loop, *yo, pull yarn through 2 loops; rep from * until 1 loop remains on the needle—25 sts.

Row 2 (Forward Pass): Tks across row.

Row 2 (RetP): Yo, pull yarn through 1 loop, *yo, pull through 2 loops; rep from * until 1 loop remains on the needle—25 sts.

Rows 3–29: Rep Row 2. MC block should measure approx 5½ in. / 14 cm.

STRIPE SEQUENCE

Row 30: Work as for Row 2 until last st, yo with CC and complete st. Work RetP with CC.

Rows 31 and 32: With CC, rep Row 2.

Row 33: Work as for Row 2 until last st, yo with MC and complete st. Work RetP with MC.

Rows 34 and 35: With MC, rep Row 2.

Row 36: Rep Row 30.

Rows 37 and 38: Rep Rows 31 and 32.

Row 39: Rep Row 33.

*Work next 30 rows as Row 2. Rep Stripe sequence over next 10 rows.

Rep from *, until you have completed 10 solid blocks of MC and 9 sections of stripes. On Row 30 of the 10th MC block, BO.

FINISHING

Weave in all ends.

Cut fifty pieces of MC, each approx. 4 in. / 10 cm long. Using crochet hook and working through each edge, attach a piece of yarn in each st across. Trim evenly.

Wet or damp block work to minimize the natural curling of Tunisian pieces.

Behind the Magic

In *Harry Potter and the Sorcerer's Stone*, costume designer Judianna Makovsky undertook the task of designing the Hogwarts uniforms for the cast. She started with ideas inspired by a classic British boys' school outfit, but "then this had to be the wizarding world, too. So we gave the children traditional British school uniforms with the various colors for the different houses, and gave the professors traditional gowns, but with a twist."

"YER A WIZARD, HARRY."

Hagrid, *Harry Potter and the Sorcerer's Stone*

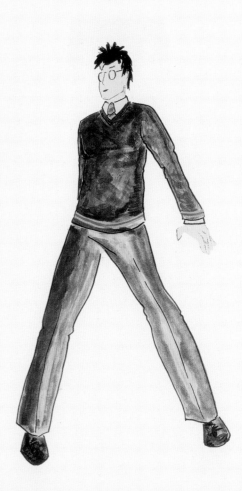

ABOVE: Daniel Radcliffe and Emma Watson film a scene as Harry and Hermione in their Gryffindor scarves in *Harry Potter and the Goblet of Fire.* RIGHT: A costume sketch of the Hogwarts uniform by Jany Temime, drawn by Laurent Guinci.

RON'S THREE BROOMSTICKS SWEATER

Designed by **SARA DUDEK**

SKILL LEVEL ⚡⚡

An outing to Hogsmeade outside Hogwarts School is a big deal for wizarding students. It means a walk into the scenic village and a visit to its many establishments, including the popular Three Broomsticks pub. For Harry, Ron, and Hermione, who visit the pub in a memorable scene in *Harry Potter and the Half-Blood Prince*, it also means taking a break from wearing their formal wizard robes and getting a chance to show off each of their personal styles.

Costume designer Jany Temime designed Ron's look with the overall Weasley aesthetic in mind. From the start, the Weasley color palette consisted of contrasting greens, oranges, and reds. And the sweater Ron wears to the Three Broomsticks is no exception.

Ron's Three Broomsticks Sweater is made with different shades of oranges, browns, navy blues, and creams. Crocheted in panels and seamed together, the sweater uses the classic granny stripe stitch to re-create the handmade look of a sweater that was likely made by Molly herself. A ribbed collar and ribbed cuffs add a cozy finishing touch to this zip-up.

SIZES

S (M, L, XL) (2X, 3X, 4X, 5X)

Shown in size M.

Instructions are written for the smallest size, with larger sizes given in parentheses; when only one number is given, it applies to all sizes.

FINISHED MEASUREMENTS

Bust/Chest: 36 (40, 44, 48) (52, 56, 60, 64) in. / 91.5 (101.5, 112, 122) (132, 142, 152.5, 162.5) cm

Length (Center Front): 26 (26, 28, 28) (28, 30, 30, 30) in. / 66 (66, 71, 71) (71, 76, 76, 76) cm

Pattern is designed to be worn with 2–4 in. / 5–10 cm positive ease (see schematic).

YARN

Worsted weight (medium #4) yarn, shown in WeCrochet *Wool of the Andes* (100% Peruvian Highland wool; 110 yd. / 100 m per 1¾ oz. / 50 g skein)

Main Color (MC): #25073 Bramble Heather, 3 (3, 4, 4) (5, 5, 6, 6) skeins

Contrast Color 1 (C1): #23893 Amber Heather, 2 (2, 3, 3) (3, 4, 4, 4) skeins

Contrast Color 2 (C2): #24075 Camel Heather, 2 (2, 3, 3) (3, 4, 4, 4) skeins

Contrast Color 3 (C3): #25066 Solstice Heather, 2 (2, 2, 3) (3, 3, 3, 4) skeins

Contrast Color 4 (C4): #24077 Dove Heather, 3 (3, 4, 4) (4, 5, 5, 6) skeins

Contrast Color 5 (C5): #24280 Persimmon Heather, 2 (2, 2, 3) (3, 3, 3, 4) skeins

Continued on page 70

HOOK

- US J-10 / 6 mm crochet hook or size needed to obtain gauge

NOTIONS

- Tapestry needle
- Locking stitch markers
- Separating zipper in color to match MC 26 (26, 28, 28) (28, 30, 30, 30) in. / 66 (66, 71, 71) (71, 76, 76, 76) cm long
- Sewing needle and thread in color to match MC

GAUGE

15 sts and 16 rows = 4 in. / 10 cm in linen st (both sc and ch are included in st count)

Make sure to check your gauge.

NOTES

- Sweater is worked from the bottom up in one piece and separated for back and fronts, then seamed at the top of the shoulders. The sleeves are worked directly onto the cardigan in joined, turned rounds down to the cuffs. Collar and zipper panels are worked onto the sweater after.
- Follow the directions by row while at the same time striping colors according to the color chart. As you stripe the colors, carry the yarn up the side for short color changes. Cut and rejoin the color if there are long gaps.
- Sweater is worked in linen stitch. Each row starts with a ch 2 and ends with a sc.

SPECIAL STITCHES

linen stitch (multiple of 2 sts)

Row 1: Sc in third ch from hook (skipped chs count as ch-1 sp), *sc in next ch, ch 1, sk next ch; rep from * across to last ch, sc in last ch, turn.

Row 2: Ch 2 (counts as first ch-1 sp), *sk sc, sc in ch-1 sp of previous row, ch 1; rep from * to last ch-1 sp, sc in last ch-1 sp, turn.

Rep Row 2 for patt.

sc, sc in ch-sp; cont in linen st across the row, turn.

Begin working rows in corresponding color in the color striping chart.

Rows 1–60: Ch 2, sc in ch-sp, cont in linen st across, turn.

RIGHT FRONT

Rows 1–24 (24, 28, 28) (28, 34, 34, 34): Ch 2, work linen st over next 34 (36, 40, 44) (48, 52, 56, 60) sts, turn—17 (18, 20, 22) (24, 26, 28, 30) ch-sps, 17 (18, 20, 22) (24, 26, 28, 30) sc.

Fasten off.

SHAPE NECK

Row 1 (RS): Join yarn (color according to striping chart) 4 (4, 5, 5) (5, 6, 6, 6) ch-sps from front edge, work linen st over 26 (28, 30, 34) (38, 40, 44, 48) sts, turn—13 (14, 15, 17) (19, 20, 22, 24) ch-sps, 13 (14, 15, 17) (19, 20, 22, 24) sc.

Row 2 (WS): Ch 2, linen st over 24 (26, 28, 32) (36, 38, 42, 46) sts, turn—12 (13, 14, 16) (18, 19, 21, 23), ch-sps, 12 (13, 14, 16) (18, 19, 21, 23) sc.

Row 3: Ch 2, sk (sc, ch-sp, sc), sc in 2nd ch-sp, work linen st across, turn—11 (12, 13, 15) (17, 18, 20, 22) ch-sps, 11 (12, 13, 15) (17, 18, 20, 22) sc.

Row 4: Ch 2, linen st over 20 (22, 24, 28) (32, 34, 38, 42) sts, turn—10 (11, 12, 14) (16, 17, 19, 21) ch-sps, 10 (11, 12, 14) (16, 17, 19, 21) sc.

BOTTOM RIBBING

With MC, ch 9.

Row 1: Sc in 2nd ch from hook and in each ch across, turn—8 sc.

Row 2: Ch 1, sc blo in each ch across, turn.

Rows 3–136 (148, 164, 180) (196, 208, 224, 240): Rep Row 2.

Do not fasten off.

SWEATER BODY

Setup Row 1 (RS): Ch 2, rotate ribbing panel 90 degrees to start working in ends of ribbing rows, sk first sc row, *sc in next sc row, ch 1, sk next sc row; rep from * across, ending with a sc in final sc row, turn—68 (74, 82, 90) (98, 104, 112, 120) ch-sps, 68 (74, 82, 90) (98, 104, 112, 120) sc.

Setup Row 2 (WS): Ch 2 (counts as first ch-sp here and throughout), sk first

SHAPE SHOULDER SLOPE

Row 1 (RS): Ch 2, linen st to next to last ch-sp, turn—9 (10, 11, 13) (15, 16, 18, 20) ch-sps, 9 (10, 11, 13) (15, 16, 18, 20) sc.

Row 2 (WS): Ch 2, sk ch-sp, begin linen st in second ch-sp, cont linen st across, turn—8 (9, 10, 12) (14, 15, 17, 19) ch-sps, 8 (9, 10, 12) (14, 15, 17, 19) sc.

Row 3: Ch 2, linen st to next to last ch-sp, turn—7 (8, 9, 11) (13, 14, 16, 18) ch-sps, 7 (8, 9, 11) (13, 14, 16, 18) sc.

Row 4: Ch 2, sk ch-sp, begin linen st in second ch-sp, cont linen st across—6 (7, 8, 10) (12, 13, 15, 17) ch-sps, 6 (7, 8, 10) (12, 13, 15, 17) sc.
Fasten off.

BACK

Join yarn in next color according to the color striping chart, in the same st as final sc of Right Front.

Rows 1–28 (28, 32, 32) (32, 38, 38, 38): Ch 2, linen st over next 68 (76, 84, 92) (100, 104, 112, 120) sts ending with a sc, turn—34 (38, 42, 46) (50, 52, 56, 60) ch-sps, 34 (38, 42, 46) (50, 52, 56, 60) sc.

SHAPE BACK SHOULDER SLOPE

Row 1 (RS): Ch 2, sk ch-sp, begin working linen st in second ch-sp, linen st across to next to last ch-sp, turn—32 (36, 40, 44) (48, 50, 54, 58) ch-sps, 32 (36, 40, 44) (48, 50, 54, 58) sc.

Rows 2–4: Rep Row 1—26 (30, 34, 38) (42, 44, 48, 52) ch-sps, 26 (30, 34, 38) (42, 44, 48, 52) sc after Row 4.
Fasten off.

LEFT FRONT

Join yarn in next color according to the color striping chart, in the same st as final sc of Row 1 of back.

Rows 1–24 (24, 28, 28) (28, 34, 34, 34): Ch 2, linen st over 34 (36, 40, 44) (48, 52, 56, 60) sts, ending with sc, turn—17 (18, 20, 22) (24, 26, 28, 30) ch-sps, 17 (18, 20, 22) (24, 26, 28, 30) sc.

SHAPE NECK

Row 1 (RS): Ch 2, linen st across 26 (28, 30, 34) (38, 40, 44, 48) sts, leaving the rem unworked, turn—13 (14, 15, 17) (19, 20, 22, 24) ch-sps, 13 (14, 15, 17) (19, 20, 22, 24) sc.

Row 2 (WS): Ch 2, sk ch-sp, begin linen st in second ch-sp and continue linen

st across, turn—24 (26, 28, 32) (36, 38, 42, 46) sts; 12 (13, 14, 16) (18, 19, 21, 23), ch-sps, 12 (13, 14, 16) (18, 19, 21, 23) sc.

Row 3: Ch 2, linen st across to next to last ch-sp, turn—22 (24, 26, 30) (34, 36, 40, 44) sts; 11 (12, 13, 15) (17, 18, 20, 22) ch-sps, 11 (12, 13, 15) (17, 18, 20, 22) sc.

Row 4: Ch 2, sk ch-sp, begin linen st in second ch-sp and continue linen st across, turn—20 (22, 24, 28) (32, 34, 38, 42) sts; 10 (11, 12, 14) (16, 17, 19, 21) ch-sps, 10 (11, 12, 14) (16, 17, 19, 21) sc.

SHAPE SHOULDER SLOPE

Row 1 (RS): Ch 2, sk ch-sp, beg linen st in second ch-sp, linen st across, turn—9 (10, 11, 13) (15, 16, 18, 20) ch-sps, 9 (10, 11, 13) (15, 16, 18, 20) sc.

Row 2 (WS): Ch 2, linen st across to next to last ch-sp, turn—8 (9, 10, 12) (14, 15, 17, 19) ch-sps, 8 (9, 10, 12) (14, 15, 17, 19) sc.

Row 3: Ch 2, sk ch-1 sp, beg linen st in second ch-sp and cont linen st across, turn—7 (8, 9, 11) (13, 14, 16, 18) ch-sps, 7 (8, 9, 11) (13, 14, 16, 18) sc.

Row 4: Ch 2, linen st across to next to last ch-sp—6 (7, 8, 10) (12, 13, 15, 17) ch-sps, 6 (7, 8, 10) (12, 13, 15, 17) sc.
Fasten off.
Seam both shoulders with a sl st seam, ensuring the seam is on the WS of the work.

SLEEVES (MAKE 2)

Note: You will work linen st up and around the sleeve, skipping rows when you ch as you would for linen st. This section is worked in joined, turned rnds.

Using yarn with final color before you started shaping the neck for the two fronts, and working the color striping chart in reverse for the sleeves (so it resembles the same color pattern as the body), join yarn in the side of the row (in a starting ch-sp) at front outer edge where fronts and back were divided.

Rnd 1: Ch 2, sk sc, sc in ch-sp, continue working linen st into the edges of the body rows, when you reach the point where you have started, ending with a sc, join in starting ch-2 with a sl st, turn—28 (28, 32, 32) (32, 38, 38, 38) ch-sps, 28 (28, 32, 32) (32, 38, 38, 38) sc.

Rnd 2: Ch 2, sk sc, sc in ch-sp, continue working linen st around, ending with a sc, join in starting ch-2 with sl st, turn—28 (28, 32, 32) (32, 38, 38, 38) ch-sps, 28 (28, 32, 32) (32, 38, 38, 38) sc.

Rnds 3–10: Rep Rnd 2.

Rnd 11 (dec rnd): Ch 2, sk first ch-sp, linen st around, ending with sc in next to last ch-sp, join in starting ch-2 with sl st, turn—26 (26, 30, 30) (30, 36, 36, 36) ch-sps, 26 (26, 30, 30) (30, 36, 36, 36) sc.

Rnds 12–20: Rep Rnd 2.

Rnd 21 (dec rnd): Rep Rnd 11—24 (24, 28, 28) (28, 34, 34, 34) ch-sps, 24 (24, 28, 28) (28, 34, 34, 34) sc.

Rnds 22–30: Rep Rnd 2.

Rnd 31 (dec rnd): Rep Rnd 11—22 (22, 26, 26) (26, 32, 32, 32) ch-sps, 22 (22, 26, 26) (26, 32, 32, 32) sc.

Rnds 32–40: Rep Rnd 2.

Rnd 41 (dec rnd): Rep Rnd 11—20 (20, 24, 24) (24, 30, 30, 30) ch-sps, 20 (20, 24, 24) (24, 30, 30, 30) sc.

Rnds 42–50: Rep Rnd 2.

Rnd 51: Rep Rnd 11—18 (18, 22, 22) (22, 28, 28, 28) ch-sps, 18 (18, 22, 22) (22, 28, 28, 28) sc.

Rnds 52–60: Rep Rnd 2.

Rnd 61: Rep Rnd 11—16 (16, 20, 20) (20, 26, 26, 26) ch-sps, 16 (16, 20, 20) (20, 26, 26, 26) sc.

Rnd 62: Rep Rnd 2.

SLEEVE RIBBING

Join MC and ch 7.

Row 1: Sc in second ch from hook and each ch across—6 sc.

Row 2: Sl st in sc of sleeve, sl st in ch-sp of linen st of sleeve, turn, work sc blo in sc from previous row, turn—6 sc.

Row 3: Ch 1, sc blo in each sc across, turn.

Rep Rows 2–3, continuing to work around the bottom of the sleeve until ribbing lines the entire cuff. Join ribbing with a sl st seam, ensuring that the seam appears on the WS of the work. Fasten off.

NECKLINE

With MC, join yarn on the edge of right front along neckline.

Row 1: Ch 2, work linen st up right neckline, up over right shoulder, across back, across left shoulder, and around neckline of left front, ensuring linen st is worked evenly in such a way that it doesn't cause puckering (not enough sts skipped) or holes (too many sts skipped), ending with a sc, turn.

Row 2: Ch 2, work linen st across, working sc2tog into sts on each side of the two shoulder seams (working in the ch-sps and skipping the sc), turn.

Row 3: Rep Row 2.

NECKLINE RIBBING

Ch 9 (9, 11, 11) (11, 13, 13, 13).

Row 1: Sc in 2nd ch from hook and in each ch across toward neckline—8 (8, 10, 10) (10, 12, 12, 12) sc.

Row 2: Sl st in sc of neckline, sl st in ch-sp of linen st of neckline, turn, work sc blo in sc from previous row, turn.

Row 3: Ch 1, sc blo in each sc across.

Rep Rows 2–3 across the neckline. Fasten off.

ZIPPER BAND

Join MC in a corner of one of the fronts. Work 2 rows of linen st into the edges of the linen st rows of the bottom ribbing, body, and neckline edge, taking care to work over any yarns that were carried up the sides and tuck them to the inside of the cardigan. Fasten off. Rep on the opposite side.

FINISHING

Weave in all remaining ends and block to measurements. Linen st will stretch easily with a wet block, so mist blocking is recommended. If you wet block, do not let the cardigan dry with sts stretched too much.

With separating zipper, and with sewing needle and thread, sew zipper onto each side of the cardigan. Make sure the color stripes are aligning by zipping the zipper closed as you sew. Do not stretch the crochet as you sew on the zipper as this will cause the zipper to pucker.

ʙᴇʜɪɴᴅ ᴛʜᴇ ᴍᴀɢɪᴄ

Costume designer Jany Temime counts Ron as one of her favorite characters to dress. His costumes followed the Weasley color palette of orange, green, and brown and included plaids, checks, and stripes for texture.

"Dɪᴅ ʏᴏᴜ ʜᴇᴀʀ ᴡʜᴀᴛ ꜱʜᴇ ᴡᴀꜱ ꜱᴀʏɪɴɢ ʙᴀᴄᴋ ᴀᴛ ᴛʜᴇ ᴘᴜʙ ᴀʙᴏᴜᴛ ᴍᴇ ᴀɴᴅ ʜᴇʀ ꜱɴᴏɢɢɪɴɢ? Aꜱ ɪꜰ."

Ron Weasley, *Harry Potter and the Half Blood Prince*

ABOVE: Ron Weasley, Harry Potter, and Hermione Granger in *Harry Potter and the Half-Blood Prince*.

CHART

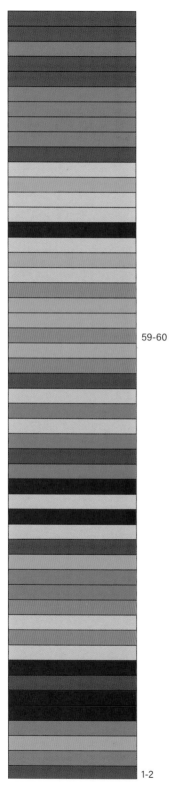

59-60

1-2

KEY

■ linen st in MC

■ linen st in C1

■ linen st in C2

■ linen st in C3

□ linen st in C4

■ linen st in C5

DIRECTIONS

- Each box in the color stripe chart reperesents 2 rows of linen stitch.

- The chart is worked from the bottom up for the body, and from the end point for the body down for the sleeves.

- Work the color chart as far as needed while aslo working the directions for the sweater. Smaller sizes will not make it all the eay up to the color stripe chart.

ABOVE: Harry, Ron, and Hermione in Professor McGonagall's office after discovering the cursed necklace on their way back from the Three Broomsticks in *Harry Potter and the Half-Blood Prince*.

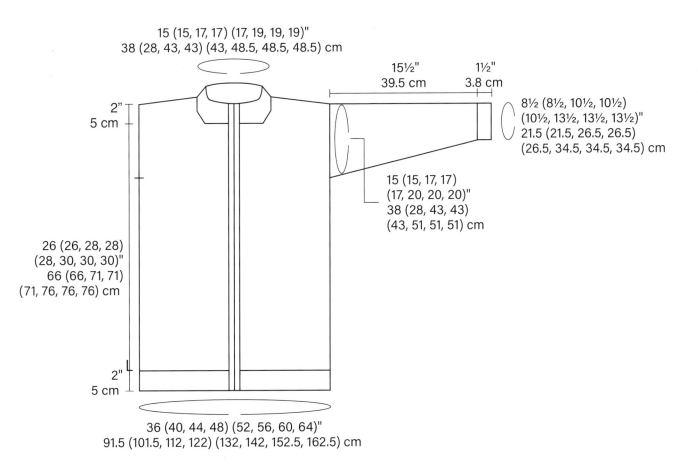

15 (15, 17, 17) (17, 19, 19, 19)"
38 (28, 43, 43) (43, 48.5, 48.5, 48.5) cm

15½"
39.5 cm

1½"
3.8 cm

2"
5 cm

8½ (8½, 10½, 10½)
(10½, 13½, 13½, 13½)"
21.5 (21.5, 26.5, 26.5)
(26.5, 34.5, 34.5, 34.5) cm

15 (15, 17, 17)
(17, 20, 20, 20)"
38 (28, 43, 43)
(43, 51, 51, 51) cm

26 (26, 28, 28)
(28, 30, 30, 30)"
66 (66, 71, 71)
(71, 76, 76, 76) cm

2"
5 cm

36 (40, 44, 48) (52, 56, 60, 64)"
91.5 (101.5, 112, 122) (132, 142, 152.5, 162.5) cm

HERMIONE'S GODRIC'S HOLLOW SET

Designed by **BRITT SCHMIESING**

SKILL LEVEL ⚡⚡

Harry and Hermione visit the village of Godric's Hollow—Harry's birthplace—in *Harry Potter and the Deathly Hallows – Part 1*. Searching for more answers in their hunt for Horcruxes, they arrive in the late evening to a quaint Tudor village gently enveloped in fresh snow. While there, the pair quietly make their way to a little village graveyard surrounded by trees to pay respect to the past, including Harry's parents, Lily and James.

The set for Godric's Hollow was built on the back lot of Pinewood Studios, which housed its own garden. "Pinewood has a magnificent cedar tree, and I wanted it as the centerpiece for the graveyard," production designer Stuart Craig explains. "We built a big set: two streets, a pub, a church, a churchyard, gravestones, a lych-gate, and the derelict cottages of Bathilda Bagshot and the Potters."

While walking in the graveyard, Hermione wears a pretty hat-and-mittens set in soft purple and pink hues. A replica of this cozy set, this project features Hermione's wonderfully textured crochet hat with a slight halo to the fabric and her colorful fingerless mittens, perfect for a stroll through a snowfall.

SIZE
One size

FINISHED MEASUREMENTS
HAT
Brim Circumference: 20½ in. / 52 cm
Length: 9 in. / 23 cm
MITTS
Hand Circumference: 7½ in. / 19 cm
Length: 11½ in. / 29 cm
Note: Will stretch to fit a circumference of 8–8½ in. / 20.5–21.5 cm

YARN
HAT
DK weight (light #3) yarn, shown in Berroco *Ultra Wool DK* (100% superwash wool; 292 yd. / 267 m per 3½ oz. / 100 g ball) in color #83157 Lavender, 1 ball
MITTS
DK weight (light #3) yarn, shown in Berroco *Pixel* (100% superwash wool; 328 yd. / 300 m per 3½ oz. / 100 g per hank) in color #2232 Cupcake, 1 hank

HOOKS
- US G-6 / 4 mm crochet hook or size needed to obtain gauge
- US I-9 / 5.5 mm crochet hook or size needed to obtain gauge

NOTIONS
- Removable stitch marker

Continued on page 78

GAUGE

GAUGE

HAT

5½ (sc, 3 dc) groups and 14 rnds = 4 in. / 10 cm in pattern with larger hook

MITTS

22 sts and 25 rnds = 4 in. / 10 cm in pattern with smaller hook

Make sure to check your gauge.

NOTES

- Brim is worked in rib pattern on smaller hook. Body of hat is worked in continuous spiral with larger hook.
- Move stitch marker up as work progresses.
- Mitts are worked in the round from the bottom up in a continuous spiral.
- *Pixel* works up in wide fading stripes of color. To achieve look in photo, separate each color change into small balls. Alternate colors at random intervals of 1–4 rounds, changing color in the last pull through of a single crochet. Due to the nature of crochet, the first stitch of the round will shift slightly to the left (or right depending on your stitching hand). Try to keep color changes aligned vertically.

SPECIAL ABBREVIATIONS

dc dec (double crochet decrease): [Yarn over, insert hook in indicated stitch, yarn over, pull through, yarn over, pull through 2 loops] twice, yarn over, pull through remaining 3 loops on hook—1 stitch decreased.

sc dec (single crochet decrease): Insert hook in indicated sp, yarn over, draw through loop, insert hook in next indicated sp, yarn over, draw through loop, yarn over, draw through 3 loops on hook.

HAT

BRIM

With smaller hook, ch 79.

Rnd 1: Dc in 3rd ch from hook (skipped sts count as first dc) and in each ch across; join with sl st in top of beg ch-2—78 dc.

Rnd 2: Ch 1 loosely, fpdc around first dc, bpdc around next dc, [fpdc around next dc, bpdc around next dc] around, join with sl st in top of beg fpdc.

Rnd 3: Ch 1 loosely, [fpdc around each fpdc, bpdc around each bpdc] around, join with sl st in top of beg fpdc.

BODY

Rnd 1: With larger hook, ch 1, (sc, 3 dc) in first st, *(sc, 3 dc) in next st, sk next st, [(sc, 3 dc) in next st, sk next 2 sts] 12 times**, (sc, 3 dc in next st); rep from * around, ending at **, pm for beg of rnd (see Notes), do not join—28 (sc, 3 dc) groups.

Rnd 2: (Sc, 3 dc) in each sc around.

Rep Rnd 2 for approximately 6 in. / 15 cm from base of brim.

SHAPE CROWN

Rnd 1: *(Sc, 2 dc) in next sc, [(sc, 3 dc) in next sc] 3 times; rep from * around—7 (sc, 2 dc) groups, 21 (sc, 3 dc) groups.

Rnd 2: *[(Sc, 2 dc) in next sc] twice, [(sc, 3 dc) in next sc] twice; rep from * around—14 (sc, 2 dc) groups, 14 (sc, 3 dc) groups.

Rnd 3: *[(Sc, 2 dc) in next sc] 3 times, (sc, 3 dc) in next sc; rep from * around—21 (sc, 2 dc) groups, 7 (sc, 3 dc) groups.

Rnd 4: [(Sc, 2 dc) in next sc] around—28 (sc, 2 dc) groups.

Rnd 5: [(Sc, dc) in next sc, (sc, 2 dc) in next sc] around—14 (sc, dc) groups, 14 (sc, 2 dc) groups.

Rnd 6: (Sc, dc) in next sc around—28 (sc, dc) groups.

Rnd 7: [Sc in next sc, (sc, dc) in next sc] around—14 sc, 14 (sc, dc) groups.

Rnd 8: [Sk next sc, (sc, dc) in next sc] around—14 (sc, dc) groups.

Rnd 9: [Dc dec in next sc and dc] around—7 dc.

Fasten off. Weave tail around 7 dc twice; pull taut. Weave in ends.

ABOVE: Wearing her warm hat and mitts, Hermione finds the sign of the Deathly Hallows in the cemetery of Godric's Hollow in *Harry Potter and the Deathly Hallows – Part 1.*

MITTS

RIGHT MITT

With smaller hook, ch 44.

Row 1: Sc in 2nd ch from hook and in each ch across—43 sc.

Rnd 2: Being careful not to twist sts, place st marker to mark beg of rnd moving marker up as work progresses, sc in first sc, [ch 1, sk next sc, sc in next sc] around—22 sc, 21 ch-1 sps.

Rnd 3: [Ch 1, sk next sc, sc in next sp] around.

Rep Rnd 3, alternating colors (see Notes) as you prefer until mitt measures approximately 8 in. / 20.5 cm.

THUMBHOLE

Next rnd: [Ch 1, sc in next sp] until 4 sc and 4 ch-1 sps rem, ch 7, sk 7 sts, sc in last sp.

Next rnd: [Ch 1, sc in next sp] around to last sc before chs, ch 1, sk next sc, [sc in next ch, ch 1, sk 1 ch] 4 times.

Rep Rnd 3 until mitt measures approximately 11½ in. / 29 cm from beg.

Fasten off.

THUMB

Rnd 1: Join with a sl st in ch sp at center top of thumbhole, ch 1, sc in same sp, ch 1, sk next st, [sc in next sp, ch 1, sk next st] to corner, sc in corner of thumbhole, ch 1, [sc in next sp, ch 1, sk next sc] to next corner, sc in corner of thumbhole, ch 1, [sc in next sp, ch 1, sk next st] to beg—10 sc, 9 ch-1 sps.

Rnd 2: [Sc in next sp, ch 1] around.

Rep Rnd 2 for approximately 1 in. / 2.5 cm.

Dec rnd: Sc dec in next sp and following sp, ch 1, [sc in next sp, ch 1] around—9 sc, 8 ch-1 sps.

Rep Rnd 2 until thumb measures approximately 2 in. / 5 cm or desired length.

Fasten off. Weave in ends.

LEFT MITT

Rep instructions for Right Mitt to thumbhole.

Next rnd: Ch 7, sk next 7 sts, sc in next sp, [ch 1, sc in next sp] around.

Next rnd: [Ch 1, sk next ch, sc in next ch] 4 times, [ch 1, sc in next sp] around.

Rep instructions for right mitt for remainder.

FINISHING

Weave in ends.

LUNA'S CROPPED CARDIGAN

Designed by **BRITT SCHMIESING**

SKILL LEVEL ⚡⚡

First introduced in *Harry Potter and the Order of the Phoenix*, Luna Lovegood is a special witch in a number of ways. For one, she can see Thestrals, which comes in handy when Harry sees them for the first time and gets a bit of a shock. Later in the fifth film, Harry finds Luna out on the Hogwarts grounds, taking a closer look at the mysterious magical animals. While the two chat, Harry asks Luna about her missing shoes, giving the audience a chance to appreciate Luna's beautiful but eccentric fashion choices. "Everything is mismatched," says costume designer Jany Temime, who always thought of Luna as "living in her own handmade world. She can see things that nobody else sees, and so I wanted to reflect that."

Luna's cropped cardigan is a replica of the purple cardigan Luna wears while visiting the Thestrals in *Order of the Phoenix*. Luna often wears layers, and this cardigan is the perfect layering piece. Featuring filet crochet in the underarms and beautiful ribbing around the hem, this button-up cardigan is ready to be paired with any pattern in your wardrobe, no matter how eccentric.

SIZES

XS (S, M, L, XL, 2XL, 3XL)

Shown in size S.

Instructions are written for the smallest size, with larger sizes given in parentheses; when only one number is given, it applies to all sizes.

FINISHED MEASUREMENTS

Chest: 34 (38, 42, 46, 50, 54, 58) in. / 86.5 (96.5, 106.5, 117, 127, 137, 147.5) cm in circumference

Length: 12¼ (12¾, 13, 13¼, 13¾, 14¾, 15) in. / 31 (32, 33, 33.5, 35, 37.5, 38) cm

YARN

DK weight (light #3) yarn, shown in Cascade Yarns *Ultra Pima* (100% pima cotton; 220 yd. / 200 m per 3½ oz. / 100 g hank) in color #3709 Wood Violet, 3 (3, 3, 3, 4, 4, 4) hanks

HOOKS

- US F-5 / 3.75 mm crochet hook
- US G-6 / 4 mm crochet hook or size needed to obtain gauge

NOTIONS

- Removable stitch markers
- Tapestry needle

GAUGE

16 sts and 10 rows = 4 in. / 10 cm in dc with larger hook

Make sure to check your gauge.

Continued on page 84

NOTES

- Cardigan is worked from the top down using raglan increases.
- Ribbed hem is worked side to side separately and then whipstitched to bodice.
- Lace triangles create the flutter sleeve effect.

SPECIAL ABBREVIATIONS

dc dec (double crochet decrease):
[Yo, insert hook in indicated stitch, yo, pull through, yarn over, pull through 2 lps] twice, yo, pull through remaining 3 lps on hook—
1 st decreased.

picot: Ch 3, sl st into first ch of ch-3.

puff st (puff stitch): [Insert hook into indicated st, yo, pull up lp, yo] 3 times, pull through 6 lps on hook.

CARDIGAN

BODICE

With larger hook, ch 89 (89, 93, 93, 97, 97, 101).

Row 1 (RS): Dc in 3rd ch from hook and each ch across, turn—88 (88, 92, 92, 96, 96, 100) dc.

Place a st marker in the 16th (16th, 17th, 17th, 18th, 18th, 19th) dc in from each front edge (fronts) and 13th (13th, 13th, 13th, 15th, 15th, 15th) dc toward center from previous markers (sleeves).

Row 2: Ch 2 (*counts as first dc here and throughout*), [dc in each dc to marked st, 2 dc in marked st (*place st marker in 2nd dc*), 2 dc in next st, dc in each st to 1 st before next marked st, 2 dc in next st, 2 dc in marked st (*place st marker in first dc*)] twice, dc in each st to end, turn—8 dc inc'd; 96 (96, 100, 100, 104, 104, 108) dc.

Row 3 (buttonhole row): Ch 2, [dc in each dc to marked st, 2 dc in marked st (*from this point forward move st markers up as in Row 2*), 2 dc in next st, dc in each st to 1 st before next marked st, 2 dc in next st, 2 dc in marked st] twice, dc in each st to last 3 sts, ch 1, sk next st (*buttonhole made*), dc in last 2 sts, turn—8 dc inc'd; 104 (104, 108, 108, 112, 112, 116) dc.

Rows 4–11 (4–12, 4–13, 4–14, 4–15, 4–17, 4–18): Rep Row 2, working a buttonhole approximately every 8 (8, 9, 9, 7, 7, 8) rows on bodice edge, turn—168 (176, 188, 196, 208, 224, 236) dc.

Rows 12–14 (13–15, 14–16, 15–17, 16–18, 18–20, 19–21): Ch 2, [dc in each dc to marked st, 2 dc in marked st, dc in each st to next marked st, 2 dc in marked st] twice, dc in each st to end, turn—4 dc inc'd; 180 (188, 200, 208, 220, 236, 248) dc.

LACE SECTION

Note: Cont to work buttonholes every 8 (8, 9, 9, 7, 7, 8) rows on bodice edge, being sure to work the final buttonhole on the last row of bodice. You will have a total of 4 (4, 4, 5, 5, 5) buttonholes.
Remove all st markers.

Row 1: Ch 2, dc in next 20 (22, 25, 27, 30, 34, 37) sts, ch 3, sk next dc, [dc in next 23 sts, ch 3, sk next dc] twice, dc in next 40 (44, 50, 54, 60, 68, 74) sts, ch 3, sk next dc, [dc in next 23 sts, ch 3, sk next dc] twice, dc to last st, turn—174 (182, 194, 202, 214, 230, 242) dc, 6 ch-3 sps.

Row 2: Ch 2, [dc in next st and each st to 1 st before ch-3 sp, ch 3, puff st in ch-3 sp, ch 3, sk next dc] 6 times, dc in each st to end, turn—162 (170, 182, 190, 202, 218, 230) dc, 12 ch-3 sps, 6 puff sts.

LUNA LOVEGOOD: "THEY'RE CALLED THESTRALS. THEY'RE QUITE GENTLE, REALLY, BUT PEOPLE AVOID THEM, BECAUSE THEY'RE A BIT . . ."
HARRY POTTER: "DIFFERENT."

Harry Potter and the Order of the Phoenix

Row 3: Ch 2, [dc in next st and each st to 1 st before ch-3 sp, ch 3, sc in ch-3 sp, ch 3, sc in next ch-3 sp, ch 3, sk next dc] 6 times, dc in each st to end, turn—150 (158, 170, 178, 190, 206, 218) dc, 18 ch-3 sps, 12 sc.

Row 4: Ch 2, [dc in next st and each st to 1 st before ch-3 sp, ch 3, (puff st, ch 1, picot, ch 2) in each ch-3 sp to last ch-3 sp, puff st in last ch-3 sp, ch 3, sk next dc] 6 times, dc in each st to end, turn—138 (146, 158, 166, 178, 194, 206) dc, 12 ch-3 sps, 18 puff sts, 12 picots, 12 ch-1 sps, 12 ch-2 sps.

Row 5: Ch 2, [dc in next st and each st to 1 st before ch-3 sp, ch 3, sc in ch-3 sp, ch 3, (sc, ch 3) in each ch-2 sp to last ch-3 sp, sc in last ch-3 sp, ch 3, sk next dc] 6 times, dc in each st to end, turn—126 (134, 146, 154, 166, 182, 194) dc, 30 ch-3 sps, 24 sc.

Rows 6–12: Rep Rows 4 and 5 alternately, ending last rep after Row 4—42 (50, 62, 70, 82, 98, 110) dc, 12 ch-3 sps,66 puff sts, 60 picots, 60 ch-1 sps, 60 ch-2 sps after Row 12.
Fasten off.

HEM

With smaller hook, ch 8.
Row 1: Sc in 2nd ch from hook and in each ch across—7 sc.
Row 2: Ch 1, sc in back lp of each sc across.
Rep Row 2 until hem measures approximately 34 (38, 42, 46, 50, 54, 58) in. / 86.5 (96.5, 106.5, 117, 127, 137, 147.5) cm.
Fasten off. Weave in ends.

FINISHING

Lay bodice flat with front edges meeting in the center and buttonholes overlapping opposite edge. Fold hem in half lengthwise, center it on the back, and pin in place. Fold the hem so that its short edges match up with the front edges and pin in place at those points. Hem is now folded in the same manner as the cardigan. On each folded side of the hem, measure in 1½ (1½, 1½, 1½, 2, 2, 2) in. / 4 (4, 4, 4, 5, 5, 5) cm (*underarm section*) and place pins on hem on both front and back. Align these pins with the bodice and pin hem and bodice together, leaving 1½ (1½, 1½, 1½, 2, 2, 2) in. / 4 (4, 4, 4, 5, 5, 5) cm on each side of folded hem open. Pin hem in place between all markers to hold in place for seaming. Whipstitch tog.

NECKLINE EDGE

Starting at the bottom right front hem edge, join yarn with a sl st, ch 2, dc in each sc of hem, 2 dc in end of each dc row to neckline, work 3 hdc in first st of neckline, [work hdc in base of each st across to 1 st before raglan corner, dc dec in next 2 sts] 4 times, hdc to last st of neckline, work 3 hdc in last st, 2 dc in end of each dc row to hem, dc in each sc of hem. Fasten off.

BUTTONS
[MAKE 4 (4, 4, 4, 5, 5, 5)]

Rnd 1: With smaller hook and leaving a 6 in. / 15 cm tail, ch 3, sl st to join into a ring, ch 1, work 6 sc into ring—6 sc.
Rnd 2: 2 sc in each st around—12 sc.
Rnd 3: [Sc dec] around—6 sc.
Fasten off, leaving a long tail.
Close starting ring with yarn tail and straight sts, then stuff tail into button. Run ending tail through last sts twice and pull snug. Work a couple of straight sts to lock in place. Use tail to align button across from buttonhole and sew in place.
Weave in ends.

ABOVE: Luna Lovegood visits Hogwarts' herd of Thestrals in the Forbidden Forest in *Harry Potter and the Order of the Phoenix.*

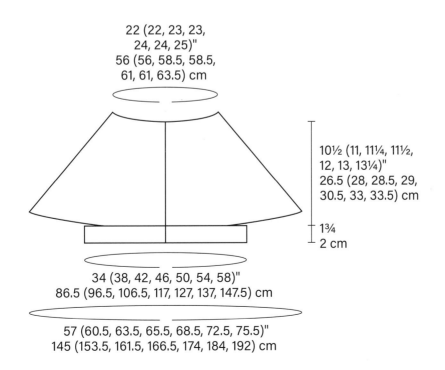

HERMIONE'S ROOM OF REQUIREMENT SWEATER

Designed by **SARA DUDEK**

SKILL LEVEL ⚡⚡⚡

I n *Harry Potter and the Order of the Phoenix*, Harry and his friends need a place to practice Defense Against the Dark Arts—somewhere Professor Umbridge won't find them. After coming up with some less-than-ideal solutions, the students finally find the Room of Requirement. The members of Dumbledore's Army are able to sneak into the room to practice their spells together during school hours, and also after hours, when dress codes are no longer in effect. This is another great opportunity for fans to catch a glimpse of Hermione's sense of style.

Costume designer Judianna Makovsky's idea for Hermione Granger's look was to keep it "classically British. I dressed her in pleated skirts, knee socks, and lovely handmade Fair Isle sweaters." We get a chance to see one of these sweaters in action in the Room of Requirement in *Order of the Phoenix*.

Hermione's Room of Requirement sweater is a stunning yoke pullover, worked in gorgeous browns and creams. Worked from the top down with a ribbed collar, this sweater features easy increases around the yoke. The sleeves are separated and finished with a ribbed cuff.

SIZES
XS (S, M, L) (XL, 2X, 3X, 4X, 5X)
Shown in size S.
Instructions are written for the smallest size, with larger sizes given in parentheses; when only one number is given, it applies to all sizes.

FINISHED MEASUREMENTS
Bust: 29½ (34, 38, 41½) (46, 50, 54, 58, 64) in. / 75 (86.5, 96.5, 105.5) (117, 127, 137, 147.5, 162.5) cm
Pattern is designed to be worn with 2–4 in. / 5–10 cm positive ease (see schematic).

YARN
Fingering weight (super fine #1) yarn, shown in WeCrochet *Bare Palette* (100% Peruvian Highland wool; 436 yd. / 399 m per 3½ oz. / 100 g hank)
Main Color (MC): #23851 Bare, 3 (3, 4, 4) (5, 5, 6, 6, 6) hanks
Fingering weight (super fine #1) yarn, shown in WeCrochet *Palette* (100% Peruvian Highland wool; 231 yd. / 211 m per 1¾ oz. / 50 g ball)
Contrast Color 1 (C1): #25532 Grizzly Heather, 1 (2, 2, 2) (2, 3, 3, 3, 4) ball(s)
Contrast Color 2 (C2): #24560 Almond, 1 (1, 1, 2) (2, 2, 2, 2, 2) ball(s)

HOOKS
- US C-2 / 2.75 mm crochet hook
- US D-3 / 3.25 mm crochet hook or size needed to obtain gauge

Continued on page 90

NOTIONS

- Tapestry needle
- Locking stitch marker

GAUGE

22 sts and 18 rnds = 4 in. / 10 cm in esc
with larger hook

Make sure to check your gauge.

NOTES

- Sweater is worked top down and in
  the round with a circular yoke and
  gradual increases. It is then separated
  for body and sleeves. Body is worked
  top down first, and then each sleeve is
  worked top down individually.
- Circular yoke is worked off the color
  chart in extended single crochet.
  Change colors according to the chart,
  and work increases where you see an
  extra box added to the chart.
- An increase is 2 esc in the next stitch.
- Starting chain for each new round
  should be in same color as first esc
  according to colorwork chart.
- Circular yoke may pucker as it
  is worked; this flattens with wet
  blocking.

SPECIAL TECHNIQUE

To work a color change with esc, work
until the stitch before the color
change. In the stitch before the color
change, with the original color,
insert hook in next st, yarn over and
pull up a loop (2 loops on hook), yarn
over and pull through 1 loop (still 2
loops on hook), change to new color
for final yarn over and pull through
2 loops.

SPECIAL ABBREVIATIONS

esc (extended single crochet): Insert
hook in next st, yarn over, pull up a
loop (2 loops on hook), yarn over and
pull through one loop (still 2 loops
on hook), yarn over and pull through
2 loops.

**esc2tog (extended single crochet 2
together):** Insert hook under front
loop only of next 2 sts, yo and pull
through 2 front loops, yo and pull
through 1 loop on hook, yo and pull
through remaining 2 loops on hook.

the colorwork charts (see notes); join
with sl st—264 (288, 312, 336) (372,
408, 444, 468, 504) esc after final rnd.

SEPARATE FOR BODY AND SLEEVES

With MC and larger hook, ch 1, esc in
next 38 (44, 49, 53) (58, 63, 68, 72, 81)
sts, ch 6 (6, 8, 8) (10, 12, 14, 16, 16) and
sk 57 (57, 59, 62) (70, 79, 87, 91, 91) to
create sp for first sleeve, esc in next
75 (87, 97, 106) (116, 125, 135, 143, 161)
sts across front, ch 6 (6, 8, 8) (10, 12,
14, 16, 16) and sk 57 (57, 59, 62) (70,
79, 87, 91, 91) to create sp for second
sleeve, esc in remaining 37 (43, 48, 53)
(58, 62, 67, 71, 80) sts; join with sl st.
Do not fasten off.

BODY

With MC and larger hook:

Rnd 1: Ch 1, esc in next 38 (44, 49, 53)
(58, 63, 68, 72, 81) sts, esc in next 6 (6,
8, 8) (10, 12, 14, 16, 16) ch, esc in next
75 (87, 97, 106) (116, 125, 135, 143, 161)
sts, esc in next 6 (6, 8, 8) (10, 12, 14, 16,
16) ch, esc in rem 37 (43, 48, 53) (58, 62,
67, 71, 80) sts; join with sl st—162 (186,
210, 228) (252, 274, 298, 318, 354) esc.

Rnd 2: Ch 1, esc around; join with sl st.
Rep Rnd 2 until body measures 10½ (11,
11½, 11½) (12, 12, 12½, 12½, 12½) in. /
26.5 (28, 29, 29) (30.5, 30.5, 32, 32, 32)
cm from end of circular yoke.

Next 5 rnds: Join C1. Work the next 5
rnds in esc according to the edging
colorwork chart. Note the colorwork
pattern won't rep evenly for all sizes.
Do not fasten off; cont to body ribbing.

BODY RIBBING

With smaller hook and MC, ch 13.

Row 1: Turn, working in chs moving
toward the body sc in 2nd ch from
hook and in each ch across—12 sc.

Row 2: Sl st in esc of body, sl st in next
esc st of body, turn, begin working in
the sc of body ribbing Row 1, sc blo in
next 12 sc, turn—12 sc.

SWEATER

NECK RIBBING

With smaller hook and MC, ch 9.

Row 1: Sc in 2nd ch from hook and in
each ch across, turn—8 sc.

Row 2: Ch 1, sc blo in each sc across,
turn.

**Rows 3–110 (120, 130, 140) (155, 170, 185,
195, 210):** Rep Row 2.
Join neck band in a circle with sl st
seam on WS.

CIRCULAR YOKE

Switch to larger hook and join the color
of Rnd 1 according to colorwork
chart.

Rnd 1: Ch 1, moving to the left of seam
with RS of seam facing, work an esc
in end of each sc row of neck band
according to Rnd 1 of the colorwork
chart.

**Rnds 2–37 (37, 41, 41) (46, 46, 50, 50,
54):** Ch 1, work esc around, working
color changes and inc according to

Row 3: Ch 1, sc blo in each st across—12 sc. Rep Rows 2–3 around the bottom of the body. Once you have worked ribbing around the entire body, work a sl st seam to join the ribbing, ensuring that the seam appears on WS.

SLEEVE (MAKE 2)

With MC and larger hook, join yarn in the center of chs in the underarm, working in the rnd so you cont to show the RS of the st in the same way as for yoke and body.

Rnd 1: Ch 1, esc in next 3 (3, 4, 4) (5, 6, 7, 8, 8) chs, esc in edge of separation for body and sleeve rnd, esc in next 57 (57, 59, 62) (70, 79, 87, 91, 91) sts, esc in edge of separation for body and sleeve rnd, esc in next 3 (3, 4, 4) (5, 6, 7, 8, 8) chs; join with sl st—65 (65, 69, 72) (82, 93, 103, 109, 109) esc.

Rnd 2: Ch 1, esc around; join with sl st.

Rnds 3–9: Rep Rnd 2.

Rnd 10 (dec rnd): Ch 1, esc2tog, esc around to last 2 sts, esc2tog—63 (63, 67, 70) (80, 91, 101, 107, 107) esc.

Rnds 11–19: Rep Rnd 2.

Rnd 20 (dec rnd): Rep Rnd 10—61 (61, 65, 68) (78, 89, 99, 105, 105) esc.

Rnds 21–60 (70, 70, 70) (70, 70, 70, 70, 70): Rep Rnds 11–20 four (5, 5, 5) (5, 5, 5, 5, 5) more times—53 (51, 55, 58) (68, 79, 89, 95, 95) esc.

SIZES XS, XL, 2XL, 3XL, 4XL, AND 5XL ONLY

Rep Rnds 11–15 once more.

ALL SIZES

Next 5 rnds: Join C1, work the next 5 rnds in esc according to the edging colorwork chart. Note the colorwork pattern won't rep evenly for all sizes. Do not fasten off; cont to sleeve ribbing.

ABOVE: Hermione sports her classic British cream-and-brown pullover in *Harry Potter and the Order of the Phoenix*.

SLEEVE RIBBING

With smaller hook and MC, ch 13.

Row 1: Turn, working in chs moving toward the sleeve, sc in 2nd ch from hook and in each ch across—12 sc.

Row 2: Sl st in esc of sleeve, sl st in next esc st of sleeve, turn, begin working in the sc of sleeve ribbing Row 1, sc blo in next 12 sc, turn—12 sc.

Row 3: Ch 1, sc blo in each st across—12 sc. Rep Rows 2–3 around the bottom of the sleeve. Once you have worked ribbing around the entire sleeve, work a sl st seam to join the ribbing, ensuring that the seam appears on the WS.

FINISHING

Weave in ends. Soak project in cool water for 20 minutes, then block to measurements.

CHARTS

KEY

☐ esc in MC

■ esc in C1

■ esc in C2

EDGING COLORWORK

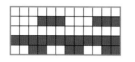

XS AND S

M AND L

XL AND 2XL

3XL AND 4XL

5XL

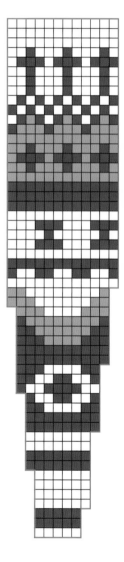

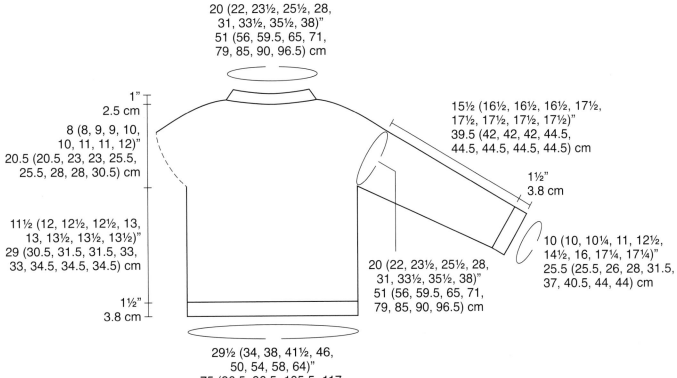

20 (22, 23½, 25½, 28,
31, 33½, 35½, 38)"
51 (56, 59.5, 65, 71,
79, 85, 90, 96.5) cm

1"
2.5 cm

8 (8, 9, 9, 10,
10, 11, 11, 12)"
20.5 (20.5, 23, 23, 25.5,
25.5, 28, 28, 30.5) cm

15½ (16½, 16½, 16½, 17½,
17½, 17½, 17½, 17½)"
39.5 (42, 42, 42, 44.5,
44.5, 44.5, 44.5, 44.5) cm

1½"
3.8 cm

11½ (12, 12½, 12½, 13,
13, 13½, 13½, 13½)"
29 (30.5, 31.5, 31.5, 33,
33, 34.5, 34.5, 34.5) cm

20 (22, 23½, 25½, 28,
31, 33½, 35½, 38)"
51 (56, 59.5, 65, 71,
79, 85, 90, 96.5) cm

10 (10, 10¼, 11, 12½,
14½, 16, 17¼, 17¼)"
25.5 (25.5, 26, 28, 31.5,
37, 40.5, 44, 44) cm

1½"
3.8 cm

29½ (34, 38, 41½, 46,
50, 54, 58, 64)"
75 (86.5, 96.5, 105.5, 117,
127, 137, 147.5, 162.5) cm

situated in the midst of rice
manufactures silks and
(1859) in which the allie
the Austrians (see ITAL
a monument were erect
purple aniline dye, di
given from it the na

The latter spies,
h was addressed by Pigafetta,
that extend alo
is in
northe
the S
easter
Sesto
by r
Luig
Lug
Sh
sh
sh

MAGGIORE, L

Lac Majeur: Ge
Its area is abo
5¾ m., and j
about sea-le
River, flow
way to jo
important
through
implon
in is
in th

Paris
(see below), who believes the
text. See the *Primo viaggio
gation et descouverment de la
boyme Pigapheta, Vincentin.
in 1524 (in August of that
his book in Venice). Of the
gly supposed by Thomassy.
o have been the MS. of
ce, Marie Louise of Savoy,
MS., often called the MS. of
S., Phillips 16,405. The
Milan. From this Carlo
lished his Italian edition
n of this, by Amoretti

An English version of
rcades of the Newe Worlde
apparently in the
tion de Colines of Paris
534 (or 1536).

an unknown Portu-
the *Derrotero* or Log-
the work of Francisco
he "Trinidad": this
the narrative of the
tuguese, and printed
isbon Academy. (4
e Seville Archives,
r of Maximilian of
to the cardinal of
ra, often based on
to other records.
translated at
(1) executed at
of his departure
of August, 1519.
are both of some

round the World
akluyt Society
gems de Ferndo
de Magalhães
fe of Magellan
mbrosian MS.,
ography, &c.,
e the appear-
tta had been
with
bblicati nella
sto (Rome,
(C. R. B.)

Magellan),
constella-
5° 40' of
their stars
rs of the
as magi
of magic

vince of
sea-level
ance, see

For E. B. Tylor the distinguishing characteristic of magic
ality; it is a confused mass of beliefs and practices, and
consists in the absence of the ordinary nexus of natural
Under the general head of magic he distinguishes
(i) a non-spiritual element.   (i) The former is
ons or gods; hence, in Tylor's view,
s involve the intervention of spiritual beings,
and correspondences in nature:
mistaking of an ideal connexion
dian medicine man draws the
expects that shooting at
next day, he mistakes a real
the sorcerer for a real

the law of sympathy
her at a distance
t there is some
ve at one time
other. These
"homoeo-
or imita-
ontagious
nciple
belief
uring
the
the

be common to
group does no
magical: cons
under the hea
tinguishing cha
mind is marke
not more so, i
ment in human
nology can be
magie the resu
results of the cr
between magic
religion is to b
former, nor in a
nor yet in its ma
an organized cul
mitted, without n
traced in the ma
flows along chan
contrast of the c
but these laws do
are the demonolog
in the objects used
magic is dynamical
(see below), of whic
operates in a *milie
distance is no obstac
but law reigns in th
ceived as existing.
of magic is even mo
sanctity enters into i
her than quantitat
ending on their d
ive periods of t
ciousness) by
reason of o
Lehmann
magic i
lism for
else pe
view

may be regarded a
al is responsible, whi
ant lines, growing as it g
objects, among which were m
geniuses or idiots; and such
powers for the good of society;
essional medicine man; man or
and not vice versa. Priest and
the former, learning humility in
own, discarded the spell for the p
a higher power.

Definition of Magic.—To ar
may either follow the a priori
decline to recognize the distinc
societies between magical and
ask what magic and correspon
Frazer's method ignores the fac
an institution, i.e. a produ

(iii) Individuals are found
whose will rules the
bring rain or sunshine, and whose
Sometimes it is bound up with the office
who controls
an with magical
be performed by all
or other conditions may
power (*mana*), whose will rules the
to the fields. In many cases the magical powers of both men and
their objects, animate and inanimate, are put down to the fact that
a god resides in them.
d. Hubert and Mauss have made the most complete and sys-
tematic study of magic which has yet appeared. They hold that
implicitly at any rate, magic is everywhere distingui
systems of social facts,
vidual

FANTASTIC FASHION

"I DON'T BELONG HERE! I BELONG IN
YOUR WORLD—AT HOGWARTS!"

Harry Potter, *Harry Potter and the Chamber of Secrets*

STUDENT WIZARD HOODED PONCHO

Designed by **LEE SARTORI**

SKILL LEVEL ⚡⚡

W hen fans are first introduced to Harry Potter in *Harry Potter and the Sorcerer's Stone*, Harry is wearing oversized hand-me-down clothes that once belonged to his cousin, Dudley. But when Harry goes shopping for school on Diagon Alley with Hagrid, he purchases brand new robes and a Hogwarts uniform that fits him just right. Robes are the loose-fitting outer garments most commonly worn by wizards and witches. They come in many forms, patterns, designs, and colors, and they are available in standard and dress varieties, among others. At Hogwarts, students are required to purchase and bring three sets of standard black robes to school with them as part of their school uniform. The robes are sleek, formal, and a point of great pride for students. When Harry arrives to Hogwarts in his newly purchased robes, we see him finally fitting in, dressed in the same robes as his new fellow classmates.

Inspired by the Hogwarts students' elegant black robes, this hooded poncho is worked top down in the raglan style. With easy shaping and increases throughout the shoulders, the poncho then grows and flows out in a loose-fitting circle around the body. Sleeves are then separated so that armholes can be added in the traditional robe style.

SIZES

S (M, L, XL, 2XL/3XL)

Shown in size S.

Instructions are written for the smallest size, with larger sizes given in parentheses; when only one number is given, it applies to all sizes.

FINISHED MEASUREMENTS

To Fit Bust: 34 (38, 42, 46, 52) in. / 86.5 (96.5, 106.5, 117, 132) cm

Note: Poncho is designed with positive ease. Choose a size according to your bust measurement.

Length: 22 (22, 23, 23½, 24½) in. / 56 (56, 58.5, 59.5, 65) cm

YARN

Worsted weight (medium #4) yarn, shown in WeCrochet *Brava Worsted* (100% premium acrylic; 218 yd. / 199 m per 3½ oz. / 100 g skein) in color #28413 Black, 7 (7, 9, 11, 12) skeins

HOOK

- US G-6 / 4 mm crochet hook
- US K-10½ / 6.5 mm crochet hook or size needed to obtain gauge

NOTIONS

- Tapestry needle
- Locking stitch markers

GAUGE

10 sts and 10 rows = 4 in. / 10 cm in hdc with larger hook

Make sure to check your gauge.

NOTES

- Ch 2 at start of round counts as 1 hdc.
- Ch 1 does not count as a stitch.

HOOD

With smaller hook, ch 60 (60, 60, 72, 72).

Row 1: Sc in 2nd ch from hook and in each st across, turn—59 (59, 59, 71, 71) sc.

Rows 2 and 3: Ch 1, sc across, turn.

Rows 4–13: Ch 1, [2 sc in next sc] 4 times, sc across, turn—99 (99, 99, 111, 111) sts after Row 13.

Rows 14–23: Ch 1, [2 sc in next sc] 3 times, sc across, turn—129 (129, 129, 141, 141) sts.

Mark edges of Row 16 with st markers.

Rows 24–31: Ch 1, 2 sc in first sc, sc across to last sc, 2 sc in last sc, turn—145 (145, 145, 157, 157) sc.

Row 32: Ch 1, sc across, turn.

Row 33: Ch 1, 2 sc in first sc, sc across to last sc, 2 sc in last sc, turn—147 (147, 147, 159, 159) sc.

Rows 34–37: Rep Rows 32 and 33—151 (151, 151, 163, 163) sc.

Rows 38–40: Rep Row 32.

Row 41: Rep Row 33—153 (153, 153, 165, 165) sc.

Rows 42–49: Rep Rows 38–41—157 (157, 157, 169, 169) sc.

Row 50: Ch 1, sc in first 2 sc, sc2tog, sc across to last 4 sc, sc2tog, sc in last 2 sc, turn—155 (155, 155, 167, 167) sc.

Rows 51–53: Ch 1, sc across, turn.

Rows 54–61: Rep Rows 50–53—151 (151, 151, 163, 163) sc.

Row 62: Ch 1, sc across.

Fasten off.

Seam hood by folding piece in half and meeting at Row 16. Starting at Row 16, sc through both thicknesses, working up and across Row 1 toward the crease. Leave Rows 17–62 unworked for neck opening.

YOKE

With larger hook, ch 56 (60, 64, 68, 72); join to first ch with a sl st.

Rnd 1: Ch 2, hdc in each ch around, join, turn—56 (60, 64, 68, 72) hdc.

Rnd 2: Ch 2, hdc in each st around, join, turn.

Rnds 3 and 4: Rep Rnd 2.

Rnd 5: Ch 2, hdc in same, hdc in next 6 (5, 9, 1, 6) sts, [2 hdc in next, hdc in next 6 (5, 5, 5, 4) sts] around, join, turn—64 (70, 74, 80, 86) hdc.

Insert 8 st markers after the following sts: 1st marker after the 10 (10, 10, 11, 12)th st, 2nd marker after the next 2 sts, 3rd marker after the next 8 (10, 12, 14, 14) sts, 4th marker after next 2 sts, 5th marker after next 20 (21, 22, 23, 26) sts, 6th marker after next 2 sts, 7th marker after next 8 (10, 12, 14, 14) sts, 8th marker after next 2 sts, leaving 10 (11, 10, 10, 12) hdc rem.

Rnd 6: Ch 2, [hdc around to 1 st before marked st, 2 hdc in st before marked st, move marker to space after these 2 hdc] 8 times, hdc to end of rnd, join, turn—72 (78, 82, 88, 94) hdc.

Rnds 7–17 (17, 19, 19, 21): Rep Rnd 6—160 (166, 186, 192, 214) hdc.

YOKE CONTINUED

Rnd 1: Ch 2, [hdc around to hdc **before** marked sp, 2 hdc in hdc before marked sp, move marker to sp **after** these 2 hdc] 8 times, hdc to end of rnd, join, turn—168 (174, 194, 200, 222) hdc.

Rnd 2: Ch 2, hdc in each st around, join, turn.

Rnd 3: Ch 2, [hdc around to hdc **after** marked sp, 2 hdc in hdc after marked sp, move marker to sp **before** these 2 hdc] 8 times, hdc to end of rnd, join, turn—176 (182, 202, 208, 230) hdc.

Rnd 4: Ch 2, hdc in each st around, join, turn.

Rnds 5–20: Rep Rnds 1–4—240 (246, 266, 272, 294) hdc after Rnd 19.

"YOU TWO BETTER CHANGE INTO YOUR ROBES. I EXPECT WE'LL BE ARRIVING SOON."

Hermione Granger, *Harry Potter and the Sorcerer's Stone*

BEHIND THE MAGIC

Before filming the first movie, there was some debate as to whether Hogwarts students would wear uniforms or modern clothes. In order to decide, Daniel Radcliffe was tested in both, and it was agreed that the uniforms looked better. This was a great relief to costume designer Judianna Makovsky, who otherwise would have had to individually dress four hundred students!

ABOVE: Harry Potter, Hermione Granger, and their fellow students in their Hogwarts robes in *Harry Potter and the Order of the Phoenix.*

Remove the 1st, 4th, 5th, and 8th st markers. Sleeves (between new 1st and 2nd markers and 3rd and 4th markers) will have 30 (32, 36, 38, 40) sts. Move each st marker out toward body by 3 (2, 2, 1, 0) sts on each side so that sleeves now have 36 (36, 40, 40, 40) sts.

Rnd 21: Ch 2, [hdc in each st to next marker, skip next 36 (36, 40, 40, 40) hdc twice, hdc in each hdc to end, join, turn—168 (174, 186, 192, 214) hdc.

Leave markers in place to mark sleeve placement.

Rnds 22–24: Ch 2, hdc around, join, turn.

Fasten off.

FRONT

Pm on each side with 84 (87, 93, 96, 107) hdc between marker for front and back.

Row 1: Sk 1st 2 sts after side marker and join in 3rd st, ch 3 (*does not count as a st*), hdc in next hdc, [hdc2tog] twice, hdc across to last 8 sts before next marker, [hdc2tog] 3 times, leave remaining 2 sts unworked, turn—74 (77, 83, 86, 97) hdc.

Row 2: Ch 3 (does not count as st), hdc in first hdc, [hdc2tog] twice, hdc to last 6 sts, [hdc2tog] 3 times, turn—69 (72, 78, 81, 92) hdc.

Rows 3–9 (9, 9, 11, 11): Rep Row 2—34 (37, 43, 36, 47) sts.

Fasten off.

BACK

Rep as for Front.

EDGE

Join in any st around.

Rnds 1–5: Ch 2, *hdc in each st around to end of row, hdc into row ends on each side; rep from * around; join, turn.

Fasten off.

SLEEVES

Rnd 1: Join to first st of marked off sleeve, ch 1, hdc around, join, turn—36 (36, 40, 40, 40) sts.

Rnd 2: Ch 2, hdc around, join, turn.

Rep Rnd 2 until sleeve measures approximately 8 in. / 10 cm.

Fasten off.

FINISHING

Sew remaining sts under arm closed. Join hood to neckline of poncho using preferred joining method. Weave in ends.

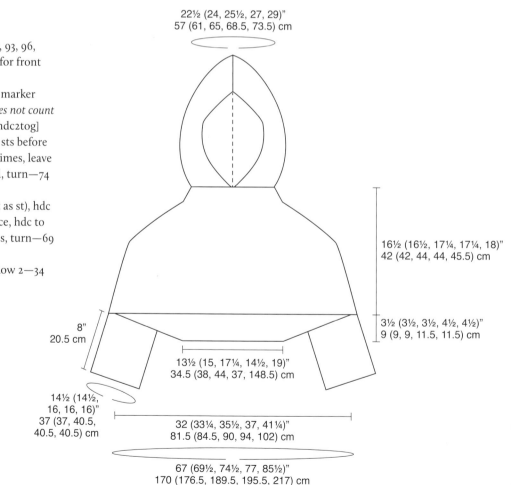

22½ (24, 25½, 27, 29)"
57 (61, 65, 68.5, 73.5) cm

16½ (16½, 17¼, 17¼, 18)"
42 (42, 44, 44, 45.5) cm

3½ (3½, 3½, 4½, 4½)"
9 (9, 9, 11.5, 11.5) cm

8"
20.5 cm

13½ (15, 17¼, 14½, 19)"
34.5 (38, 44, 37, 148.5) cm

14½ (14½, 16, 16, 16)"
37 (37, 40.5, 40.5, 40.5) cm

32 (33¼, 35½, 37, 41¼)"
81.5 (84.5, 90, 94, 102) cm

67 (69½, 74½, 77, 85½)"
170 (176.5, 189.5, 195.5, 217) cm

BERTIE BOTT'S EVERY-FLAVOUR SOCKS

Designed by **JULIE DESJARDINS**

SKILL LEVEL ⚡⚡⚡

With Bertie Bott's Every-Flavour Beans, there's risk with every bite! The Every-Flavour Beans are one of the most popular treats in the wizarding world. They're similar to real-world jelly beans, but the difference with Bertie Bott's is that they come in every flavor imaginable, even the bad ones—and the *really* bad ones.

Characterized by their colorful packaging, Bertie Bott's Every-Flavour Beans come in a rectangular box with a peaked top that is striped red and white like a circus tent. This eye-catching packaging was designed by the graphics department headed by Miraphora Mina and Eduardo Lima, who created, printed, and applied hundreds of labels and other packaging for the culinary delights of the wizarding world.

These Bertie Bott's-inspired socks feature the red and white stripes of the packaging of Bertie Bott's Every-Flavour Beans. Work in rows for the body of these socks, adding the heel, toe, and cuff in yellow to finish them off. They're the perfect, subtle way to show off some Harry Potter flair.

SIZE

To Fit Shoe Size: Baby/Todder/Child/ Youth 0–4 (5–9, 10–13, 1–3, 4–6) (Women's 4–6½, 7–9½, 10–12½) (Men's 6–8½, 9–11½, 12–14)
Shown in size Women's 10–12½
Instructions are written for the smallest size, with larger sizes given in parentheses; when only one number is given, it applies to all sizes.

FINISHED MEASUREMENTS

Foot Circumference: 4¼ (4¼, 5½, 5½, 5½) (5½, 6½, 6½) (6½, 7¾, 7¾) in. / 11 (11, 14, 14, 14) (14, 16.5, 16.5) (16.5, 19.5, 19.5) cm
Leg Length: 3 (4, 5, 6¾, 7½) (8, 8, 9) (9, 9, 9½) in. / 8 (10, 13, 17, 19) (20, 20, 23) (23, 23, 24) cm

YARN

Fingering weight (super fine #1) yarn, shown in Fibrelya *Kassou* (80% superwash merino, 20% nylon; 420 yd. / 385 m per 4 oz. / 115 g hank)
Color A: Rouge 1 hank
Color B: Natural, 1 hank
Color C: Jaune, 1 hank

HOOK

- US E-4 / 3.5 mm crochet hook or size needed to obtain gauge

NOTIONS

- 2 stitch markers in different colors
- Tapestry needle

GAUGE

13 sts and 14 rows = 2 in. / 5 cm in patt
Make sure to check your gauge.

Continued on page 104

SPECIAL ABBREVIATIONS

bpdc (back post double crochet): Yo, insert hook from back to front to back around post of indicated st, yo and pull up a loop, [yo and draw through 2 loops] twice.

fpdc (front post double crochet): Yo, insert hook from front to back to front around post of indicated st, yo and pull up a loop, [yo and draw through 2 loops] twice.

NOTES

- When working in chains, work in the back bump. This will create a much less visible seam on foot and leg.
- Ch 1 or ch 2 at start of rows and rounds do not count as a stitch.
- Change colors by making the last yarn over of the last stitch of the row with the new color. Do not cut old color until you are instructed to fasten off. Carry the yarn loosely.
- Socks are worked in rows in three sections, each building on the previous section. See figure 1.

The resulting piece is folded at the arrows and sewn to create the foot and leg.

The toes, heel, and cuff are then added to their respective opening and worked in rounds.

SOCKS (MAKE 2)

FOOT AND FRONT OF LEG

With A, ch 21 (27, 27, 30, 33) (33, 36, 36) (36, 36, 42).

Row 1: Working in back bumps of ch, sc in 2nd ch from hook and in each ch across, change to B, turn—20 (26, 26, 29, 32) (32, 35, 35) (35, 35, 41) sts.

Row 2: Ch 1, sl st-blo in each st across, turn.

Row 3: Ch 1, hdc-blo in each st across, change to A, turn.

Row 4: Ch 1, sl st-blo in each st across, turn.

Row 5: Ch 1, sc-blo in each st across, change to B, turn.

Rows 6–15 (6–15, 6–19, 6–19, 6–19) (6–19, 6–23, 6–23) (6–23, 6–27, 6–27): Rep Rows 2–5, ending last rep on Row 3. At the end of last row and with A, ch 19 (26, 33, 41, 45) (45, 45, 51) (51, 51, 56), turn.

Working instep and front of leg:

Row 16 (16, 20, 20, 20) (20, 24, 24) (24, 28, 28): Working in back bumps, sc in 2nd ch from hook, sc in each ch across, sc in each sc across, change to B, turn—38 (51, 58, 69, 76) (76, 79, 85) (85, 85, 96) sts.

Rows 17–30 (17–30, 21–38, 21–38, 21–38) (21–38, 25–46, 25–46) (25–46, 29–54, 29–54): Rep Rows 2–5, ending last rep on Row 3.

Fasten off.

BACK OF LEG

With RS facing, and counting from toe edge of foot, join A to 21st (27th, 27th, 30th, 33rd) (33rd, 36th, 36th) (36th, 36th, 42nd) st with sl st-blo.

Row 31 (31, 39, 39, 39) (39, 47, 47) (47, 55, 55): Sl st-blo in next 17 (24, 31, 39, 43) (43, 43, 49) (49, 49, 54) sts, turn—18 (25, 32, 40, 44) (44, 44, 50) (50, 50, 55) sts.

Row 32 (32, 40, 40, 40) (40, 48, 48) (48, 56, 56): Ch 1, sc in each st across, change to B, turn.

Rows 33–46 (33–46, 41–58, 41–58, 41–58) (41–58, 49–70, 49–70) (49–70, 57–82, 57–82): Rep Rows 2–5 ending last rep on Row 3.

Fasten off.

ASSEMBLY

Crochet sole starting ch to instep's last row as follows: With A and WSs facing, fold foot in half. *Working through both thicknesses, insert hook from outside to inside of inner loop of first ch, pull up a loop, insert hook from outside to inside of inner loop of corresponding st on last row, pull up a loop, yo and complete sl st.** Rep in each st across foot—20 (26, 26, 29, 32) (32, 35, 35) (35, 35, 41) sl sts. Fasten off.

Crochet front of leg starting ch to back of leg's last row as follows:
With A and WS facing, fold leg in half. Rep from * to ** in each st across leg—18 (25, 32, 40, 44) (44, 44, 50) (50, 50, 55) sl sts. Fasten off.

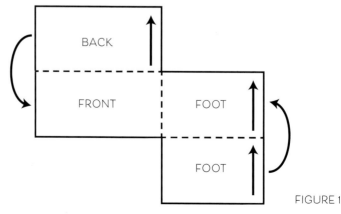

FIGURE 1

"I WAS MOST UNFORTUNATE IN MY YOUTH TO
COME ACROSS A VOMIT-FLAVORED ONE, AND
SINCE THEN I'M AFRAID I'VE LOST MY LIKING
FOR THEM. BUT I THINK I COULD BE SAFE WITH
A NICE TOFFEE. MMM, ALAS, EARWAX."

Professor Dumbledore, *Harry Potter and the Sorcerer's Stone*

ABOVE: Professor Dumbledore vists Harry in the hospital wing in *Harry Potter and the Sorcerer's Stone*.

TOE

With RS facing, join A to toe opening with sl st.

Rnd 1: Ch 1, working in row ends, sc in each row end; join with sl st in 1st sc—30 (30, 38, 38, 38) (38, 46, 46) (46, 54, 54) sts. Fasten off.

With RS facing, join C to 1st stitch with sl st.

Rnd 2: Ch 1, sc-blo in each st around; do not join.

Rnd(s) 3 (3-4, 3-4, 3-5, 3-5) (3-5, 3-6, 3-6) (3-6, 3-6, 3-6): Sc in each st around, do not join. Pm in 1st and 16th (16th, 20th, 20th, 20th) (20th, 24th, 24th) (24th, 28th, 28th) sts.

Rnd 4 (5, 5, 6, 6) (6, 7, 7) (7, 7, 7): Sc2tog over 1st 2 sts, sc in each st until 2 sts rem before next marker, [sc2tog] twice, sc in each st until 2 sts rem, sc2tog over last 2 sts, do not join—26 (26, 34, 34, 34) (34, 38, 38) (38, 50, 50) sts.

Rnds 5-7 (6-8, 6-9, 7-10, 7-10) (7-10, 8-12, 8-12) (8-12, 8-14, 8-14): Rep Rnd 4 (5, 5, 6, 6) (6, 7, 7) (7, 7, 7)—14 (14, 18, 18, 18) (18, 20, 20) (20, 22, 22) sts rem after last rnd.

Fasten off, leaving a long tail for sewing.

HEEL

With RS facing, join A to heel opening with sl st.

Rnd 1: Ch 1, working in row ends, sc in sl st and sc row ends, 2 sc in hdc row ends; join with sl st in 1st sc—38 (38, 48, 48, 48) (48, 58, 58) (58, 68, 68) sts. Fasten off.

With RS facing, join C to first st with sl st.

Rnd 2: Ch 1, *sc-blo in next 3 sts, sc2tog-blo over next 2 sts; rep from * until 8 sts rem, [sc-blo in next 2 sts, sc2tog-blo over next 2 sts] twice, do not join—30 (30, 38, 38, 38) (38, 46, 46) (46, 54, 54) sts.

Rnd 3: Sc in each st around; do not join.

Pm in 1st and 16th (16th, 20th, 20th, 20th) (20th, 24th, 24th) (24th, 28th, 28th) sts.

Rnd 4: Sc2tog over 1st 2 sts, sc in each st until next marker, sc2tog over next 2 sts, sc in each st to end, do not join—28 (28, 36, 36, 36) (36, 44, 44) (44, 52, 52) sts.

Rnd 5: Sc in each st around; do not join.

Rnds 6-9 (6-11, 6-11, 6-11, 6-13) (6-13, 6-15, 6-15) (6-15, 6-19, 6-19): Rep Rnds 4 and 5—24 (22, 30, 30, 28) (28, 34, 34) (34, 38, 38) sts rem after last rnd.

Fasten off, leaving a long tail for sewing.

CUFF

With RS facing, join A to top of sock with sl st.

Rnd 1: Ch 1, working in row ends, hdc in sl st and sc row ends, 2 hdc in hdc row ends; join with sl st in 1st sc—38 (38, 48, 48, 48) (48, 58, 58) (58, 68, 68) sts. Fasten off.

With RS facing, join C to first st with sl st.

Rnd 2: Ch 2, [fpdc around each of next 3 sts, bpdc around next st] around; join with sl st in 1st fpdc.

Rnd 3: Ch 2, fpdc around ch 2 and first fpdc, fpdc around each of next 2 sts, bpdc around next st, [fpdc around each of next 3 fpdc, bpdc around next bpdc] around; join with sl st in first fpdc.

Fasten off for baby, toddler, child, and youth sizes.

WOMEN'S AND MEN'S SIZES ONLY

Rnds 4-6: Rep Rnd 3.
Fasten off.

FINISHING

With tapestry needle and long tail, and with RSs facing, place toe ends tog. Insert tapestry needle from outside to inside of first st on instep, then from outside to inside of opposite st on sole; pull tight. Rep across. Fasten off.

With tapestry needle and long tail, and with RSs facing, place heel ends tog. Insert tapestry needle from outside to inside of first stitch on leg, and from outside to inside of opposite st on foot; pull tight. Rep across. Fasten off.

Weave in ends. Block lightly if desired.

THE DUMBLEDORE HAT

Designed by **CORRINE TURNER**

SKILL LEVEL ⚡⚡

A lbus Dumbledore is a longtime professor and headmaster at Hogwarts School of Witchcraft and Wizardry. Often described as one of the greatest wizards of all time, he develops a close relationship with Harry during his time at Hogwarts, offering guidance, support, and mentorship. While he's not infallible, it is Professor Dumbledore who ultimately gives Harry the key to defeating Voldemort, though he tragically does not live to see his student's victory.

In the films, there is no doubt that Professor Dumbledore is one of the most elaborately dressed characters. The role was first played by Richard Harris, who wore more traditional wizard's robes and a hat in a beautiful maroon shade. After the sad news of Harris's death, the role was taken up by Michael Gambon, and the costume changed as well. Gambon's Dumbledore wears intricately detailed robes crafted in silvers and grays, and the traditional wizard's hat is replaced with a smoking cap.

This everyday take on Dumbledore's hat makes it a staple winter accessory. Worked from the brim up, Dumbledore's hat features elegant colorwork as well as intricate beading to add grandness. Continue with easy shaping for a slouchy fit, and finish with a clever tassel to top it off.

SIZE
One size

FINISHED MEASUREMENTS
Brim Circumference: 21 in. / 53.5 cm
Length: 9 in. / 23 cm

YARN
DK weight (light #3) yarn, shown in WeCrochet *Capra DK* (85% fine merino wool, 15% cashmere; 123 yd. / 112 m per 1¾ oz. / 50 g ball)
Color A: #68 Adriatic Heather, 3 balls
Color B: #61 Tansy Heather, 1 ball
Color C: #65 Angelite Heather, 1 ball

HOOK
- US J-10 / 6 mm crochet hook or size needed to obtain gauge

NOTIONS
- Stitch marker
- Hildie & Jo rainbow opaque glass seed beads: .7 oz. (20 g) size 10/0 in Gold AB
- Hildie & Jo glass seed beads: .7 oz. (20 g) size 10/0 in Transparent Crystal AB
- Tapestry needle
- DMC embroidery hand needle size 1–5
- Sewing thread
- Clover large tassel maker

GAUGE
14 sts and 20 rnds = 4 in. / 10 cm in center single crochet
Make sure to check your gauge.

Continued on page 110

SPECIAL ABBREVIATION

csc (center single crochet): Single crochet into the V of the stitch from the previous round.

NOTES

- Rounds are worked continuously without joining unless stated otherwise.
- When you get to a color change, insert your hook into the indicated stitch, yarn over and draw up a loop in the specified color, then yarn over and finish your stitch with the color of the next stitch.
- Use a stitch marker to mark the beginning of each round.
- As you complete the colorwork, carry colors A, B, and C up the side of the work until needed again.

HAT

With A, ch 72 and join in the rnd with a slip st.

Rnd 1: Sc in the back bump of each ch—72 sc.

Rnds 2–17: Csc in each st around.

Rnd 18: [Csc C, csc B] around.

Rnd 19: With A, csc in each st around.

Rnd 20: With B, csc in each st around.

Rnd 21: [Csc C, csc 3 sts with B] around.

Rnd 22: With B, csc in each st around.

Rnd 23: [Csc A, csc 3 sts with B] around.

Rnd 24: [Csc 2 sts with A, csc B, csc 3 sts with A, csc B, csc A] around.

Rnd 25: [Csc 2 sts with A, csc B, csc A, csc C, csc A, csc B, csc A] around.

Cut C.

Rnd 26: With A, csc in each st around.

Rnd 27: [Csc 2 sts with A, csc B, csc 3 sts with A, csc B, csc A] around.

Cut B.

Rnds 28 and 29: With A, csc in each st around.

Before proceeding to Rnd 30, sew one seed bead to the center of each specified st:

Rnd 18: Sew rainbow beads to color B sts; sew crystal beads to color C sts.

Rnds 21 and 25: Sew crystal beads to color C sts.

Rnd 27: Sew rainbow beads to color B sts.

Rnd 30 (brim): Fold the edge of the brim up to the current round so that the wrong sides are facing each other and each stitch of the current round and beginning round are lined up. Sc each stitch together to close the brim.

Rnds 31–46: Csc in each st around—72 sts.

Rnd 47: [Csc 16 sts, csc2tog] around—68 sts.

Rnd 48: Csc in each st around.

Rnd 49: [Csc 15 sts, csc2tog] around—64 sts.

Rnd 50: Csc in each st around.

Rnd 51: [Csc 14 sts, csc2tog] around—60 sts.

Rnd 52: Csc in each st around.

Rnd 53: [Csc 13 sts, csc2tog] around—56 sts.

Rnd 54: Csc in each st around.

Rnd 55: [Csc 12 sts, csc2tog] around—52 sts.

Rnd 56: Csc in each st around.

Rnd 57: [Csc 11 sts, csc2tog] around—48 sts.

Rnd 58: Csc in each st around.

Rnd 59: [Csc 10 sts, csc2tog] around—44 sts.

Rnd 60: Csc in each st around.

Rnd 61: [Csc 9 sts, csc2tog] around—40 sts.

Rnd 62: Csc in each st around.

Rnd 63: [Csc 8 sts, csc2tog] around—36 sts.

Rnd 64: Csc in each st around.

Fasten off. Sew top of hat closed by weaving yarn through the remaining stitches and cinch close. Weave in ends.

FINISHING

Using B and the tassel maker, create a tassel. Thread the tail of the tassel through the center of the top of the hat and secure it at the length you desire. Weave in ends.

CHART

KEY

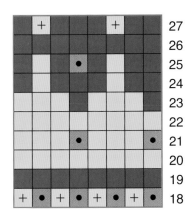

- ▧ csc in color A
- ☐ csc in color B
- ☐ csc in color C
- ⊙ crystal bead
- ⊞ rainbow bead

ʙEHIND THE ᴍAGIC

Dumbledore is rarely sighted without a hat in the first several Harry Potter films, wearing it nearly everywhere he goes. It isn't until *Harry Potter and the Half-Blood Prince* that he is seen with a longer beard and no hat. Costume designers wanted the great wizard to appear at his most vulnerable for this chapter of the story.

RIGHT: A promotional image of Michael Gambon as Professor Dumbledore for *Harry Potter and the Prisoner of Azkaban.*

Unbreakable Vow Sweater

Designed by **VINCENT WILLIAMS**

SKILL LEVEL ⚡⚡

I n *Harry Potter and the Half-Blood Prince*, Draco Malfoy is given an unthinkable task by Lord Voldemort—one that will likely put him in mortal danger. In a bid of desperation, Draco's mother, Narcissa, and her sister Bellatrix make their way to the home of Professor Snape, where Narcissa begs Snape for his help and protection. "And therefore she betrays, really, what she believes is the true cause in order to try to secure her son's safety," says actress Helen McCrory, who plays Narcissa. "So she's somebody who puts her children first, before her. She might be a baddie, but she's a good mother." Much to the sisters' surprise, Snape agrees to help, and, under the ever-suspicious eye of Bellatrix, makes an Unbreakable Vow to protect Draco with his life.

The spell's unique visual presentation inspires this dramatic pullover, which is worked in a raglan style with easy shaping. On a background of black fading to green, the spell stands out in dramatic white colorwork, seemingly casting light onto the body of the sweater itself.

SIZES

S (M, L, XL, 2X) (3X, 4X, 5X, 6X)

Shown in size M with 4 in. / 10 cm of positive ease.

Instructions are written for the smallest size, with larger sizes given in parentheses; when only one number is given, it applies to all sizes.

FINISHED MEASUREMENTS

Chest: 34 (38, 42, 46, 50) (54, 58, 62, 66) in. / 86.5 (96.5, 106.5, 117, 127) (137, 147.5, 157.5, 167.5) cm

Designed to be worn with 4 in. / 10 cm positive ease.

YARN

DK weight (light #3) yarn, shown in Hazel Knits *Lively DK* (90% superwash wool, 10% nylon; 275 yd. / 251 m per 4 oz. / 113 g hank)

Color A: Carbon Fiber, 3 (3, 4, 4, 5)(6, 7, 8, 9) hanks

DK weight (light #3) yarn, shown in Madelinetosh *Tosh DK* (100% superwash merino wool; 225 yd. / 205 m per 3½ oz. / 100 g hank)

Color B: Cactus, 2 (2, 3, 3, 4) (5, 6, 7, 8) hanks

Color C: Joshua Tree, 2 (2, 3, 3, 4) (5, 6, 7, 8) hanks

Color D: Natural (undyed), 1 (1, 1, 1, 1) (1, 2, 2, 2) hanks

HOOK

• US I-9 / 5.5 mm crochet hook

Continued on page 114

NOTIONS

- Tapestry needle
- 5 locking/removable stitch markers
- 2 bobbins per sleeve (optional)

GAUGE

13 sts and 19 rnds = 4 in. / 10 cm in patt, blocked

NOTES

- Sweater is worked in the round from the top down.
- When making an increase (inc) in a marked stitch, remove the marker, work the first stitch as a standard sc, work the second stitch as a csc, then place your marker into the csc before proceeding in pattern.
- When working the charted spell motif, color D will be worked via intarsia in the round. The total yardage of color D should be split in half so two balls/bobbins can be worked separately during the sleeve. Small floats will be created on the wrong side of the work when color D is being pulled up into action. Color D should not be crocheted over and carried through the entire round.

SPECIAL ABBREVIATIONS

csc (center single crochet): Insert hook through center of next st (between the legs of the st rather than through the top front and back loops), yo, pull up a loop, yo, draw through both loops on hook.

csc inc: Work standard sc under two loops of st, work a csc in same stitch

cscRdec (center single crochet decrease to the right): Insert hook into st, yo, pull up a loop (2 loops on hook). Insert hook into next st, yo, pull up a loop (3 loops on hook). Switch the 2nd and 3rd loop on the hook to create a right-leaning decrease. Yo and pull through all 3 loops on hook.

csc2tog (center single crochet 2 together): Insert hook through center of indicated st (between the legs of the st rather than through the top front and back loops), yo, pull up a loop. Insert hook through center of next st, yo, pull up a loop. Yo and draw through all 3 loops on hook.

st of inc, inc in next st; rep from * twice more, csc to EOR marker, csc in st with EOR marker—8 sts inc'd.

Rnds 3 & 4: Csc in each st around.

Rep Rnds 2–4 twelve (13, 14, 16, 17) (18, 19, 20, 21) times more—164 (172, 182, 198, 210) (220, 228, 240, 248) sts.

For size S only: Sk Rnds 5–7; proceed to "For sizes S, 3X, & 6X."

For sizes M, L, XL, 2X, 3X, 4X, 5X & 6X only: Proceed to Rnd 5.

Rnd 5: Csc to first marker, inc in marked st, pm in 2nd st of inc, csc to next marker, csc in marked st, inc in next st, pm in 2nd st of inc, csc to next marker, inc in marked st, pm in 2nd st of inc, csc to next marked st, csc in marked st, inc in next st, pm in 2nd st of inc, csc to next marked st, csc in st marked with EOR marker—4 sts inc'd.

Rnd 6-7: Csc in each st around.

Rep Rnds 5–7 - (1, 2, 2, 4)(5, 7, 8, 10) times more — - (180, 194, 210, 230) (244, 260, 276, 292) sts.

For sizes M, 4X, & 5X: Proceed to body.

For sizes S, 3X, & 6X: Csc to first marked st, csc in first marked st, inc in next st, pm in 2nd st of inc, csc to next marker, csc in next marked st, inc in next st, pm in 2nd st of inc, *csc to next marker, inc in marked st, pm in 2nd st of inc; rep from * once more, csc to EOR marker, csc in st with EOR marker—4 sts inc'd; 168 (-, -, -, -) (248, -, -, 296) sts.

For size L: Csc to first marked st, csc in first marked st, inc in next st, pm in 2nd st of inc, csc to 4th marker, inc in marked st, pm in 2nd st of inc, csc to EOR marker, csc in st with EOR marker—2 sts inc'd; - (-, 196, -, -) (-, -, -, -) sts.

For sizes XL & 2X: Csc to 2nd marked st, csc in 2nd marked st, inc in next st, pm in 2nd st of inc, csc to next marker, inc in marked st, pm in 2nd st of inc, csc to EOR marker, csc in st with EOR marker—2 sts inc'd; - (-, -, 212, 232) (-, -, -, -) sts.

YOKE

With color A, loosely ch 60 (60, 62, 62, 66) (68, 68, 72, 72); place EOR marker in last st, join rnd with sl st, ch 1.

Rnd 1: Csc in first 11 (11, 11, 11, 12) (12, 12, 13, 13) ch, pm in last st worked [back right shoulder], csc in next 10 (10, 10, 10, 11) (11, 11, 12, 12) ch, pm in last st worked [front right shoulder], csc in next 19 (19, 20, 20, 21) (22, 22, 23, 23) ch, pm in last st worked [front left shoulder], csc in next 10 (10, 10, 10, 11) (11, 11, 12, 12) ch, pm in last st worked [back left shoulder], csc in last 10 (10, 11, 11, 11) (12, 12, 12, 12) ch—60 (60, 62, 62, 66) (68, 68, 72, 72) sts.

Note: Work in continuous rnds; do not join.

Rnd 2: Csc to 1st marker, inc in marked st, csc inc in next st, *csc to next marker, inc in marked st, pm in 2nd

BODY

Note: Work in continuous rnds; do not join.

Rnd 1: Csc to first marker [back right shoulder], fsc 9 (10, 11, 12, 13) (14, 15, 16, 17), rm, sk 37 (38, 41, 44, 47) (50, 51, 54, 57) sts [right sleeve], csc in 2nd marked st, csc to 3rd marked st, csc in 3rd marked st, rm, fsc 9 (10, 11, 12, 13) (14, 15, 16, 17), sk 37 (38, 41, 44, 47) (50, 51, 54, 57) sts [left sleeve], csc in st after 4th marker, rm, csc to EOR marker, csc in st with EOR marker—112 (124, 136, 148, 164) (176, 188, 200, 216) sts.

Csc in each st around for 10 (11, 12, 12, 13) (13, 13, 14, 14) rnds.

Transition Rnd 1: With color B, csc in each st around.

Transition Rnd 2: With color A, csc in each st around.

Transition Rnds 3–6: Rep Transition Rnds 1 & 2.

With color B, csc in each st around for 27 (29, 30, 30, 33) (33, 36, 37, 37) rnds.

Using color C in place of color B and color B in place of color A, rep Transition Rnds 1–6.

With color C, csc in each st around for 35 (35, 36, 36, 38) (40, 40, 41, 41) rnds.

Body measures 15½ (16, 16½, 17, 17½) (18, 18½, 19, 19) in. / 39.5 (40.5, 42, 43, 44.5) (45.5, 47, 48.5, 48.5) cm from underarm.

SLEEVES (MAKE 2)

Leaving a 5 in. / 12.5 cm tail and counting from the rightmost underarm st, join color A at the 5th (6th, 7th, 7th, 8th) (8th, 9th, 9th, 10th) underarm st.

Note: Work in continuous rnds; do not join.

Rnd 1: Csc 5 (5, 5, 6, 6) (7, 7, 8, 8) underarm sts, place BOR marker in the first underarm st, csc across 37 (38, 41, 44, 47) (50, 51, 54, 57) sleeve sts, csc in each of the rem 4 (5, 6, 6, 7) (7, 8, 8, 9) underarm sts, place EOR marker in the last underarm st—46 (48, 52, 56, 60) (64, 66, 70, 74) total sleeve sts.

Proceed to your selected size and **at the same time** work a color transition from color A to B beginning on Rnd 46 (48, 52, 56, 60) (64, 66, 70, 74) as follows: *1 rnd color B, 1 rnd color A; rep from * twice more. Cont in patt with color B.

Note for ALL sizes: Work a csc in each st around for rnds between the sleeve dec rnds.

For size S: Dec rnd: CscRdec, csc to last 2 sts, csc2tog—2 sts dec'd.

Rep dec rnd on every 6th rnd 4 more times—10 total sts dec'd.

Work Spell Chart 1.

For size M: Dec rnd: CscRdec, csc to last 2 sts, csc2tog—2 sts dec'd.

Rep Dec Rnd on every 6th rnd 3 more times, then on every 8th rnd 1 time—10 total sts dec'd.

Work Spell Chart 2.

For size L: Dec rnd: CscRdec, csc to last 2 sts, csc2tog—2 sts dec'd.

Rep dec rnd every 6 rnds 5 more times—12 total sts dec'd.

Work Spell Chart 3.

For size XL: Dec rnd: CscRdec, csc to last 2 sts, csc2tog—2 sts dec'd.

Rep dec rnd every 6 rnds 6 more times—14 total sts dec'd.

Work Spell Chart 4.

For size 2X: Dec rnd: Csc in first st, cscRdec, csc to last 2 sts, csc2tog—2 sts dec'd.

Rep dec rnd every 4 rnds 2 more times, then every 6 rnds 5 times—16 total sts dec'd.

Work Spell Chart 5.

For size 3X: Dec rnd: Csc in first st, cscRdec, csc to last 2 sts, csc2tog—2 sts dec'd.

Rep dec rnd every 4 rnds 7 more times, then every 6 rnds 2 times—20 total sts dec'd.

Work Spell Chart 5.

For size 4X: Dec rnd: Csc in first st, cscRdec, csc to last 2 sts, csc2tog—2 sts dec'd.

Rep dec rnd every 4 rnds 7 more times, then every 6 rnds 2 times—20 total sts dec'd.

Work Spell Chart 6.

For size 5X: Dec rnd: Csc in first st, cscRdec, csc to last 2 sts, csc2tog—2 sts dec'd.

Rep dec rnd every 4 rnds 11 more times—24 total sts dec'd.

Work Spell Chart 6.

For size 6X: Dec rnd: Csc in first st, cscRdec, csc to last 2 sts, csc2tog—2 sts dec'd.

Rep dec rnd every 4 rnds 12 more times—26 total sts dec'd.

Work Spell Chart 7.

All sizes: Fasten off.

FINISHING

Weave in all remaining ends on WS of work. Steam or wet block to measurements.

"Swear to it. Make the Unbreakable Vow."

Bellatrix Lestrange, *Harry Potter and the Half-Blood Prince*

ABOVE: Severus Snape makes an Unbreakable Vow to Narcissa Malfoy, while her sister Bellatrix Lestrange casts the charm in *Harry Potter and the Half-Blood Prince*.

CHARTS

KEY

- ■ csc in color B
- ■ csc in color C
- □ csc in color D
- ⌃ cscRdec in color indicated

CHART 1

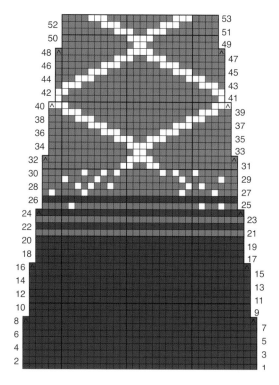

CHART 2

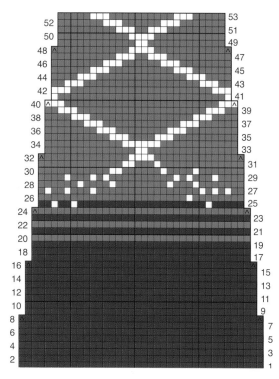

CHART 3

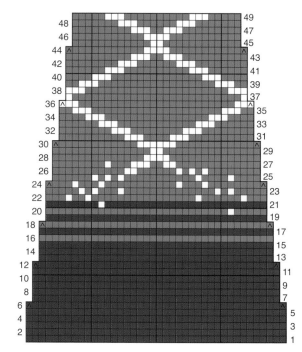

CHARTS

KEY

- ■ csc in color B
- ▣ csc in color C
- □ csc in color D
- ⟨Λ⟩ cscRdec in color indicated

CHART 4

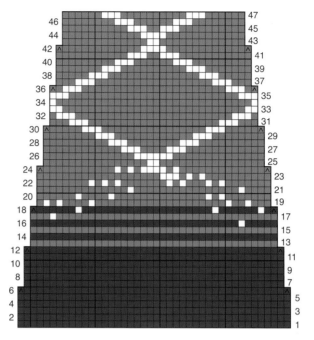

CHART 6

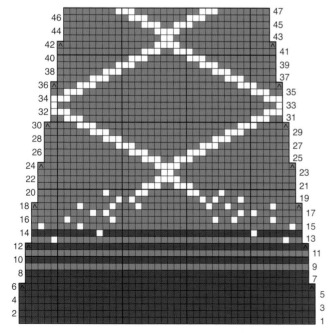

CHART 7

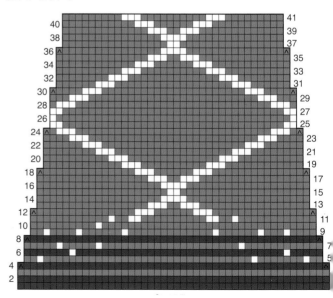

CHART 5

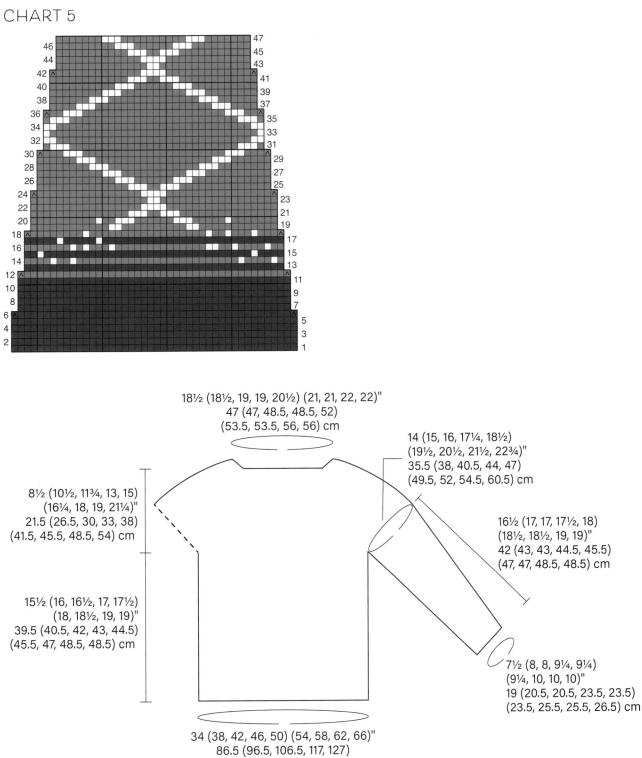

18½ (18½, 19, 19, 20½) (21, 21, 22, 22)"
47 (47, 48.5, 48.5, 52)
(53.5, 53.5, 56, 56) cm

14 (15, 16, 17¼, 18½)
(19½, 20½, 21½, 22¾)"
35.5 (38, 40.5, 44, 47)
(49.5, 52, 54.5, 60.5) cm

8½ (10½, 11¾, 13, 15)
(16¼, 18, 19, 21¼)"
21.5 (26.5, 30, 33, 38)
(41.5, 45.5, 48.5, 54) cm

16½ (17, 17, 17½, 18)
(18½, 18½, 19, 19)"
42 (43, 43, 44.5, 45.5)
(47, 47, 48.5, 48.5) cm

15½ (16, 16½, 17, 17½)
(18, 18½, 19, 19)"
39.5 (40.5, 42, 43, 44.5)
(45.5, 47, 48.5, 48.5) cm

7½ (8, 8, 9¼, 9¼)
(9¼, 10, 10, 10)"
19 (20.5, 20.5, 23.5, 23.5)
(23.5, 25.5, 25.5, 26.5) cm

34 (38, 42, 46, 50) (54, 58, 62, 66)"
86.5 (96.5, 106.5, 117, 127)
(137, 147.5, 157.5, 168) cm

Keepsakes & Curios

"Welcome home.."

Ron Weasley to Harry, *Harry Potter and the Chamber of Secrets*

THE BURROW BLANKET

Designed by **EMILY DAVIS**

SKILL LEVEL ⚡

H arry visits The Burrow, the Weasley home, for the first time in *Harry Potter and the Chamber of Secrets*, after Ron and his brothers rescue Harry from the Dursleys' house on Privet Drive. The Burrow, with its many leaning additions and structures, is the exact opposite of Privet Drive, full of warm colors, mismatched furniture, fanciful oddities, and, unsurprisingly, a lot of magic.

Set decorator Stephenie McMillan was called upon to decorate the Weasley home twice: once to introduce it, and then for a second time after the home was set ablaze by Death Eaters in *Harry Potter and the Half-Blood Prince*. "We completely changed the furniture and gave them a new kitchen. We gave them a piano. We kept the cast-iron fireplace, which would have survived, but otherwise we replaced it all," she said. McMillan and her team went thrift store shopping to replace much of the decor, surmising that Molly Weasley would take the opportunity to surround herself with comfort items—much like this traditional cozy blanket, inspired by The Burrow's earthy color palette and homey aesthetic.

The Burrow Blanket is a granny square motif blanket, pieced together in a color palette suitable to Molly Weasley's eclectic tastes. Molly leans toward browns, oranges, and greens in her decorating, and this blanket combines them to show how they unexpectedly work. A lovely edge is worked around the Blanket after seaming to bring all the squares together.

SIZE
One size

FINISHED MEASUREMENTS
Length: 60 in. / 152.5 cm
Width: 52 in. / 132 cm

YARN
DK weight (light #3) yarn, shown in WeCrochet *City Tweed DK* (55% merino wool, 25% superfine alpaca, 20% Donegal tweed; 123 yd. / 112 m per 1¾ oz. / 50 g ball), 6 balls each
Color A: #28198 Artichoke
Color B: #24546 Habanero
Color C: #24982 Blue Blood
Color D: #24543 Plum Wine
Color E: #24980 Snowshoe
Color F: #24550 Tabby

HOOK
- US H-8 / 5 mm crochet hook or size needed to obtain gauge

NOTIONS
- Blocking mat and pins
- Tapestry needle

GAUGE
14 sts and 8 rows = 4 in. / 10 cm in double crochet
Gauge is not critical for this pattern, but the yarn weight and hook size used will affect the finished measurements.

Continued on page 126

NOTES

- This blanket comprises various colored granny squares sewn together.
- Tabby is the contrast color used to border each square. It is also used for seaming and the blanket border.
- You will make 168 squares total.

SPECIAL TERM

picot: Ch 4, sl st to first ch. This st is worked in the same sp as a sc.

SPECIAL TECHNIQUE

Mattress Stitch

Mattress stitch creates an invisible seam along vertical edges. It can join any two edges, including turning chain edges, top edges, or bottom edges.

Place the pieces being sewn together side by side on a flat surface with the right sides facing you. Thread a piece of yarn about 3 times longer than the seam to be sewn into a tapestry needle.

Beginning at the bottom edge, insert the tapestry needle under first edge stitch on one piece, then under the corresponding stitch on the other piece.

*Insert the tapestry needle under the next stitch of the first piece, then under the next stitch of the other piece. Repeat from *, alternating sides until the seam is complete, ending on the last stitch on the first piece. Weave in ends on the wrong side to secure.

SQUARES (MAKE 34 WITH A, 34 WITH B, 34 WITH C, 33 WITH D, 33 WITH E)

Ch 4; join with sl st in first ch to form a ring.

Rnd 1: Ch 3 (counts as first dc here and throughout the pattern), 2 dc in ring, ch 2, [3 dc in ring, ch 2] 3 times; join with sl st in top of beg ch—12 dc, 4 ch-2 sp.

Rnd 2: Turn, sl st in ch-2 sp, (ch 3, 2 dc) in same ch-2 sp, *(3 dc, ch 2, 3 dc) in next ch-2 sp (corner made); rep from * 2 more times; (3 dc, ch 2) in first ch-2 sp, join with sl st in top of beg ch—24 dc, 4 ch-2 sp.

Rnd 3: Turn, sl st in ch-2 sp, (ch 3, 2 dc) in same ch-2 sp, *3 dc in sp between next 2 dc groups, (3 dc, ch 2, 3 dc) in next ch-2 sp; rep from * 2 more times, 3 dc in sp between next 2 dc groups; (3 dc, ch 2) in first ch-2 sp, join with sl st in top of beg ch—36 dc, 4 ch-2 sp.

Rnd 4: Turn, sl st in ch-2 sp, (ch 3, 2 dc) in same ch-2 sp, *[3 dc in sp between next 2 dc groups] twice, (3 dc, ch 2, 3 dc) in next ch-2 sp; rep from * 2 more times, [3 dc in sp between next 2 dc groups] twice, (3 dc, ch 2) in first ch-2 sp, join with sl st in top of beg ch—48 dc, 4 ch-2 sp.
Fasten off.

Rnd 5: Attach F in first dc of any side, ch 1, *sc in each st across, 3 sc in ch-2 sp; rep from * around, join with sl st to first sc—60 sc.
Fasten off.

ASSEMBLY

Block squares to 4¼ in. x 4¼ in. / 11 cm x 11 cm before joining. (Sample was steam blocked.) Using the Assembly Color Chart as a guide, and using F and mattress st, seam squares together.

BORDER

With WS facing, attach F on the bottom right corner of the blanket, ch 1.

Rnd 1: Sc 144 along the bottom edge, (sc 3) in corner, sc 168 along the left edge, (sc 3) in corner, sc 144 along the top edge, (sc 3) in corner, sc 168 along right edge, (sc 3) in corner; join with sl st to first sc—636 sc.

Rnd 2: Ch 1, turn, *sc 4, picot; rep from * around, join with sl st to first sc—636 sc, 159 picot.
Fasten off.

FINISHING

Weave in all ends.

CHART

KEY

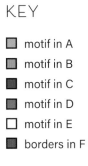 motif in A
 motif in B
 motif in C
 motif in D
 motif in E
 borders in F

52"
132 cm

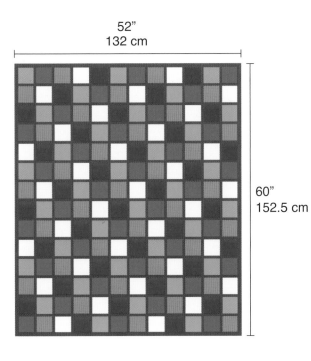

60"
152.5 cm

ABOVE: A behind-the-scenes photo of
The Burrow set.

Hogwarts Acceptance Letter Cross-Body Bag

Designed by **MARANATHA ENOIU**

SKILL LEVEL ⚡⚡

When a young witch or wizard turns eleven, they receive a very special letter by Owl Post: their Hogwarts acceptance letter. In order to create the scene where Harry receives thousands of duplicates of his letter in *Harry Potter and the Sorcerer's Stone*, special effects supervisor John Richardson went for a practical effect rather than producing the letters digitally. "We built machines that would fling the envelopes out at a very rapid but controlled speed," he explains. "These were built into the top of the set. We had another mechanism that fired them down the chimney using an air device." After showing director Chris Columbus the setup for the letters, Richardson recalls him exclaiming, "Gosh, it works! That's great!"

This bag is a cross-body purse that features details from the Hogwarts acceptance letter. Worked in one piece and seamed together at the sides, the bag is crocheted in the color of parchment paper with details such as the wax seal for the closure. Add a long strap to finish and be ready to wear this functional crochet piece that celebrates your love of all things Hogwarts.

SIZE
One size

FINAL MEASUREMENTS
Width: 10 in. / 25.5 cm
Length: 8 in. / 20 cm after seaming

YARN
Fingering weight (super fine #1), shown in WeCrochet *Stroll* (75% fine superwash merino wool, 25% nylon; 231 yds. / 211 m per 1¾ oz. / 50 g skein)
Color A: Bare, 3 skeins
Color B: #23701 Black, 1 skein
Color C: #27234 Hollyberry, 1 skein

HOOK
• US B-1 / 2.25 mm crochet hook or size needed to obtain gauge

NOTIONS
• Stitch marker
• Tapestry needle

GAUGE
35 sts and 40 rows = 4 in. / 10 cm in sc
Make sure to check your gauge.

NOTES
• The colorwork rows are worked on the right side.
• The strap is created with a Romanian cord. Remember to always turn cord clockwise.

Continued on page 130

SPECIAL TECHNIQUE

Romanian Cord

A Romanian cord is a flat reversible cord that can be used for straps and ties. When turning at the end of each row, always turn work clockwise.

Ch 2.

Row 1: Sc in 2nd ch from hook, turn—1 sc.

Row 2: Sc in horizontal bar at the end of row (cord edge), turn.

Row 3: Sc in 2 horizontal bars at the end of row (cord edge), turn.

Repeat Row 3 until cord is desired length. Fasten off.

BAG

Fsc 90.

Rows 2–162: Ch 1, sc across, turn—90 sc. Piece should measure 15 in. / 38 cm in length.

COLORWORK

Note: Refer to the chart or written instructions below. You will be working with the RS facing throughout the entire colorwork section. For all rows, join yarn on RS; at end of each row, fasten off and break yarn.

Row 1: With A, sc in first 27 sc; with B, sc in next 37 sc; with A, sc in last 26 sc—90 sc.

Row 2: With A, sc in first 26 sc; with B, sc in next sc; with A, sc in next 37 sc; with B, sc in next sc; with A, sc in last 25 sc.

Row 3: With A, sc in first 25 sc; with B, sc in next sc; with A, sc in next 11 sc; with B, sc in next 4 sc; with A, sc in next sc; with B, sc in next sc; with A, sc in next 3 sc; with B, sc in next sc; with A, sc in next sc; with B, sc in next 4 sc; with A, sc in next sc; with B, sc in next 4 sc; with A, sc in next 7 sc; with B, sc in next 2 sc; with A, sc in last 24 sc.

Row 4: With A, sc in first 24 sc; with B, sc in next sc; with A, sc in next 8 sc; with B, sc in next 3 sc; with A, sc in next sc; with B, sc in next sc; with A, sc in next 4 sc; with B, sc in next sc; with A, sc in next 3 sc; with B, sc in next sc; with A, sc in next sc; with B, sc in next sc; with A, sc in next 2 sc; with B, sc in next sc; with A, sc in next sc; with B, sc in next sc; with A, sc in next 2 sc; with B, sc in next sc; with A, sc in next sc; with B, sc in next 3 sc; with A, sc in next 4 sc; with B, sc in next 2 sc; with A, sc in last 23 sc.

Row 5: With A, sc in first 23 sc; with B, sc in next sc; with A, sc in next sc; with B, sc in next 3 sc; with A, sc in next sc; with B, sc in next 3 sc; [with A, sc in next sc; with B, sc in next sc] 3 times; with A, sc in next sc; with B, sc in next 2 sc; [with A, sc in next sc, with B, sc in next sc] 3 times; [with A, sc in next sc, with B, sc in next 4 sc] 2 times; with A, sc in next 2 sc; with B, sc in next sc; with A, sc in next 2 sc; with B, sc in next 3 sc; with A, sc in next sc; with B, sc in next sc; with A, sc in last 23 sc.

Row 6: With A, sc in first 23 sc; with B, sc in next sc; with A, sc in next 2 sc; with B, sc in next sc; with A, sc in next 3 sc; with B, sc in next sc; with A, sc in next 2 sc; with B, sc in next sc; [with A, sc in next sc, with B, sc in next sc] 2 times; with A, sc in next 2 sc; with B, sc in next sc; with A, sc in next sc; with B, sc in next 5 sc; with A, sc in next sc; with B, sc in next sc; with A, sc in next 2 sc; [with B, sc in next sc, with A, sc in next sc] 2 times; with B, sc in next sc; with A, sc in next 3 sc; with B, sc in next sc; with A, sc in next 2 sc; with B, sc in next sc; with A, sc in next 3 sc; with B, sc in next sc; with A, sc in last 23 sc.

Row 7: With A, sc in first 23 sc; with B, sc in next sc; with A, sc in next 2 sc; with B, sc in next 5 sc; with A, sc in next 2 sc; [with B, sc in next sc; with A, sc in next sc] 2 times; with B, sc in next 4 sc; [with A, sc in next sc, with B, sc in next sc] 4 times; with A, sc in next 2 sc; with B, sc in next sc; with A, sc in next sc; with B, sc in next sc; [with A, sc in next 2 sc; with B, sc in next sc] 2 times; with A, sc in next 2 sc; with B, sc in next 3 sc; with A, sc in next sc; with B, sc in next 2 sc; with A, sc in last 22 sc.

Row 8: With A, sc in first 22 sc; with B, sc in next 2 sc; with A, sc in next 2 sc; with B, sc in next sc; with A, sc in next 3 sc; with B, sc in next sc; with A, sc in next 2 sc; with B, sc in next 3 sc; with A, sc in next 23 sc; with B, sc in next sc; with A, sc in next 4 sc; with B, sc in next sc; with A, sc in next sc; with B, sc in next 3 sc; with A, sc in last 21 sc.

Row 9: With A, sc in first 21 sc; [with B, sc in next 3 sc; with A, sc in next sc] 2 times; with B, sc in next 3 sc; with A, sc in next 5 sc; with B, sc in next 16 sc; with A, sc in next 9 sc; with B, sc in next 3 sc; with A, sc in next sc; with B, sc in next sc; with A, sc in next sc; with B, sc in next 2 sc; with A, sc in last 20 sc.

Row 10: With A, sc in first 20 sc; with B, sc in next 2 sc; with A, sc in next sc; with B, sc in next sc; with A, sc in next 8 sc; with B, sc in next 5 sc; with A, sc in next 16 sc; with B, sc in next 6 sc; with A, sc in next 7 sc; with B, sc in next sc; with A, sc in last 23 sc.

Row 11: With A, sc in first 24 sc; with B, sc in next 2 sc; with A, sc in next 3 sc; with B, sc in next 3 sc; with A, sc in next 5 sc; with B, sc in next 2 sc; with A, sc in next 12 sc; with B, sc in next 2 sc; with A, sc in next 6 sc; with B, sc in next 2 sc; with A, sc in next 3 sc; with B, sc in next 2 sc; with A, sc in next 2 sc; with B, sc in next 2 sc; with A, sc in last 20 sc.

Row 12: With A, sc in first 21 sc; with B, sc in next 8 sc; with A, sc in next 5 sc; with B, sc in next 4 sc; with A, sc in next sc; with B, sc in next sc; with A, sc in next 10 sc; with B, sc in next sc; with A, sc in next 2 sc; with B, sc in next 3 sc; with A, sc in next 5 sc; with B, sc in next 8 sc; with A, sc in last 21 sc.

Row 13: With A, sc in first 23 sc; with B, sc in next sc; with A, sc in next 2 sc; with B, sc in next sc; with A, sc in next 6 sc; with B, sc in next 8 sc; with A, sc in next 8 sc; with B, sc in next sc; with A, sc in next 5 sc; with B, sc in next 2 sc; with A, sc in next 6 sc; with B, sc in next sc; with A, sc in next 2 sc; with B, sc in next sc; with A, sc in last 23 sc.

Row 14: With A, sc in first 22 sc; with B, sc in next 2 sc; with A, sc in next sc; with B, sc in next sc; with A, sc in next 6 sc; with B, sc in next sc; with A, sc in next sc; with B, sc in next sc; with A, sc in next 6 sc; with B, sc in next 2 sc; with A, sc in next 5 sc; with B, sc in next sc; with A, sc in next sc; with B, sc in next 4 sc; with A, sc in next 2 sc; with B, sc in next 2 sc; with A, sc in next 6 sc; with B, sc in next sc; with A, sc in next sc; with B, sc in next 2 sc; with A, sc in last 22 sc.

Row 15: With A, sc in first 21 sc; with B, sc in next 2 sc; with A, sc in next sc; with B, sc in next sc; with A, sc in next 6 sc; [with B, sc in next sc; with A, sc in next sc] 2 times; [with B, sc in next 2 sc; with A, sc in next sc] 2 times; with B, sc in next sc; with A, sc in next sc; [with B, sc in next 2 sc; with A, sc in next sc] 2 times; with B, sc in next sc; with A, sc in next sc; with B, sc in next 4 sc; with A, sc in next 3 sc; with B, sc in next sc; with A, sc in next 6 sc; with B, sc in next sc; with A, sc in next sc; with B, sc in next 2 sc; with A, sc in last 21 sc.

Row 16: With A, sc in first 21 sc; with B, sc in next 3 sc; with A, sc in next 7 sc; with B, sc in next 3 sc; with A, sc in next 2 sc; with B, sc in next sc; with A, sc in next sc; with B, sc in next sc; with A, sc in next 2 sc; with B, sc in next 2 sc; with A, sc in next 2 sc; with B, sc in next 2 sc; with A, sc in next sc; [with B, sc in next sc, with A, sc in next sc] 2 times; with B, sc in next 4 sc; with A, sc in next sc; with B, sc in next 2 sc; with A, sc in next 3 sc; with B, sc in next sc; with A, sc in next 7 sc; with B, sc in next 3 sc; with A, sc in last 21 sc.

Row 17: With A, sc in first 31 sc; with B, sc in next 4 sc; with A, sc in next sc; with B, sc in next 3 sc; with A, sc in next 2 sc; with B, sc in next 2 sc; [with A, sc in next sc, with B, sc in next sc] 2 times; with A, sc in next sc; with B, sc in next 3 sc; with A, sc in next sc; with B, sc in next 2 sc; with A, sc in next 4 sc; with B, sc in next sc; with A, sc in last 31 sc.

Row 18: With A, sc in first 31 sc; with B, sc in next sc; with A, sc in next sc; with B, sc in next 3 sc; with A, sc in next sc; with B, sc in next sc; with A, sc in next sc; with B, sc in next 3 sc; with A, sc in next 2 sc; with B, sc in next sc; with A, sc in next sc; with B, sc in next sc; with A, sc in next 4 sc; with B, sc in next 2 sc; with A, sc in next 2 sc; with B, sc in next 3 sc; with A, sc in next sc; with B, sc in next sc; with A, sc in last 30 sc.

Row 19: With A, sc in first 31 sc; with B, sc in next sc; with A, sc in next 3 sc; with B, sc in next 6 sc; with A, sc in next 3 sc; with B, sc in next sc; with A, sc in next sc; with B, sc in next sc; with A, sc in next 4 sc; with B, sc in next 4 sc; with A, sc in next 4 sc; with B, sc in next sc; with A, sc in last 30 sc.

Row 20: With A, sc in first 30 sc; with B, sc in next sc; with A, sc in next sc; with B, sc in next 3 sc; with A, sc in next sc; with B, sc in next 2 sc; with A, sc in next sc; with B, sc in next 13 sc; with A, sc in next 2 sc; with B, sc in next sc; with A, sc in next 2 sc; with B, sc in next 2 sc; with A, sc in last 31 sc.

Row 21: With A, sc in first 30 sc; with B, sc in next sc; with A, sc in next 3 sc; with B, sc in next 2 sc; with A, sc in next 2 sc; with B, sc in next 2 sc; with A, sc in next 11 sc; [with B, sc in next sc; with A, sc in next 2 sc] 2 times; with B, sc in next sc; with A, sc in last 32 sc.

Row 22: With A, sc in first 31 sc; with B, sc in next 2 sc; with A, sc in next sc; with B, sc in next 2 sc; with A, sc in next 2 sc; with B, sc in next 2 sc; [with A, sc in next sc; with B, sc in next 4 sc] 2 times; with A, sc in next sc; with B, sc in next sc; with A, sc in next 2 sc; with B, sc in next sc; with A, sc in last 35 sc.

Row 23: With A, sc in first 32 sc; with B, sc in next sc; with A, sc in next sc; with B, sc in next sc; with A, sc in next 4 sc; with B, sc in next sc; with A, sc in next 2 sc; with B, sc in next 2 sc; with A, sc in next 3 sc; with B, sc in next 2 sc; with A, sc in next 2 sc; with B, sc in next sc; with A, sc in next 2 sc; with B, sc in next sc; with A, sc in last 35 sc.

Row 24: With A, sc in first 34 sc; with B, sc in next 5 sc; with A, sc in next 3 sc; [with B, sc in next 2 sc; with A, sc in next 3 sc] 2 times; with B, sc in next 4 sc; with A, sc in last 34 sc.

Row 25: With A, sc in first 34 sc; with B, sc in next sc; with A, sc in next 5 sc; with B, sc in next 11 sc; with A, sc in next 5 sc; with B, sc in next sc; with A, sc in last 33 sc.

Row 26: With A, sc in first 34 sc; with B, sc in next 5 sc; [with A, sc in next 3 sc, with B, sc in next 2 sc] 2 times; with A, sc in next 3 sc; with B, sc in next 5 sc; with A, sc in last 33 sc.

Row 27: With A, sc in first 34 sc; with B, sc in next sc; with A, sc in next 4 sc; with B, sc in next sc; with A, sc in next 2 sc; with B, sc in next 2 sc; with A, sc in next 3 sc; with B, sc in next 2 sc; with A, sc in next 2 sc; with B, sc in next sc; with A, sc in next 4 sc; with B, sc in next sc; with A, sc in last 33 sc.

Row 28: With A, sc in first 32 sc; with B, sc in next 3 sc; with A, sc in next 4 sc; with B, sc in next sc; [with A, sc in next sc; with B, sc in next 4 sc] 2 times; with A, sc in next sc; with B, sc in next sc; with A, sc in next 4 sc; with B, sc in next 3 sc; with A, sc in last 31 sc.

Row 29: With A, sc in first 32 sc; with B, sc in next sc; with A, sc in next 6 sc; with B, sc in next sc; with A, sc in next 11 sc; with B, sc in next sc; with A, sc in next 6 sc; with B, sc in next sc; with A, sc in last 31 sc.

Row 30: With A, sc in first 31 sc; with B, sc in next sc; with A, sc in next sc; with B, sc in next 2 sc; with A, sc in next 2 sc; with B, sc in next sc; with A, sc in next sc; with B, sc in next 13 sc; with A, sc in next sc; with B, sc in next 2 sc; with A, sc in next 2 sc; with B, sc in next sc; with A, sc in next sc; with B, sc in next sc; with A, sc in last 30 sc.

Row 31: With A, sc in first 29 sc; with B, sc in next 2 sc; with A, sc in next 2 sc; with B, sc in next sc; with A, sc in next sc; with B, sc in next 4 sc; with A, sc in next 5 sc; with B, sc in next sc; with A, sc in next sc; with B, sc in next sc; with A, sc in next 5 sc; with B, sc in next sc; with A, sc in next sc; with B, sc in next sc; with A, sc in next sc; with B, sc in next 3 sc; with A, sc in next sc; with B, sc in next 2 sc; with A, sc in last 28 sc.

Row 32: With A, sc in first 29 sc; [with B, sc in next 2 sc; with A, sc in next 2 sc] 2 times; with B, sc in next 3 sc; with A, sc in next 4 sc; with B, sc in next sc; with A, sc in next sc; with B, sc in next sc; with A, sc in next 2 sc; with B, sc in next sc; with A, sc in next sc; with B, sc in next 8 sc; with A, sc in next sc; with B, sc in next 2 sc; with A, sc in last 28 sc.

Row 33: With A, sc in first 29 sc; with B, sc in next 2 sc; with A, sc in next 2 sc; with B, sc in next 3 sc; with A, sc in next 3 sc; with B, sc in next 2 sc; with

A, sc in next 3 sc; [with B, sc in next sc; with A, sc in next sc] 2 times; with B, sc in next 2 sc; with A, sc in next sc; with B, sc in next sc; with A, sc in next 5 sc; with A, sc in next 2 sc; with B, sc in next 2 sc; with A, sc in last 28 sc.

Row 34: With A, sc in first 29 sc; with B, sc in next 3 sc; with A, sc in next 2 sc; with B, sc in next 6 sc; with A, sc in next 4 sc; [with B, sc in next sc; with A, sc in next sc] 2 times; with B, sc in next 3 sc; with A, sc in next sc; with B, sc in next 4 sc; with A, sc in next sc; with B, sc in next sc; with A, sc in next sc; with B, sc in next 3 sc; with A, sc in last 28 sc.

Row 35: With A, [dec over next 2 sc] 2 times, sc in next 27 sc; with B, sc in next sc; with A, sc in next 2 sc; with B, sc in next 4 sc; with A, sc in next 6 sc; [with B, sc in next sc, with A, sc in next sc] 2 times; with B, sc in next 8 sc; [with A, sc in next sc; with B, sc in next sc] 2 times; with A, sc in next 26 sc, [dec over next 2 sc] 2 times—86 sc.

Row 36: With A, [dec over next 2 sc] 2 times, sc in next 25 sc; with B, sc in next 2 sc; with A, sc in next sc; with B, sc in next 5 sc; with A, sc in next 5 sc; [with B, sc in next sc, with A, sc in next sc] 2 times; with B, sc in next 3 sc; with A, sc in next sc; with B, sc in next 4 sc; with A, sc in next 2 sc; with B, sc in next 2 sc; with A, sc in next 24 sc, [dec over next 2 sc] 2 times—82 sc.

Row 37: With A, dec over first 2 sc, sc in next 17 sc; with B, sc in next 4 sc; with A, sc in next 5 sc; with B, sc in next 8 sc; with A, sc in next 4 sc; [with B, sc in next sc, with A, sc in next sc] 2 times; with B, sc in next 2 sc; with A, sc in next 3 sc; with B, sc in next 2 sc; with A, sc in next 2 sc; with B, sc in next 2 sc; with A, sc in next 5 sc; with B, sc in next 4 sc; with A, sc in next 16 sc, dec over last 2 sc—80 sc.

Row 38: With A, [dec over next 2 sc] 2 times, sc in next 14 sc; with B, sc in

next sc; with A, sc in next 2 sc; with B, sc in next 2 sc; with A, sc in next 6 sc; with B, sc in next 6 sc; with A, sc in next 4 sc; with B, sc in next sc; with A, sc in next sc; with B, sc in next sc; with A, sc in next 2 sc; with B, sc in next sc; with A, sc in next 3 sc; with B, sc in next 2 sc; with A, sc in next sc; with B, sc in next sc; with A, sc in next 6 sc; with B, sc in next 2 sc; with A, sc in next 2 sc; with B, sc in next sc; with A, sc in next 13 sc, [dec over next 2 sc] 2 times—76 sc.

Row 39: With A, [dec over next 2 sc] 2 times, sc in next 13 sc; with B, sc in next sc; with A, sc in next 2 sc; with B, sc in next 2 sc; with A, sc in next 5 sc; with B, sc in next 6 sc; with A, sc in next 4 sc; with B, sc in next sc; with A, sc in next sc; with B, sc in next sc; with A, sc in next 5 sc; with B, sc in next 5 sc; with A, sc in next 5 sc; with B, sc in next 2 sc; with A, sc in next 2 sc; with B, sc in next sc; with A, sc in next 12 sc, [dec over next 2 sc] 2 times—72 sc.

Row 40: With A, dec over first 2 sc, sc in next 12 sc; with B, sc in next sc; with A, sc in next 4 sc; with B, sc in next 3 sc; with A, sc in next 8 sc; with B, sc in next 2 sc; with A, sc in next 3 sc; with B, sc in next sc; with A, sc in next sc; with B, sc in next sc; with A, sc in next 3 sc; with B, sc in next 2 sc; with A, sc in next 8 sc; with B, sc in next 3 sc; with A, sc in next 4 sc; with B, sc in next sc; with A, sc in next 11 sc, dec over last 2 sc—70 sc.

Row 41: With A, [dec over next 2 sc] 2 times, sc in next 8 sc; with B, sc in next 5 sc; with A, sc in next 3 sc; with B, sc in next 2 sc; with A, sc in next 9 sc; with B, sc in next 9 sc; with A, sc in next 9 sc; with B, sc in next 2 sc; with A, sc in next 3 sc; with B, sc in next 5 sc; with A, sc in next 7 sc, [dec over next 2 sc] 2 times—66 sc.

Row 42: With A, dec over first 2 sc, sc in next 12 sc; with B, sc in next 2 sc; with A, sc in next 3 sc; with B, sc in

next 5 sc; with A, sc in next 6 sc; with B, sc in next 7 sc; with A, sc in next 6 sc; with B, sc in next 5 sc; with A, sc in next 3 sc; with B, sc in next 2 sc; with A, sc in next 11 sc, dec over last 2 sc—64 sc.

Row 43: With A, [dec over next 2 sc] 2 times, 10 sc; with B, sc in next 2 sc; with A, sc in next 6 sc; with B, sc in next sc; [with A, sc in next 9 sc; with B, sc in next sc] 2 times; with A, sc in next 6 sc; with B, sc in next 2 sc; with A, sc in next 9 sc, [dec over next 2 sc] 2 times—60 sc.

Row 44: With A, [dec over next 2 sc] 3 times, sc in next 7 sc; with B, sc in next 3 sc; with A, sc in next 3 sc; with B, sc in next 2 sc; with A, sc in next 19 sc; with B, sc in next 2 sc; with A, sc in next 3 sc; with B, sc in next 3 sc; with A, sc in next 6 sc, [dec over next 2 sc] 3 times—54 sc.

Row 45: With A, [dec over next 2 sc] 2 times, sc in next 8 sc; with B, sc in next 2 sc; with A, sc in next sc; with B, sc in next sc; with A, sc in next 2 sc; with B, sc in next 19 sc; with A, sc in next 2 sc; with B, sc in next sc; with A, sc in next sc; with B, sc in next 2 sc; with A, sc in next 7 sc, [dec over next 2 sc] 2 times—50 sc.

Row 46: With A, [dec over next 2 sc] 3 times, sc in next 5 sc; with B, sc in next 3 sc; with A, sc in next 23 sc; with B, sc in next 3 sc; with A, sc in next 4 sc, [dec over next 2 sc] 3 times—44 sc.

Row 47: With A, [dec over next 2 sc] 2 times, sc in next 7 sc; with B, sc in next 5 sc; with A, sc in next 13 sc; with B, sc in next 5 sc; with A, sc in next 6 sc, [dec over next 2 sc] 2 times—40 sc.

Row 48: With A, dec over first 2 sc, sc in next 11 sc; with B, sc in next 2 sc; with A, sc in next 11 sc; with B, sc in next 2 sc; with A, sc in next 10 sc, dec over last 2 sc—38 sc.

Row 49: With A, [dec over next 2 sc] 3 times, sc in next 8 sc; with B, sc in next 11 sc; with A, sc in next 7 sc, [dec over next 2 sc] 3 times—32 sc.

Row 50: With A, [dec over next 2 sc] 3 times, sc in next 20 sc, [dec over next 2 sc] 3 times—26 sc.

Row 51: With A, [dec over next 2 sc] 3 times, sc in next 14 sc, [dec over next 2 sc] 3 times—20 sc.

Row 52: With A, [dec over next 2 sc] 3 times, sc in next 8 sc, [dec over next 2 sc] 3 times—14 sc.

Row 53: With A, [dec over next 2 sc] 2 times, sc in next 6 sc, [dec over next 2 sc] 2 times—10 sc.

Rows 54-79: With A, sc across.

WAX SEAL

With C, make a magic ring.
Rnd 1: 10 sc into magic ring—10 sc.
Rnd 2: [Sc in next sc, inc in next sc] evenly around—15 sc.
Rnd 3: [Sc in next 2 sc, inc in next sc] around—20 sc.
Rnd 4: [Sc in next 3 sc, inc in next sc] around—25 sc.

Rnd 5: [Sc in next 4 sc, inc in next sc] around—30 sc.
Rnd 6: [Sc in next 5 sc, inc in next sc] around—35 sc.
Rnd 7: [Sc in next 6 sc, inc in next sc] around—40 sc.
Rnd 8: [Sc in next 7 sc, inc in next sc] around—45 sc.
Rnd 9: [Sc in next 8 sc, inc in next sc] around—50 sc.
Rnd 10: Sc in blo around.
Using surface sl sts, stitch an H on front.

STRAP

Make a Romanian cord: With two strands of B held tog, ch 2.
Row 1: Sc in 2nd ch from hook, turn—1 sc.
Row 2: Sc in horizontal bar at the end of row, turn.
Row 3: Sc in 2 horizontal bars at the end of the row, turn.
Rep Row 3 until the strap measures 50 in. / 127 cm.

ASSEMBLY

Fold bag with RS tog so that the edge meets the top of the flap. Sc through both layers up each side of bag to seam. Sew strap to either side of the bag at top seam.
Attach A to the top of either side of flap piece and sc evenly around for a clean border.
Sew wax seal on front of bag at bottom center, sewing only along the sides of the wax seal to enable the tongue flap to fit through.
Weave in ends.

CHART

KEY

☐ sc in color A

■ sc in color B

⬚⟨∧⟩ sc2tog in color A

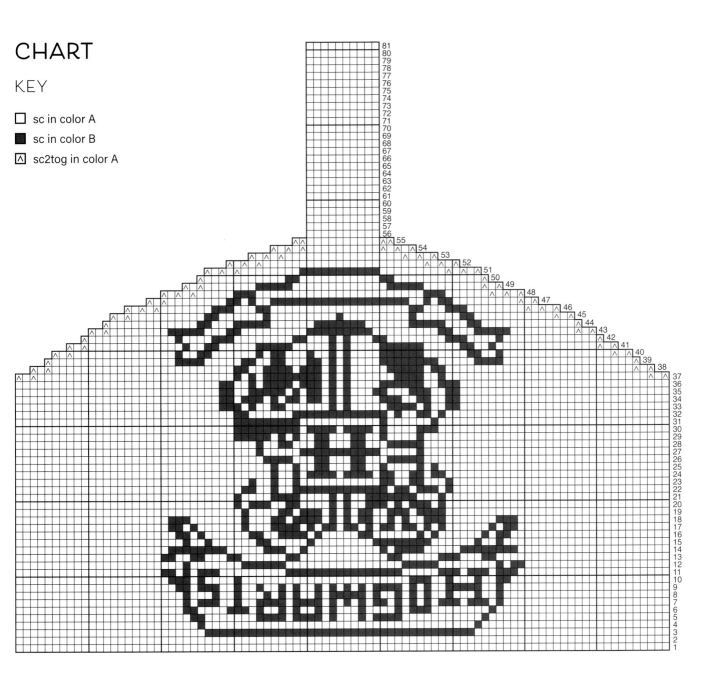

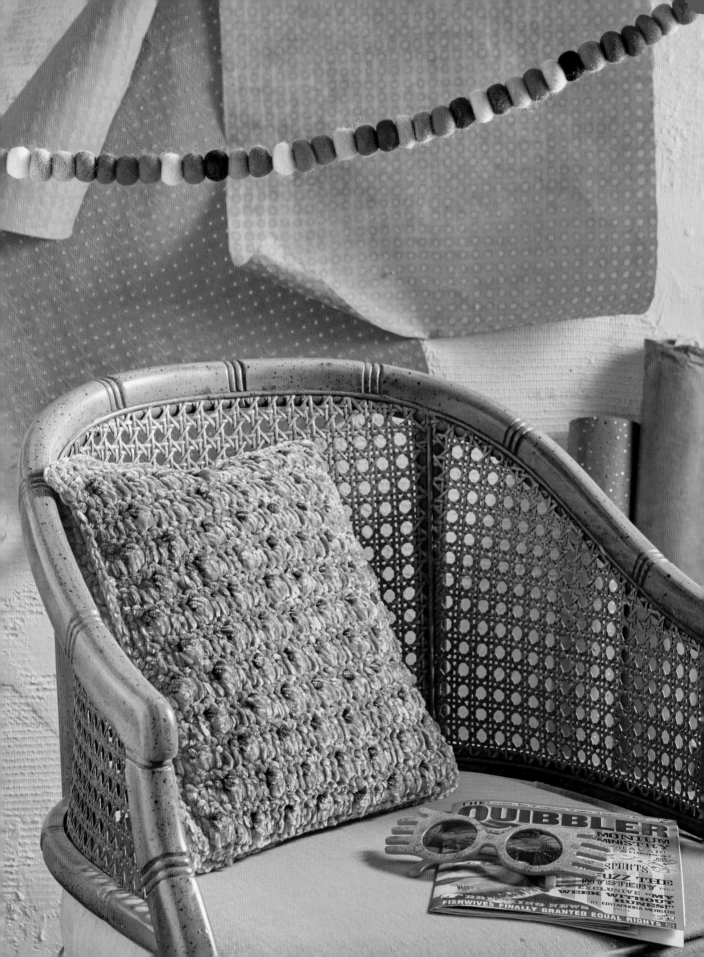

THE DIRIGIBLE PLUM PILLOW

Designed by **ALYSHA LITTLEJOHN**

SKILL LEVEL ⚡

Dirigible Plums first appear in the Harry Potter films in *Harry Potter and the Order of the Phoenix*, where Luna Lovegood wears them as earrings. A floating fruit that grows upside down from a twisted tree, the plums reappear in *Harry Potter and the Deathly Hallows – Part 1* outside the Lovegood house, a whimsical leaning tower that tapers off at the top. The house is a reflection of the Lovegoods' eclectic taste and is filled with paintings of magical creatures that Luna created herself. These paintings were in turn inspired by drawings by Evanna Lynch, who played Luna. "Evanna has a very artistic eye," said set decorator Stephenie McMillan, "and came up with some great ideas. The end result is wonderfully eclectic, but homey."

This Dirigible Plum Pillow is crocheted with ultrasoft velvet yarn in the vibrant colors of Dirigible Plums. Each plum pops from the background fabric with wonderfully textured crochet stitches. Style your pillow right side up for plums that have already been picked, or flip your pillow upside down if your plums are still growing!

SIZE
One size

FINISHED MEASUREMENTS
Length: 16 in. / 40.5 cm
Height: 16 in. / 40.5 cm

YARN
Bulky weight (bulky #5) yarn, shown in Bernat Velvet (100% polyester; 315 yd. / 288 m per 10.5 oz. / 300 g skein)
Color A: Terracotta Rose, 1 skein
Color C: Pine, 1 skein
Worsted weight (medium #4) yarn, shown in Go Handmade Bohème Velvet "Double" (100% polyester; 77 yd. / 70 m per 1.8 oz / 50 g skein)
Color B: #670 Warm Orange, 2 skeins

HOOK
- US I-9 / 5.5 mm crochet hook or size needed to obtain gauge

NOTIONS
- 16 in. / 40.5 cm square pillow form
  Tapestry needle

GAUGE
9 sts and 4 rows = 4 in. / 10 cm in dc
Make sure to check your gauge.

NOTES
- Turning chain 2 does not count as a stitch.
- Carry unused strands of yarn across the back of the work. Color changes occur in the last yarn over of a stitch.

Continued on page 138

ABOVE: Concept art of the Dirigible Plums by Adam Brockbank for *Harry Potter and the Deathly Hallows – Part 1.*

FRONT/BACK PANEL (MAKE 2)

With A, ch 36.

Row 1: Sc in 2nd ch from hook and in each ch across, turn—35 sc.

Row 2: Ch 1, sc in each st across, turn.

Row 3: Ch 2, [dc in next 3 sts (switch to B on last yarn over), bo (switch to C on last yarn over), sc4tog between each section of previously worked bo (switch to A on last yarn over)] 8 times, cut B and C, dc in last 3 sts, turn—8 bo, 27 dc.

Row 4: Ch 2, sc in each st across, turn.

Row 5: Ch 2, dc in next 5 sts (switch to B on last yarn over), [bo (switch to C on last yarn over), sc4tog between each section of previously worked bo (switch to A on last yarn over), dc in next 3 sts (switch to B on last yarn over)] 6 times, bo (switch to C on last yarn over), sc4tog between each section of previously worked bo (switch to A on last yarn over), cut B and C, dc in last 5 sts—7 bo, 28 dc.

Rows 6–21: Rep Rows 2–5 four times.

Rows 22–23: Rep Rows 2–3.

Rows 24–25: Ch 1, sc in each st across, turn. Fasten off. Weave in ends.

FINISHING

With WSs facing, place front and back pieces tog. Join A with sl st to any corner st of pillow, ch 1. Working through both thicknesses, work sc evenly around 3 sides of the cushion with 3 sc in each corner. Insert pillow form, then join last side. Join with sl st to first sc.

Fasten off. Weave in ends.

CHART

KEY

◖ chain (ch)

+ single crochet (sc)

T double crochet (dc)

⬙ bobble (bo)

⋏ single crochet 4 together (sc4tog)

REDUCED SAMPLE OF PATTERN

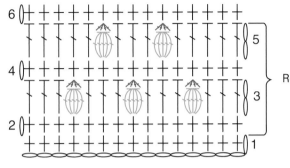

Repeat

ABOVE: Harry, Ron, and Hermione on the steps of the Lovegood house in *Harry Potter and the Deathly Hallows – Part 1*.

THE GRIM DOILY

Designed by **ROHN STRONG**

SKILL LEVEL ⚡⚡

To those in the wizarding world, the Grim is an omen of death. Taking the form of a giant spectral dog, the Grim is thought to bring about the demise of any person who is unlucky enough to encounter it. In the Harry Potter films, the Grim is first brought to Harry's attention when he attends Professor Trelawney's Divination class. In a class exercise, students study the tea leaves left at the bottom of their teacups to divine the future and predict fortunes. While Ron looks inside Harry's cup and sees a cross and a sun—surmising that Harry will suffer but be happy about it—Professor Trelawney sees something much more sinister: the Grim, indicating that Harry himself is in mortal danger.

Inspired by Professor Trelawny's alarming prediction, the Grim doily is crocheted with black yarn set against a white background to represent the tea leaves at the bottom of Harry's teacup. The doily is worked first in rows and then with an easy-to-follow chart to bring the Grim to life. Finish the doily with a beautiful scalloped border for that pretty and classic touch!

FINISHED MEASUREMENTS
Diameter: 16¾ in. / 42.5 c

YARN
Worsted weight (medium #4) yarn, shown in Premier Yarns *Premier Home* (85% recycled cotton, 15% polyester; 131 yd. / 120 m per 2.65 oz. / 75 g skein)

Main Color (MC): #01 White, 2 skeins
Contrast Color (CC): #16 Black, 1 skein

HOOK
- US D-3 / 3.25 mm crochet hook or size needed to obtain gauge

NOTIONS
- Tapestry needle

GAUGE
20 sts and 20 rows = 4 in. / 10 cm in sc
Make sure to check your gauge.

NOTES
- Doily is worked in one piece from the bottom up. Increases are then worked on either side. Decreases form the top of the doily.
- Follow the written instructions, or follow the chart from right to left for right-side rows and left to right for wrong-side rows.

With MC, ch 33.

Follow the chart or the following written instructions:

Row 1 (WS): Sc in 2nd ch from hook and in each ch across—32 sc.

Row 2 (RS): Ch 1, turn, 2 sc in 1st sc, sc in each st across to last sc, 2 sc in last sc—34 sc.

Row 3: Rep Row 2—36 sc.

Row 4: Rep Row 2—38 sc.

Row 5: Rep Row 2—40 sc.

Row 6: Rep Row 2—42 sc.

Row 7: Rep Row 2—44 sc.

Row 8: Ch 1, turn, 2 sc in 1st sc, sc in next 24 sc; with CC, sc in next sc; with MC, sc to last sc, 2 sc in last sc—46 sc.

Row 9: Ch 1, turn, with MC, 2 sc in 1st sc, sc in next 19 sc; with CC, sc in next sc; with MC, sc to last sc, 2 sc in last sc—48 sc.

Row 10: Ch 1, turn, with MC, 2 sc in 1st sc, sc in next 27 sc; with CC, sc in next 2 sc; with MC, sc to last sc, 2 sc in last sc—50 sc.

Row 11: Ch 1, turn, with MC, 2 sc in 1st sc, sc in next 16 sc, [with CC, sc in next sc; with MC, sc in next sc] twice; with CC, sc in next sc; with MC, sc to last sc, 2 sc in last sc—52 sc.

Row 12: Ch 1, turn, with MC, 2 sc in 1st sc, sc in next 30 sc; [with CC, sc in next sc; with MC, sc in next sc] twice; with CC, sc in next sc; with MC, sc to last sc, 2 sc in last sc—54 sc.

Row 13: Ch 1, turn, with MC, 2 sc in 1st sc, sc in next 19 sc; with CC, sc in next 3 sc; with MC, sc to last sc, 2 sc in last sc—56 sc.

Row 14: Ch 1, turn, with MC, 2 sc in 1st sc, sc in next 23 sc; with CC, sc in next 2 sc; with MC, sc in next 6 sc; with CC, sc in next sc; with MC, sc in next 2 sc; with CC, sc in next 2 sc; with MC, sc to last sc, 2 sc in last sc—58 sc.

Row 15: Ch 1, turn, with MC, 2 sc in 1st sc, sc in next 25 sc; with CC, sc in next sc; with MC, sc in next 3 sc; with CC, sc in next sc; with MC, sc in next 8 sc; with CC, sc in next sc; with MC,

sc to last sc, 2 sc in last sc—60 sc.

Row 16: Ch 1, turn, with MC, 2 sc in 1st sc, sc in next 16 sc; with CC, sc in next sc; with MC, sc in next 6 sc; with CC, sc in next 3 sc; with MC, sc in next 2 sc; with CC, sc in next sc; with MC, sc in next 2 sc; with CC, sc in next sc; with MC, sc in next 9 sc; with CC, sc in next sc; with MC, sc to last sc, 2 sc in last sc—62 sc.

Row 17: Ch 1, turn, with MC, 2 sc in 1st sc, sc in next 19 sc; with CC, sc in next sc; with MC, sc in next sc; with CC, sc in next 4 sc; with MC, sc in next 4 sc; with CC, sc in next sc; with MC, sc in next 5 sc; with CC, sc in next sc; with MC, sc to last sc, 2 sc in last sc—64 sc.

Row 18: Ch 1, turn, with MC, 2 sc in 1st sc, sc in next 22 sc; with CC, sc in next 2 sc; with MC, sc in next 10 sc; with CC, sc in next 2 sc; with MC, sc in next sc; with CC, sc in next sc; with MC, sc in next sc; with CC, sc in next 2 sc; with MC, sc to last sc, 2 sc in last sc—66 sc.

Row 19: Ch 1, turn, with MC, 2 sc in 1st sc, sc in next 16 sc; with CC, sc in next sc; with MC, sc in next 4 sc; with CC, sc in next sc; with MC, sc in next sc; with CC, sc in next 3 sc; with MC, sc in next sc; with CC, sc in next sc; with MC, sc in next 13 sc; with CC, sc in next sc; with MC, sc to last sc, 2 sc in last sc—68 sc.

Row 20: Ch 1, turn, with MC, sc in 1st 32 sc; with CC, sc in next 3 sc; with MC, sc in next 5 sc; with CC, sc in next 3 sc; with MC, sc in next 2 sc; with CC, sc in next 4 sc; with MC, sc in next 2 sc; with CC, sc in next 2 sc; with MC, sc to end of row.

Row 21: Ch 1, turn, with MC, 2 sc in 1st sc, sc in next 13 sc; with CC, sc in next sc; with MC, sc in next 2 sc; with CC, sc in next 3 sc; with MC, sc in next sc; with CC, sc in next 6 sc; with MC, sc in next 5 sc; with CC, sc in next 2 sc; with MC, sc in next 2 sc; with CC, sc in next 3 sc; with MC, sc in next 17 sc; with CC, sc in next

sc; with MC, sc to last sc, 2 sc in last sc—70 sc.

Row 22: Ch 1, turn, with MC, sc in 1st 31 sc; with CC, sc in next sc; with MC, sc in next 6 sc; with CC, sc in next sc; with MC, sc in next 2 sc; with CC, sc in next 10 sc; with MC, sc in next sc; with CC, sc in next 2 sc; with MC, sc to end of row.

Row 23: Ch 1, turn, with MC, 2 sc in 1st sc, sc in next 13 sc; with CC, sc in next sc; with MC, sc in next sc; with CC, sc in next sc; with MC, sc in next 2 sc; with CC, sc in next 10 sc; with MC, sc in next 6 sc; with CC, sc in next 2 sc; with MC, sc to last sc, 2 sc in last sc—72 sc.

Row 24: Ch 1, turn, with MC, sc in 1st 22 sc; with CC, sc in next sc; with MC, sc in next 6 sc; with CC, sc in next sc; with MC, sc in next 4 sc; with CC, sc in next 3 sc; with MC, sc in next sc; with CC, sc in next 13 sc; with MC, sc in next sc; with CC, sc in next sc; with MC, sc in next 2 sc; with CC, sc in next sc; with MC, sc to end of row.

Row 25: Ch 1, turn, with MC, 2 sc in 1st sc, sc in next 14 sc; with CC, sc in next 2 sc; with MC, sc in next 3 sc; with CC, sc in next 4 sc; with MC, sc in next sc; with CC, sc in next 8 sc; with MC, sc to last sc, 2 sc in last sc—74 sc.

Row 26: Ch 1, turn, with MC, sc in 1st 37 sc; with CC, sc in next sc; with MC, sc in next sc; with CC, sc in next 13 sc; [with MC, sc in next sc; with CC, sc in next sc] twice; with MC, sc to end of row.

Row 27: Ch 1, turn, with MC, 2 sc in 1st sc, sc in next 14 sc; with CC, sc in next 20 sc; with MC, sc to last sc, 2 sc in last sc—76 sc.

Row 28: Ch 1, turn, with MC, sc in 1st 37 sc; with CC, sc in next 2 sc; with MC, sc in next sc; with CC, sc in next 16 sc; with MC, sc in next sc; with CC, sc in next sc; with MC, sc to end of row.

Row 29: Ch 1, turn, with MC, sc in 1st 16 sc; with CC, sc in next 26 sc; with MC, sc in next 4 sc; with CC, sc in next 2 sc; with MC, sc in next 15 sc; with CC, sc in next sc; with MC, sc to end of row.

Row 30: Ch 1, turn, with MC, sc in 1st 11 sc; with CC, sc in next 2 sc; with MC, sc in next 24 sc; with CC, sc in next 22 sc; with MC, sc in next 2 sc; with CC, sc in next sc; with MC, sc to end of row.

Row 31: Ch 1, turn, with MC, sc in 1st 15 sc; with CC, sc in next sc; with MC, sc in next 2 sc; with CC, sc in next 22 sc; with MC, sc to end of row.

Row 32: Ch 1, turn, with MC, sc in 1st 27 sc; with CC, sc in next sc; with MC, sc in next 7 sc; with CC, sc in next 15 sc; with MC, sc in next sc; with CC, sc in next 11 sc; with MC, sc to end of row.

Row 33: Ch 1, turn, with MC, sc in 1st 15 sc; with CC, sc in next 8 sc; with MC, sc in next 2 sc; with CC, sc in next 17 sc; with MC, sc in next 8 sc; with CC, sc in next 3 sc; with MC, sc to end of row.

Row 34: Ch 1, turn, with MC, sc in 1st 24 sc; with CC, sc in next 4 sc; with MC, sc in next 3 sc; with CC, sc in next 20 sc; with MC, sc in next 3 sc; with CC, sc in next 5 sc; with MC, sc in next sc; with CC, sc in next sc; with MC, sc in next sc; with CC, sc in next 2 sc; with MC, sc in next sc; with CC, sc in next sc; with MC, sc to end of row.

Row 35: Ch 1, turn, with MC, sc in 1st 14 sc; with CC, sc in next sc; with MC, sc in next 2 sc; with CC, sc in next 4 sc; with MC, sc in next 3 sc; with CC, sc in next 27 sc; with MC, sc in next 7 sc; with CC, sc in next sc; with MC, sc to end of row.

Row 36: Ch 1, turn, with MC, sc in 1st 11 sc; with CC, sc in next sc; with MC, sc in next 9 sc; with CC, sc in next 3 sc; with MC, sc in next 3 sc; with CC, sc in next 26 sc; with MC, sc in next 3

sc; with CC, sc in next 2 sc; with MC, sc in next sc; with CC, sc in next 2 sc; with MC, sc in next sc; with CC, sc in next 3 sc; with MC, sc to end of row.

Row 37: Ch 1, turn, with MC, sc in 1st 10 sc; with CC, sc in next sc; with MC, sc in next sc; with CC, sc in next 8 sc; with MC, sc in next 2 sc; with CC, sc in next 26 sc; with MC, sc in next 3 sc; with CC, sc in next 5 sc; with MC, sc to end of row.

Row 38: Ch 1, turn, with MC, sc in 1st 20 sc; with CC, sc in next 6 sc; with MC, sc in next 2 sc; with CC, sc in next 27 sc; with MC, sc in next 2 sc; with CC, sc in next 5 sc; with MC, sc in next 2 sc; with CC, sc in next sc; with MC, sc to end of row.

Row 39: Ch 1, turn, with MC, sc in 1st 8 sc; with CC, sc in next sc; with MC, sc in next 3 sc; with CC, sc in next 5 sc; with MC, sc in next 4 sc; with CC, sc in next 2 sc; with MC, sc in next sc; with CC, sc in next 31 sc; with MC, sc to end of row.

Row 40: Ch 1, turn, with MC, sc in 1st 22 sc; with CC, sc in next 28 sc; [with MC, sc in next sc; with CC, sc in next sc] twice; with MC, sc in next 4 sc; with CC, sc in next sc; with MC, sc in next 2 sc; with CC, sc in next 3 sc; with MC, sc to end of row.

Row 41: Ch 1, turn, with MC, sc in 1st 12 sc; with CC, sc in next 3 sc; with MC, sc in next 6 sc; with CC, sc in next sc; with MC, sc in next sc; with CC, sc in next 30 sc; with MC, sc in next sc; with CC, sc in next sc; with MC, sc to end of row.

Row 42: Ch 1, turn, with MC, sc in 1st 9 sc; with CC, sc in next sc; with MC, sc in next 7 sc; with CC, sc in next sc; with MC, sc in next 5 sc; with CC, sc in next 22 sc; with MC, sc in next sc; with CC, sc in next 4 sc; with MC, sc in next 2 sc; with CC, sc in next sc; with MC, sc in next 2 sc; with CC, sc in next sc; with MC, sc in next 2 sc; with CC, sc in next 2 sc; with MC, sc in next sc; with CC, sc in next 4 sc;

with MC, sc in next sc; with CC, sc in next sc; with MC, sc in next 3 sc; with CC, sc in next sc; with MC, sc to end of row.

Row 43: Ch 1, turn, with MC, sc in 1st 10 sc; with CC, sc in next 2 sc; with MC, sc in next sc; with CC, sc in next 3 sc; with MC, sc in next 9 sc; with CC, sc in next sc; with MC, sc in next sc; with CC, sc in next 2 sc; with MC, sc in next 7 sc; with CC, sc in next 16 sc; with MC, sc in next 7 sc; with CC, sc in next sc; with MC, sc in next 9 sc; with CC, sc in next sc; with MC, sc to end of row.

Row 44: Ch 1, turn, with MC, sc in 1st 25 sc; with CC, sc in next 15 sc; with MC, sc in next 12 sc; with CC, sc in next sc; with MC, sc in next 3 sc; with CC, sc in next sc; [with MC, sc in next sc; with CC, sc in next sc] twice; with MC, sc in next 2 sc; with CC, sc in next sc; with MC, sc in next 5 sc; with CC, sc in next sc; with MC, sc to end of row.

Row 45: Ch 1, turn, with MC, sc in 1st 10 sc; with CC, sc in next sc; with MC, sc in next 3 sc; with CC, sc in next 2 sc; with MC, sc in next sc; with CC, sc in next sc; with MC, sc in next 2 sc; with CC, sc in next sc; with MC, sc in next 4 sc; with CC, sc in next sc; with MC, sc in next 12 sc; with CC, sc in next 14 sc; with MC, sc in next 10 sc; with CC, sc in next sc; with MC, sc to end of row.

Row 46: Ch 1, turn, with MC, sc in 1st 24 sc; with CC, sc in next 15 sc; with MC, sc in next 23 sc; with CC, sc in next sc; with MC, sc in next sc; with CC, sc in next sc; with MC, sc to end of row.

Row 47: Ch 1, turn, with MC, sc in 1st 11 sc; with CC, sc in next sc; with MC, sc in next 3 sc; with CC, sc in next sc; with MC, sc in next 5 sc; with CC, sc in next sc; with MC, sc in next 13 sc; [with CC, sc in next sc; with MC, sc in next sc] twice; with CC, sc in next 6 sc; with MC, sc in next sc; with CC, sc in next 5 sc; with MC, sc in next sc; with CC, sc in next sc; with MC, sc in next 7 sc; with CC, sc in next sc; with MC, sc to end of row.

Row 48: Ch 1, turn, with MC, sc in 1st 25 sc; with CC, sc in next 3 sc; with MC, sc in next 3 sc; with CC, sc in next 5 sc; with MC, sc in next 8 sc; with CC, sc in next sc; with MC, sc to end of row.

Row 49: Ch 1, turn, with MC, sc in 1st 11 sc; with CC, sc in next sc; with MC, sc in next 2 sc; with CC, sc in next sc; with MC, sc in next 2 sc; with CC, sc in next sc; with MC, sc in next 7 sc; with CC, sc in next sc; with MC, sc in next 15 sc; with CC, sc in next 3 sc; with MC, sc in next 4 sc; with CC, sc in next 3 sc; with MC, sc to end of row.

Row 50: Ch 1, turn, with MC, sc in 1st 15 sc; with CC, sc in next 2 sc; with MC, sc in next 6 sc; with CC, sc in next sc; with MC, sc in next 2 sc; with CC, sc in next 3 sc; with MC, sc in next 3 sc; with CC, sc in next 3 sc; with MC, sc to end of row.

Row 51: Ch 1, turn, with MC, sc in 1st 11 sc; with CC, sc in next sc; with MC, sc in next 5 sc; with CC, sc in next sc; with MC, sc in next 7 sc; with CC, sc in next sc; with MC, sc in next 16 sc; with CC, sc in next 2 sc; with MC, sc in next 4 sc; with CC, sc in next 4 sc; with MC, sc in next 8 sc; with CC, sc in next sc; with MC, sc to end of row.

Row 52: Ch 1, turn, with MC, sc in 1st 19 sc; with CC, sc in next sc; with MC, sc in next 4 sc; with CC, sc in next 3 sc; with MC, sc in next 4 sc; with CC, sc in next sc; with MC, sc in next sc; with CC, sc in next sc; with MC, sc to end of row.

Row 53: Ch 1, turn, with MC, sc in 1st 11 sc; with CC, sc in next sc, with MC, sc in next 28 sc; with CC, sc in next sc; with MC, sc in next sc; with CC, sc in next sc; with MC, sc in next 2 sc; with CC, sc in next sc; with MC, sc in next 2 sc; with CC, sc in next sc; with MC, sc in next 2 sc; with CC, sc in

next 4 sc; with MC, sc to end of row.

Row 54: Ch 1, turn, with MC, sc in 1st 14 sc; with CC, sc in next 5 sc; with MC, sc in next 3 sc; with CC, sc in next 2 sc; with MC, sc in next 9 sc; with CC, sc in next sc; with MC, sc in next sc; with CC, sc in next sc; with MC, sc in next 13 sc; with CC, sc in next sc; with MC, sc in next 12 sc; with CC, sc in next sc; with MC, sc to end of row.

Row 55: Ch 1, turn, with MC, sc in 1st 40 sc; with CC, sc in next sc; with MC, sc in next 6 sc; with CC, sc in next sc; with MC, sc in next 3 sc; with CC, sc in next 3 sc; with MC, sc in next 2 sc; with CC, sc in next sc; with MC, sc in next 3 sc; with CC, sc in next 3 sc; [with MC, sc in next sc; with CC, sc in next sc] 3 times; with MC, sc to end of row.

Row 56: Ch 1, turn, with MC, sc in 1st 8 sc; with CC, sc in next sc; with MC, sc in next 2 sc; with CC, sc in next sc; with MC, sc in next 11 sc; with CC, sc in next 2 sc; with MC, sc in next 3 sc; with CC, sc in next 3 sc; with MC, sc in next 7 sc; with CC, sc in next sc; with MC, sc to end of row.

Row 57: Ch 1, turn, with MC, sc2tog, sc in next 9 sc; with CC, sc in next sc; with MC, sc in next 32 sc; with CC, sc in next 3 sc; with MC, sc in next sc; with CC, sc in next sc; with MC, sc in next 17 sc; with CC, sc in next sc; with MC, sc in next sc; with CC, sc in next sc; with MC, sc to last 2 sc, sc2tog—74 sc.

Row 58: Ch 1, turn, with MC, sc in 1st 24 sc; with CC, sc in next sc; with MC, sc in next 3 sc; with CC, sc in next sc; with MC, sc in next sc; with CC, sc in next sc; with MC, sc to end of row.

Row 59: Ch 1, turn, with MC, sc2tog, sc in next 9 sc; with CC, sc in next sc; with MC, sc in next 12 sc; with CC, sc in next sc; with MC, sc in next 17 sc; with CC, sc in next 2 sc; with MC, sc in next 3 sc; with CC, sc in next sc; with MC, sc in next sc; with CC, sc in next sc; with MC, sc in next 3 sc;

with CC, sc in next sc; with MC, sc to last 2 sc, sc2tog—72 sc.

Row 60: Ch 1, turn, with MC, sc in 1st 22 sc; with CC, sc in next 2 sc; with MC, sc in next 3 sc; with CC, sc in next sc; with MC, sc in next 10 sc; with CC, sc in next sc; with MC, sc in next 8 sc; with CC, sc in next sc; with MC, sc in next 11 sc; with CC, sc in next sc; with MC, sc to end of row.

Row 61: Ch 1, turn, with MC, sc2tog, sc in next 26 sc; with CC, sc in next sc; with MC, sc in next 2 sc; with CC, sc in next sc; with MC, sc in next 2 sc; with CC, sc in next sc; with MC, sc to last 2 sc, sc2tog—70 sc.

Row 62: Ch 1, turn, with MC, sc in 1st 20 sc; with CC, sc in next sc; with MC, sc in next 25 sc; with CC, sc in next sc; with MC, sc in next 11 sc; with CC, sc in next sc; with MC, sc to end of row.

Row 63: Ch 1, turn, with MC, sc2tog, sc in next 10 sc; with CC, sc in next sc; with MC, sc in next 3 sc; with CC, sc in next sc; with MC, sc in next 31 sc; with CC, sc in next sc; with MC, sc to last 2 sc, sc2tog—68 sc.

Row 64: Ch 1, turn, with MC, sc in 1st 20 sc; with CC, sc in next sc; with MC, sc in next 12 sc; with CC, sc in next sc; with MC, sc to end of row.

Row 65: Ch 1, turn, with MC, sc2tog, sc in next 22 sc; with CC, sc in next sc; with MC, sc to last 2 sc, sc2tog—66 sc.

Row 66: Ch 1 turn, with MC, sc in next 6 sc; with CC, sc in next 2 sc; with MC, sc in next 17 sc; with CC, sc in next sc; with MC, sc in next 15 sc; with CC, sc in next sc; with MC, sc in next 8 sc; with CC, sc in next sc; with MC, sc in next 2 sc; with CC, sc in next sc; with MC, sc to end of row.

Row 67: Ch 1 turn, with MC, sc2tog, sc in next 20 sc; with CC, sc in next sc; with MC, sc in next 14 sc; with CC, sc in next sc; with MC, sc in next 17 sc; with CC, sc in next 3 sc; with MC, sc to last 2 sc, sc2tog—64 sc.

Behind the Magic

In *Harry Potter and the Prisoner of Azkaban*, Sirius Black is mistaken for the Grim when he transforms into his Animagus, a large black dog. While Sirius's Animagus was ultimately computer generated, the director brought a real dog named Fern to the set as reference for the part. Fern was fitted with pointy ears and learned to jump ramps and perform stunts to bring the digital dog to life.

ABOVE: A prop reference shot for *Harry Potter and the Prisoner of Azkaban* that shows the teacups used in the Divination scene where the Grim appears in Harry's cup.

Row 68: Ch 1 turn, with MC, sc2tog, sc in next 5 sc; with CC, sc in next sc; with MC, sc in next 9 sc; with CC, sc in next sc; with MC, sc in next sc; with CC, sc in next 7 sc; with MC, sc in next 24 sc; with CC, sc in next sc; with MC, sc to last 2 sc, sc2tog—62 sc.

Row 69: Ch 1 turn, with MC, sc2tog, sc in next 10 sc; with CC, sc in next sc; with MC, sc in next 20 sc; with CC, sc in next 2 sc; with MC, sc in next sc; with CC, sc in next 3 sc; with MC, sc in next sc; with CC, sc in next 2 sc; with MC, sc in next sc; with CC, sc in next sc; with MC, sc to last 2 sc, sc2tog—60 sc.

Row 70: Ch 1 turn, with MC, sc2tog, sc in next 11 sc; with CC, sc in next 4 sc; with MC, sc in next 5 sc; with CC, sc in next 6 sc; with MC, sc to last 2 sc, sc2tog—58 sc.

Row 71: Ch 1 turn, with MC, sc2tog, sc in next 25 sc; with CC, sc in next 5 sc; with MC, sc in next 2 sc; with CC, sc in next 2 sc; with MC, sc in next 2 sc; with CC, sc in next sc; with MC, sc in next 5 sc; with CC, sc in next sc; with MC, sc to last 2 sc, sc2tog—56 sc.

Row 72: Ch 1 turn, with MC, sc2tog, sc in next 15 sc; with CC, sc in next sc; with MC, sc in next 4 sc; with CC, sc in next 5 sc; with MC, sc to last 2 sc, sc2tog—54 sc.

Row 73: Ch 1 turn, with MC, sc2tog, sc in next 23 sc; [with CC, sc in next sc; with MC, sc in next sc] twice; with CC, sc in next sc; with MC, sc to last 2 sc, sc2tog—52 sc.

Row 74: Ch 1 turn, with MC, sc2tog, sc in next 28 sc; with CC, sc in next sc; with MC, sc to last 2 sc, sc2tog—50 sc.

Rows 75–83: Ch 1 turn, with MC, sc2tog, sc to last 2 sc, sc2tog—2 sts dec'd; 32 sc at end of Row 83.

BORDER

Rnd 1: Sc 222 sts evenly spaced around doily.

Rnd 2: Ch 3 (counts as 1st dc), 4 dc in same st as join, *sk next 2 sts, sc in next st**, sk next 2 sts, 5 dc in next st; rep from * around, ending last rep at **, join to top of ch-3 with a sl st. Fasten off.

FINISHING

Weave in ends. Steam to lightly block.

CHART

KEY

☐ sc in color MC

◼ sc in color CC

⊻ 2 sc in 1 sc in color MC

⋀ sc2tog in color MC

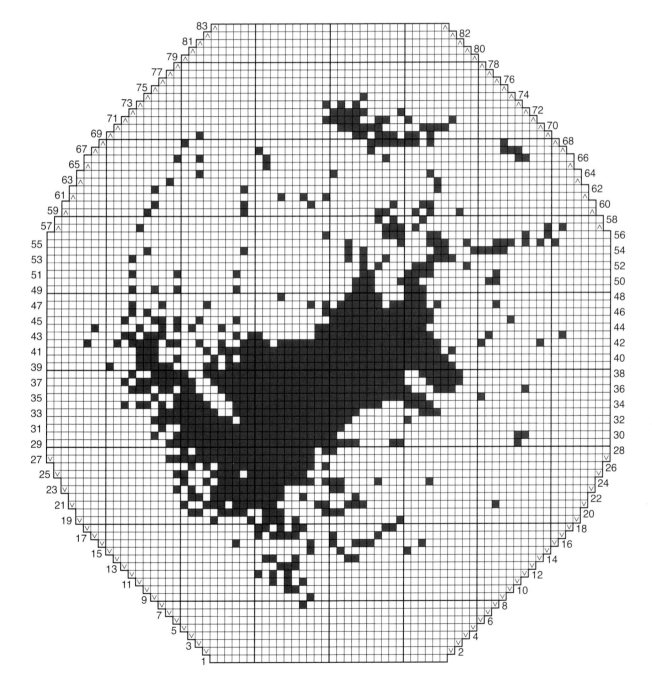

HOGWARTS CREST BLANKET

Designed by **VINCENT WILLIAMS**

SKILL LEVEL ⚡⚡

Hogwarts castle is a magical and inviting place. With moving staircases, enchanted paintings, and even ghosts, the castle seems to have a life of its own, ever evolving since the school was opened by the four founding witches and wizards. One of the key fixtures of Hogwarts in the films is the Great Hall. "We built a lot of fire into the Great Hall," says director Chris Columbus, "for it needed to be this magical, warm, loving place." To keep the founders in mind, a huge hearth decorated with the iconic Hogwarts crest was placed on one side of the room, and the walls were decorated with flambeaux held by the heraldic creatures that represent the four houses.

A must-have home accessory for any Harry Potter fan, the design for this magical, warm blanket features the iconic colors of each Hogwarts wizarding house: Slytherin, Gryffindor, Hufflepuff, and Ravenclaw. In the center is the motif of the Hogwarts crest featuring the creatures that represent each of those four houses. Working in single crochet, follow the detailed charts to crochet this warm and stunning blanket.

SIZE
One size

FINISHED MEASUREMENTS
Width: 54 in. / 137 cm
Length: 80 in. / 203 cm

YARN
Aran weight (medium #4) yarn, shown in Cascade Yarns *220 Superwash Aran* (100% superwash merino wool; 150 yd. / 137.5 m per 3½ oz. / 100 g hank), 3 hanks per house color (A–H)
Colorways:
Gryffindor: #809 Really Red (G) and #241 Sunflower (H)
Hufflepuff: #815 Black (C) and #821 Daffodil (D)
Ravenclaw: #813 Blue Velvet (A) and #875 Feather Grey (B)
Slytherin: #801 Army Green (E) and #900 Charcoal (F)
Crest Border: #817 Aran (I), 1 hank
Crest Raven and Scroll: #200 Cafe Au Lait (J), 1 hank

HOOK
• US I-9 / 5.5 mm crochet hook or size needed to obtain gauge

NOTIONS
• Tapestry needle
• Locking stitch markers

GAUGE
13 sts and 15 rows = 4 in. / 10 cm in sc
Gauge is not critical for this pattern, but the yarn weight and hook size used will affect the finished measurements.

Continued on page 150

NOTES

- Blanket is worked flat, in one piece, from the bottom up.
- Work intarsia colorwork technique with bobbins (or each full separate skein functioning as a bobbin).
- To keep track of the chart borders, markers should be removed when working a stitch, and replaced into the newly completed stitch of the same column.
- Crochet over ends as you go to make the finishing process even more seamless.

BLANKET

With A, B, and C:

Row 1 (RS): *With A, fsc 15; with B, fsc 15; rep from * two times more, with C, fsc 90, turn—180 fsc.

Row 2 (WS): With C, ch 1, sc in next 90 sts, *with B, sc in next 15 sts; with A, sc in next 15 sts; rep from * two times more, turn.

Row 3: With A, ch 1, *with A, sc in next 15 sc; with B, sc in next 15 sc; rep from * two times more, with C, sc in next 90 sc, turn.

Rows 4–15: Rep Rows 2 and 3.

With A, B, and D:

Row 16 (WS): With D, ch 1, sc in next 90 sc, *with A, sc in next 15 sc; with B, sc in next 15 sc; rep from * two times more, turn.

Row 17 (RS): With B, ch 1, *with B, sc in next 15 sc; with A, sc in next 15 sc; rep from * two times more, with D, sc in last 90 sc, turn.

Rows 18–30: Rep Rows 16 and 17.

Rows 31–90: Replacing fsc with sc, rep Rows 1–30.

Rows 91–105: Replacing fsc with sc, rep Rows 1–15.

Pm in 46th st from both the left and right edges of the blanket; you have marked sts 46 and 135.

Row 106: With D, ch 1, sc to m, [work charted motif]; with B, sc in next 15 sc; with A, sc in next 15 sc, with B, sc in last 15 sc, turn.

Row 107: With B, ch 1, sc 15; with A, sc 15; with B, sc 15, [work charted motif]; with D, sc to end, turn.

Rows 108–119: Rep Rows 106 and 107.

Row 120: Rep Row 106.

With A, B, and C:

Row 121: With A, ch 1, sc in next 15 sc; with B, sc in next 15 sc; with A, sc in next 15 sc, [work charted motif]; with C, sc to end, turn.

Row 122: With C, ch 1, sc to m, [work charted motif]; with A, sc in next 15 sc; with B, sc in next 15 sc; with A, sc in next 15 sc, turn.

Rows 123–134: Rep Rows 121 and 122.

Row 135: Rep Row 121.

With A, B, and D:

Row 136: With D, ch 1, sc to m, [work charted motif]; with B, sc in next 15 sc; with A, sc in next 15 sc; with B, sc in next 15 sc, turn.

Row 137: With B, ch 1, sc in next 15 sc; with A, sc in next 15 sc; with B, sc in next 15 sc, [work charted motif]; with D, sc to end, turn.

Rows 138–149: Rep Rows 136 and 137.

Row 150: Rep Row 136.

With F, G, and H:

Row 151: With F, ch 1, sc to m, [work charted motif]; with G, sc in next 15 sc; with H, sc in next 15 sc; with G, sc in next 15 sc, turn.

Row 152: With G, ch 1, sc in next 15 sc; with H, sc in next 15 sc; with G, sc in next 15 sc, [work charted motif]; with F, sc to end, turn.

Rows 153–164: Rep Rows 151 and 152.

Row 165: Rep Row 151.

With E, G, and H:

Row 166: With H, ch 1, sc in next 15 sc; with G, sc in next 15 sc; with H, sc in next 15 sc, [work charted motif]; with E, sc to end, turn.

Row 167: With E, ch 1, sc to m, [work charted motif]; with H, sc in next 15 sc; with G, sc in next 15 sc; with H, sc in last 15 sc, turn.

Rows 168–179: Rep Rows 166 and 167.

Row 180: Rep Row 166.

With F, G, and H:

Row 181: With F, ch 1, sc to m, [work charted motif]; with G, sc in next 15 sc; with H, sc in next 15 sc; with G, sc in next 15 sc, turn.

Row 182: With G, ch 1, sc in next 15 sc; with H, sc in next 15 sc; with G, sc in next 15 sc, [work charted motif]; with F, sc to end, turn.
Remove st markers.
Row 183: With F, ch 1, sc in next 90 sc, *with H, sc in next 15 sc; with G, sc in next 15 sc; rep from * two times more, turn.
Row 184: With G, ch 1, *with G, sc in next 15 sc; with H, sc in next 15 sc; rep from * two times more, with F, sc in next 90 sc, turn.
Rows 185–194: Rep Rows 183 and 184.
Row 195: Rep Row 183.

With E, G, and H:
Row 196: With H, ch 1, *with H, sc in next 15 sc; with G, sc in next 15 sc; rep from * two times more, with E, sc in next 90 sc, turn.
Row 197: With E, ch 1, sc in next 90 sc, *with G, sc in next 15 sc; with H, sc in next 15 sc; rep from * two times more, turn.
Rows 198–209: Rep Rows 196 and 197.
Row 210: Rep Row 196.

With F, G, and H:
Row 211: With F, ch 1, sc in next 90 sc, *with H, sc in next 15 sc; with G, sc in next 15 sc; rep from * two times more, turn.
Row 212: With G, ch 1, *with G, sc in next 15 sc; with H, sc in next 15 sc; rep from * two times more, with F, sc in next 90 sc, turn.
Rows 213–224: Rep Rows 211 and 212.
Row 225: Rep Row 211.
Rows 226–285: Rep Rows 196–225.
Rows 286–300: Rep Rows 196–210.

FINISHING

Weave in ends. Steam or wet block to measurements.

"VERY WELL. WELL, YOU ALL KNOW, OF COURSE, THAT HOGWARTS WAS FOUNDED OVER A THOUSAND YEARS AGO, BY THE FOUR GREATEST WITCHES AND WIZARDS OF THE AGE. GODRIC GRYFFINDOR, HELGA HUFFLEPUFF, ROWENA RAVENCLAW, AND SALAZAR SLYTHERIN."

Professor McGonagall, *Harry Potter and the Chamber of Secrets*

CHART

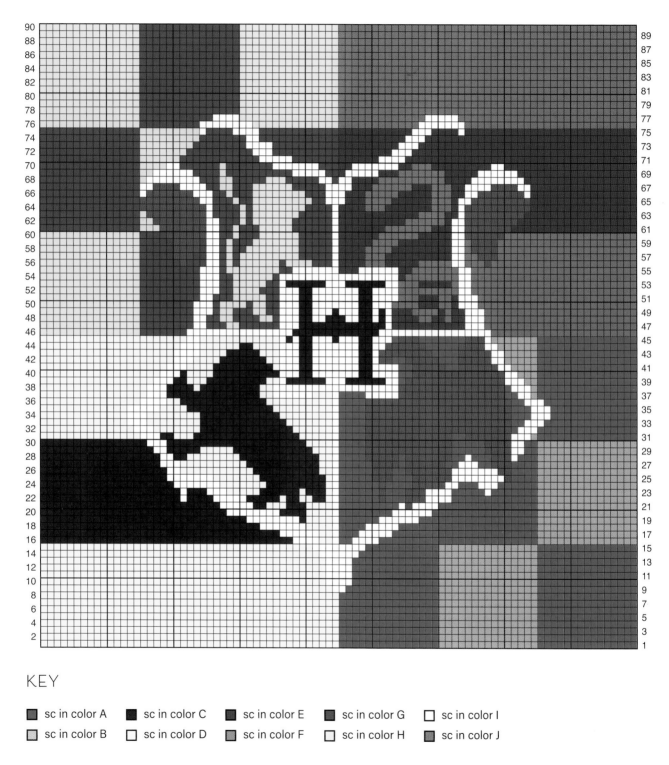

KEY

■ sc in color A   ■ sc in color C   ■ sc in color E   ■ sc in color G   □ sc in color I

■ sc in color B   □ sc in color D   ■ sc in color F   □ sc in color H   ■ sc in color J

POTIONS BASKETS

Designed by **AMINATA NDIAYE**

SKILL LEVEL ⚡⚡

P otions is a core subject taught at Hogwarts. In this class, students learn the correct way to brew potions, often in large cauldrons, each student bringing their own as part of their school supplies list. They follow specific recipes and use various magical ingredients to create the potions, starting with beginner-friendly ones and moving to more difficult potions as they advance in knowledge.

As the films progressed, getting bigger and more elaborate in scale, so too, did Professor Snape's Potions classroom. The classroom was initially filmed on location in the sacristy in Lacock Abbey, which provided locations for several of the sets at Hogwarts. Later, it was moved to Leavesden Studios. When Professor Slughorn took over as Potions Master in *Harry Potter and the Half-Blood Prince*, "the set was changed again in size and shape," says art director Hattie Storey, "but we took a similar approach." New cauldrons were brought in for the students for the Draught of Living Death assignment, and a special miniature cauldron with a little clamp was created for the vial of Felix Felicis.

In this design, three crocheted cauldron baskets await you, topped with three different colors to represent famous potions from the films. These baskets feature easy increases and sturdy sides. Worked from the bottom up, the cauldrons are then finished with their particular potion at the top, one with pink for the love potion Amortentia, one with green for the Polyjuice Potion, and one with gold for Felix Felicis.

SIZE
One size

FINISHED MEASUREMENTS
LOVE POTION BASKET
Base Diameter: 10 in. / 25.5 cm
Height: 9¾ in. / 25 cm

FELIX FELICIS BASKET
Base Diameter: 10 in. / 25.5 cm
Height: 10½ in. / 26.5 cm

POLYJUICE POTION BASKET
Base Diameter: 10 in. / 25.5 cm
Height: 11½ in. / 29 cm

YARN
Aran weight (medium #4) yarn, shown in Cascade Yarns *220 Superwash Aran* (100% superwash merino wool; 150 yd. / 137.5 m per 3½ oz. / 100 g hank)
Main Color (MC): #815 Black, 4 hanks per basket
Worsted weight (medium #4) yarn, shown in Cascade Yarns *220* (100% Peruvian Highland wool; 220 yd. / 200 m per 3½ oz. / 100 g hank)
Polyjuice Potion Cover (CC): #801 Army Green, 1 hank
Felix Felicis Cover (CC): #7826 California Poppy, 1 hank
Love Potion Cover (CC): #7804 Shrimp, 1 hank

HOOK
• US H-8 / 5 mm crochet hook or size needed to obtain gauge

NOTIONS
• Stitch marker
• Tapestry needle

Continued on page 156

GAUGE

16 sts and 16 rnds = 4 in. / 10 cm in sc
Gauge is not critical for this pattern, but the yarn weight and hook size used will affect the finished measurements.

NOTES

- The base of the basket is worked first, then the height of the basket is worked. The lined cover is worked in the round. The cover is attached to the top of the basket, then the handles are stitched and sewn to the sides of the basket.

SPECIAL ABBREVIATIONS

blsc (back loop single crochet): Work a sc in the back loop of the st.

bsc: Work sc on the bar behind the hdc.

flsc (front loop single crochet): Work a sc in the front loop of the st.

pc (popcorn stitch): Work 3 dc in same st, remove hook from last dc and insert it into the first dc of the 3 dc, grab the dropped loop with the hook and pull it through the first dc.

AMORTENTIA BASKET

BASKET BASE

Rnd 1: Make a magic ring; work 6 sc in ring, sl st to first sc, pm to mark beg of rnd—6 sc.

Note: Starting with Rnd 2, work in continuous rnds without joining.

Rnd 2: Ch 1 (does not count as a st here and throughout), 2 sc in each sc—12 sc.

Rnd 3: [Sc in next sc, 2 sc in next sc] 6 times—18 sc.

Rnd 4: Sc in next sc, 2 sc in next sc, [Sc in next 2 sc, 2 sc in next sc] 5 times, sc in last sc—24 sc.

Rnd 5: [Sc in next 3 sc, 2 sc in next sc] 6 times—30 sc.

Rnd 6: Sc in first 2 sc, 2 sc in next sc, [Sc in next 4 sc, 2 sc in next sc] 5 times, sc in last 2 sc—36 sc.

Rnd 7: [Sc in next 5 sc, 2 sc in next sc] 6 times—42 sc.

Rnd 8: Sc in first 3 sc, 2 sc in next sc, [sc in next 6 sc, 2 sc in next sc] 5 times, sc in last 3 sc—48 sc.

Rnd 9: [Sc in next 7 sc, 2 sc in next sc] 6 times—54 sc.

Rnd 10: Sc in first 4 sc, 2 sc in next sc, [sc in next 8 sc, 2 sc in next sc] 5 times, sc in last 4 sc—60 sc.

Rnd 11: [Sc in next 9 sc, 2 sc in next sc] 6 times—66 sc.

Rnd 12: Sc in first 5 sc, 2 sc in next sc, [sc in next 10 sc, 2 sc in next sc] 5 times, sc in last 5 sc—72 sc.

Rnd 13: [Sc in next 11 sc, 2 sc in next sc] 6 times—78 sc.

Rnd 14: Sc in first 6 sc, 2 sc in next sc, [sc in next 12 sc, 2 sc in next sc] 5 times, sc in last 6 sc—84 sc.

Rnd 15: [Sc in next 13 sc, 2 sc in next sc] 6 times—90 sc.

Rnd 16: Sc in first 7 sc, 2 sc in next sc, [sc in next 14 sc, 2 sc in next sc] 5 times, sc in last 7 sc—96 sc.

Rnd 17: [Sc in next 15 sc, 2 sc in next sc] 6 times—102 sc.

Rnd 18: Sc in first 8 sc, 2 sc in next sc, [sc in next 16 sc, 2 sc in next sc] 5 times, sc in last 8 sc—108 sc.

Rnd 19: [Sc in next 17 sc, 2 sc in next sc] 6 times—114 sc.

Rnd 20: Sc in first 9 sc, 2 sc in next sc, [sc in next 18 sc, 2 sc in next sc] 5 times, sc in last 9 sc—120 sc.

Do not fasten off; cont to height of basket.

RIGHT: Hermione Granger brewing Polyjuice Potion in a cauldron in the girls' bathroom, from *Harry Potter and the Chamber of Secrets.*

HEIGHT OF BASKET

Note: Cont working in the rnd without joining.

Rnds 1–24: Sc around.

Rnd 25: Blsc in each st around.

Rnds 26 and 27: Sc around.

Rnd 28: Rep Rnd 25.

Rnds 29: Sc around.

Rnd 30: Rep Rnd 25.

Rnd 31 (dec rnd): [Sc in next 18 sc, sc2tog] 6 times—114 sc.

Rnd 32 (dec rnd): [Sc in next 17 sc, sc2tog] 6 times—108 sc.

Rnd 33 (dec rnd): [Sc in next 16 sc, sc2tog] 6 times—102 sts.

Rnds 34–37: Sc around

Rnd 38: Remove marker, sl st in that marked st and in next 2 sts, ch 1, flsc in each st and in each of the 3 sl sts from beg of rnd, join to first sc, ch 1, turn—102 sts.

Rnd 39 (inc rnd): [Sc in next 16 sc, 2 sc in next st] 6 times, sl st to first sc—108 sts.

Fasten off.

BASKET COVER

Rnd 1: With CC, make a magic ring; work 6 sc in ring—6 sc.

Rnd 2: 2 sc in each sc—12 sc.

Rnd 3: [Sc in next sc, 2 sc in next sc] 6 times—18 sc.

Rnd 4: [Sc in next 2 sc, 2 sc in next sc] 6 times—24 sc.

Rnd 5: [Sc in next 3 sc, 2 sc in next sc] 6 times—30 sc.

Rnd 6: Sc in first 2 sc, 2 sc in next sc, [sc in next 4 sc, 2 sc in next sc] 5 times, sc in last 2 sc—36 sc.

Rnd 7: [Sc in next 5 sc, 2 sc in next sc] 6 times—42 sc.

Rnd 8: Sc in first 3 sc, 2 sc in next sc, [sc in next 6 sc, 2 sc in next sc] 5 times, sc in last 3 sc—48 sc.

Rnd 9: [2 sc in next sc, pc, sc in next 4 sc, 2 sc in next sc] 6 times—54 sts.

Rnd 10: Sc in first 4 sts, 2 sc in next sc, [sc in next 8 sts, 2 sc in next st] 5 times, sc in last 4 sts—60 sc.

Rnd 11: [Sc in next 9 sc, 2 sc in next sc] 6 times—66 sc.

Rnd 12: Sc in first 5 sc, 2 sc in next sc, sc in next 3 sc, pc, sc in next 6 sc, 2 sc in next sc, pc, [sc in next 9 sc, 2 sc in next sc, pc] 4 times, sc in last 4 sc—72 sts.

Rnd 13: [Sc in next 11 sts, 2 sc in next st] 6 times—78 sc.

Rnd 14: Sc in first 6 sc, 2 sc in next sc, sc in next sc, pc, sc in next 6 sc, pc, sc in next 3 sc, 2 sc in next sc, sc in next sc, pc, sc in next 10 sc, 2 sc in next sc, [sc in next 12 sc, 2 sc in next sc] 3 times, sc in last 6 sc—84 sts.

Rnd 15: Sc in first 5 sts, pc, sc in next 7 sts, 2 sc in next st, sc in next 5 sts, pc, sc in next 7 sts, 2 sc in next st, [sc in next 13 sts, 2 sc in next st] 4 times—90 sts.

Rnd 16: Sc in first 7 sts, 2 sc in next st, sc in next 4 sts, pc, sc in next 3 sts, pc, sc in next 5 sts, 2 sc in next st, sc in next 7 sts, pc, sc in next 4 sts, pc, sc in next st, [2 sc in next st, sc in next 9 sts, pc, sc in next 4 sts] twice, 2 sc in next st, sc in next st, pc, sc in next 10 sts, pc, sc in next st, 2 sc in next st, sc in last 7 sts—96 sts.

Rnd 17: [Blsc in next 15 sts, 2 blsc in next st] 6 times—102 blsc.

Do not fasten off; cont to work back of basket cover.

BACK OF BASKET COVER

Remove marker, sl st in marked st and in next 2 sts.

Rnd 1: Ch 3, dc in next 3 sts, dc2tog, [dc in next 4 sts, dc2tog) 16 times, sl st to 3rd ch - 85 sts.

Rnd 2: Ch 3, dc in next 3 sts, dc2tog, (dc in next 4 sts, dc2tog) 13 times, dc in last dc, sl st to 3rd ch - 71 sts.

Rnd 3: Ch 3, dc in next st, dc2tog, (dc in next 2 sts, dc2tog) 16 times, dc in next st, dc2tog, sl st to 3rd ch - 53 sts.

Rnd 4: Ch 3, dc in next st, dc2tog, (dc in next 2 sts, dc2 tog) 12 times, dc in last dc, sl st to 3rd ch - 40 sts.

Rnd 5: Ch 3, dc2tog, (dc in next st, dc2tog) 12 times, dc in last st, sl st to 3rd ch - 27 sts.

Rnd 6: Ch 3, dc2tog, (dc in next st, dc2tog) 8 times, sl st to 3rd ch -18 sts.

Rnd 7: Sctog around to close. Fasten off.

ATTACHING THE COVER

With RSs of basket and basket cover facing, attach yarn to any unworked back loop on Rnd 38 of the basket, insert hook in basket loop, insert hook in any st of Rnd 17 of basket cover, pull yarn through the 2 sts, yo, pull through 2 loops. Rep this sc join for the next 50 sts. Fasten off.

BASKET HANDLE

With MC, and leaving a long tail, ch 108.

Row 1: Working in the back loop of each ch, sl st in 2nd ch from hook and in each ch across, ch 1 turn— 107 sts.

Row 2: Sl st in each st, turn, sl st to 9th st to form a loop.

Fasten off, leaving a long tail for sewing handle to basket.

Sew other end of handle into 9th st to form a loop.

Sew one handle loop on side of basket, about 1 in. / 2.5 cm below top of basket join. Rep to sew opposite end of handle to opposite side of basket.

FELIX FELICIS BASKET

BASKET BASE

With MC, make a basket base as the one for Love Potion Basket.

BASKET HEIGHT

Rnd 1: Blsc in each st around—120 sts.

Rnds 2-15: Sc around.

Rnd 16 (dec rnd): [18 sc, sc2tog] 6 times—114 sts.

Rnds 17 and 18: Sc around.

Rnd 19 (dec rnd): (17 sc, sc2tog) 6 times—108 sts.

Rnds 20 and 21: Sc around.

Rnd 22 (dec rnd): (16 sc, sc2tog) 6 times—102 sts.

Rnds 23-30: Sc around.

Rnd 31: Hdc around.

Rnd 32 (work on the bar behind the hdc): Bsc in each st around.

Rnd 33: Sc around.

Rnds 34-39: Rep Rnds 31-33.

Rnd 40: Sc around.

Rnd 41: Remove marker, sl st in that st and in next 2 sts, ch 1, 1 flsc in each st and in each of the last 3 sl sts from beg of rnd, join to first sc, ch 1 turn—102 sts.

Rnd 42 (inc rnd): (Sc in next 16 flsc, 2 sc in next flsc) 6 times, sl st to first sc—108 sts.

Fasten off.

BASKET COVER

With CC, and **working in blo**, work Rnds 1-17 as Rnds 1-17 of Love Potion Basket base, then work Back of Basket Cover same as for Love Potion Back of Basket Cover.

Attach the cover to the basket using the same technique as the Love Potion Basket, sc'ing tog 51 unworked back loops of Rnd 41 of basket to 51 unworked loops of Rnd 16 of basket cover.

BASKET HANDLE

Make same handle and attach to basket the same as for Love Potion Basket.

POLYJUICE POTION BASKET

BASKET BASE

With MC, make a basket base as the one for the Love Potion Basket.

BASKET HEIGHT

Rnd 1: Blsc in each st—120 blsc.

Rnds 2-6: Sc around.

Rnd 7: Hdc around.

Rnd 8 (dec rnd): [Blsc in next 18 hdc, blsc2tog] 6 times—114 blsc.

Rnds 9 and 10: Sc around.

Rnd 11 (dec rnd): [Sc in next 17 sc, sc2tog] 6 times—108 sc.

Rnd 12: Sc around.

Rnd 13 (dec rnd): [Sc in next 16 sc, sc2tog] 6 times—102 sc.

Rnds 14-39: Sc around.

Note: The next 7 rnds are worked in tapestry crochet, joining at the end of each rnd. Work with MC and CC.

Rnd 40: Remove marker, sl st in marked st and in next 2 sts, ch 1, *with MC sc in next 4 sc, with CC sc in next sc, with MC sc in next 7 sc, with CC sc in next 3 sc, with MC sc in next 2 sc; rep from * 6 times, sl st to first sc.

Rnd 41: Ch 1, *with MC sc in next 4 sc, with CC sc in next 2 sc, with MC sc in next 2 sc, with CC sc in next 2 sts, with MC sc in next st, with CC sc in next 5 sc, with MC sc in next sc; rep from * 6 times, sl st to first sc.

Rnd 42: Ch 1, *with MC sc in next 3 sc, with CC sc in next 3 sc, with MC sc in next sc, with CC sc in next 10 sc; rep from * 6 times, sl st to first sc.

Rnd 43: Ch 1, *with MC sc in next 2 sc, with CC sc in next 15 sc; rep from * 6 times, sl st to first sc.

Cut MC.

Rnds 44 and 45: With CC only, ch 1, 1 sc in each st, sl st in first st.

Rnd 46: With CC only, ch 1, flsc in each st, sl st to first sc.

Fasten off.

POLYJUICE POTION BASKET COVER

With CC, work Rnds 1-16 as Rnds 1-16 of the base of the basket—96 sc.

Rnd 17 (work in back loop only): (15 blsc, 2 blsc in next st) 6 times—102 blsc.

Do not fasten off; cont to work the back.

Work the back as the back of the Love Potion cover.

Attach cover to basket using the same technique as the Love Potion Basket, sc'ing tog the unworked back loops of Rnd 45 of the basket to the unworked front loops of Rnd 16 of basket cover.

BASKET HANDLES (MAKE 2)

With MC, and leaving a long tail, ch 22.
Row 1 (working in back loop of the chs): Sl st in 2nd ch from hook and in next 6 ch, pc, sl st in next 13 ch, ch 1, turn—21 sts.
Row 2: Sl st in each st.
Fasten off, leaving a long tail to sew the handle to the basket.

ATTACHING THE HANDLES

Find a place on Rnd 43 of the basket height where there are 2 MC sc. Fold over the end of the handle closest to the pc and sew first 3 sts of handle to the 2 MC sc and to the row below. Sk about 4 rows down on the basket, fold the other end of the handle, and sew the last 2 sts of the handle to the basket. Sew second handle on opposite side of basket.

BEHIND THE MAGIC

By the time *Harry Potter and the Half-Blood Prince* came along, over one thousand bottles, jars, and vials had been provided by the props department to stock the Potions classrooms and offices, each of which had been fitted with a hand-lettered label created by the graphics department.

"THERE WILL BE NO FOOLISH WAND-WAVING OR SILLY INCANTATIONS IN THIS CLASS. AS SUCH, I DON'T EXPECT MANY OF YOU TO APPRECIATE THE SUBTLE SCIENCE AND EXACT ART THAT IS POTION-MAKING. HOWEVER, FOR THOSE SELECT FEW WHO POSSESS THE PREDISPOSITION, I CAN TEACH YOU HOW TO BEWITCH THE MIND AND ENSNARE THE SENSES. I CAN TELL YOU HOW TO BOTTLE FAME, BREW GLORY, AND EVEN PUT A STOPPER IN DEATH."

Professor Snape, *Harry Potter and the Sorcerer's Stone*

⭐

CLOCKWISE FROM LEFT: A set photo of Professor Slughorn's Potions classroom; Harry in his first potions class in *Harry Potter and the Sorcerer's Stone*; Seamus Finnigan blows up another potion in *Harry Potter and the Half-Blood Prince*.

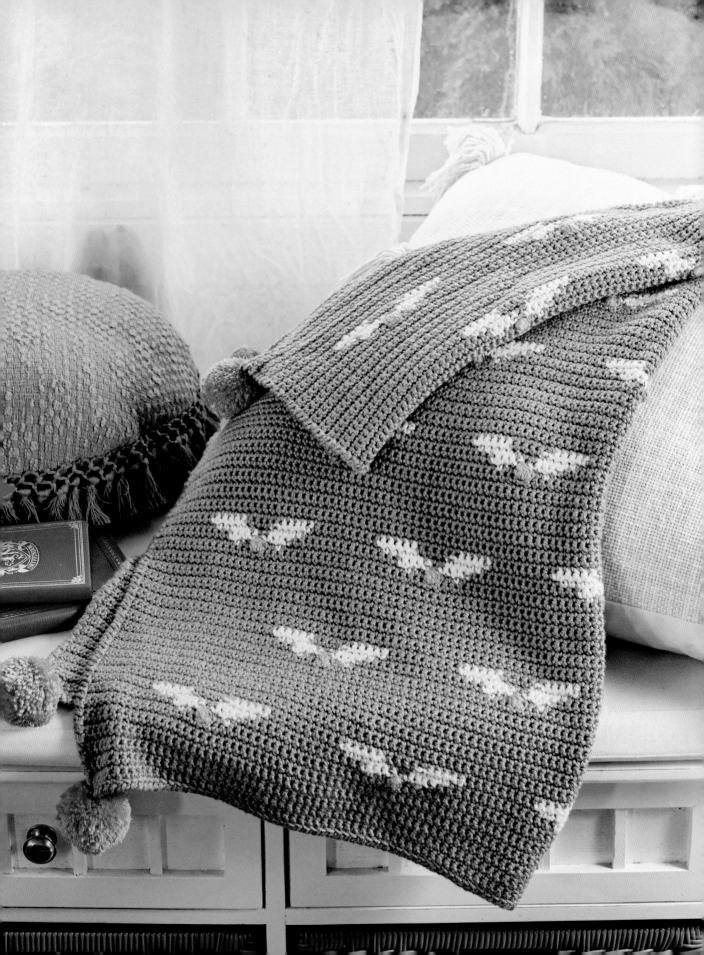

GOLDEN SNITCH BABY BLANKET

Designed by **HAILEY BAILEY**

SKILL LEVEL ⚡⚡

The Golden Snitch first makes an appearance in the Harry Potter films when Harry learns how to play Quidditch in *Harry Potter and the Sorcerer's Stone*. Harry is a natural-born Seeker, and the Snitch in turn becomes an integral part of Harry's story right up to the end, when he opens it to retrieve the Resurrection Stone hidden inside in *Harry Potter and the Deathly Hallows – Part 2*.

While the Snitch was created digitally for the films, great care was taken by designers to ensure that the Snitch itself would function properly. Many different designs were considered, and the final form featured a hollow ball and retractable wings that gently rolled up inside. "In theory," says production designer Stuart Craig, "the wings would retract into the grooves on the sphere so that it reverts back to just being a ball."

The Golden Snitch Baby Blanket features a repeating pattern of Snitches, crocheted in a textured stitch to make them pop from the fabric. Tiny wings flank each golden ball, and all the Snitches rest on a contrasting gray background. With a simple repeat, this baby blanket can easily be made bigger. Finished with a golden pom-pom in each corner, the Golden Snitch Baby Blanket is the perfect cozy home accessory for any Quidditch fan.

SIZE
One size

FINISHED MEASUREMENTS
Width: 36 in. / 91.5 cm
Length: 32 in. / 81.5 cm

YARN
Worsted weight (medium #4) yarn, shown in Berroco *Comfort* (50% super fine acrylic, 50% super fine nylon; 210 yd. / 193 m per 3½ oz. / 100 g ball):
Color A: #9770 Ash Grey, 6 balls
Color B: #9701 Ivory, 1 ball
Color C: #9743 Goldenrod, 1 ball

HOOK
- US H-8 / 5 mm crochet hook or size needed to obtain gauge

NOTIONS
- Tapestry needle
- Optional: 1⅝ in. / 45 mm pom-pom maker

GAUGE
14 sts and 20 rows = 4 in. / 10 cm in single crochet
Gauge is not critical for this pattern, but the yarn weight and hook size used will affect the finished measurements.

Continued on page 164

NOTES

- Chains do not count as a stitch throughout pattern.
- To change colors during a sc, complete the last yarn over of the stitch in the new color, and use the new color to draw through last 2 loops of the st. To change colors during a bobble, ch 1 in new color after drawing through 6 loops and completing the bobble.
- To minimize carrying yarn throughout the pattern, use small balls of yarn for the white and gold portions of each Snitch. While crocheting the Snitch, carry the gray yarn by crocheting over the strand, and pick up the strand when you switch back to gray. To improve the appearance of carried yarn, crochet over the yarn on the right side (the side with the bobbles sticking out) and drop carried yarn in front of your work on the wrong side. Then, when working the next row on the right side, crochet over the dropped yarn.

SPECIAL TERM

bobble: With C, *yarn over, insert hook into st and pull up a loop. Yarn over and draw through 2 loops; repeat from * 4 more times. You should have 6 loops on your hook. Yarn over and draw through all remaining loops. With A, ch 1.

BLANKET

With A, ch 130.

Row 1: Sc in 2nd ch from hook and in each ch across, turn—129 sc.

Rows 2–12: Ch 1, sc across, turn.

Row 13: Ch 1, sc 13, sc 1 with B, sc 2 with A, bobble with C, sc 2 with A, sc 1 with B, *sc 17 with A, sc 1 with B, sc 2 with A, bobble with C, sc 2 with A, sc 1 with B; rep from * 3 times, sc 13 with A, turn.

Row 14: Ch 1, sc 12 with A, sc 4 with B, sc 1 with A, sc 4 with B, *sc 15 with A, sc 4 with B, sc 1 with A, sc 4 with B; rep from * 3 times, sc 12 with A, turn.

Row 15: Ch 1, sc 10 with A, sc 5 with B, sc 3 with A, sc 5 with B, *sc 11 with A, sc 5 with B, sc 3 with A, sc 5 with B; rep from * 3 times, sc 10 with A, turn.

Row 16: Ch 1, sc 9 with A, sc 5 with B, sc 5 with A, sc 5 with B, *sc 9 with A, sc 5 with B, sc 5 with A, sc 5 with B; rep from * 3 times, sc 9 with A, turn.

Rows 17–28: Ch 1, sc across, turn.

Row 29: Ch 1, sc 25 with A, sc 1 with B, sc 2 with A, bobble with C, sc 2 with A, sc 1 with B, *sc 17 with A, sc 1 with B, sc 2 with A, bobble with C, sc 2 with A, sc 1 with B; rep from * 2 times, sc 25 with A, turn.

Row 30: Ch 1, sc 24 with A, sc 4 with B, sc 1 with A, sc 4 with B, *sc 15 with A, sc 4 with B, sc 1 with A, sc 4 with B; rep from * 2 times, sc 24 with A, turn.

Row 31: Ch 1, sc 22 with A, sc 5 with B, sc 3 with A, sc 5 with B, *sc 11 with A, sc 5 with B, sc 3 with A, sc 5 with B; rep from * 2 times, sc 22 with A, turn.

Row 32: Ch 1, sc 21 with A, sc 5 with B, sc 5 with A, sc 5 with B, *sc 9 with A, sc 5 with B, sc 5 with A, sc 5 with B; rep from * 2 times, sc 21 with A, turn.

Rows 33–44: Ch 1, sc across, turn.

Rows 45–140: Rep Rows 13–44 three times.

Rows 141–156: Rep Rows 13–28 once more.

Row 157: Ch 1, reverse sc around entire perimeter of blanket, working 1 st into each st, 1 st into each corner, and 1 st into even spaces when working along the sides of the blanket; sl st to first reverse sc of row when complete.

Fasten off.

FINISHING

Weave in all ends.

Optional: With C and pom-pom maker, create 4 pom-poms. Attach 1 pom-pom securely to each corner of the blanket.

"HE'S GOT THE SNITCH! HARRY POTTER RECEIVES 150 POINTS FOR CATCHING THE SNITCH!"

Lee Jordan, *Harry Potter and the Sorcerer's Stone*

CHART

KEY

- ☐ sc in color A
- ☐ sc in color B
- Ⓑ bobble in color C

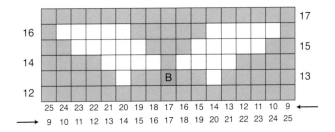

QUIDDITCH BANNER

Designed by **AMINATA NDIAYE**

SKILL LEVEL ⚡⚡

Q uidditch is a wizarding game played on broomsticks high in the air, so "the towers had to place the fans in a position where they could actually see the action," explains production designer Stuart Craig. Because the grounds of Hogwarts are essentially lush forests, the set designers felt that the Quidditch pitch should have a medieval feel, like an old-fashioned tournament. Because of this, the towers were decked out with each team's house colors and emblems in long trailing fabric banners and topped with flags. As the films progressed, the towers were made taller, and more towers were added.

This Quidditch banner is a display of tapestry crochet inspired by the Quidditch towers in the films. Work the pattern in rows using your favorite house colors, and finish off by adding a hanger to mount your house banner in a celebration of Quidditch.

FINISHED MEASUREMENTS

EACH MOTIF

Width: 9½ in. / 24 cm
Length: 6½ in. / 16.5 cm

ASSEMBLED BANNER

Width: 19 in. / 48 cm
Length: 32½ in. / 82.5 cm

YARN

Aran weight (medium #4) yarn, shown in Cascade Yarns *220 Superwash Aran* (100% superwash merino wool; 150 yd. / 137.5 m per 3½ oz / 100 g hank), 3 hanks each

GRYFFINDOR

Color A: #809 Really Red
Color B: #241 Sunflower

HUFFLEPUFF

Color A: #821 Daffodil
Color B: #815 Black

RAVENCLAW

Color A: #813 Blue Velvet
Color B: #875 Feather Grey

SLYTHERIN

Color A: #801 Army Green
Color B: #900 Charcoal

HOOK

- US H-8 / 5 mm or size needed to obtain gauge

NOTIONS

- ⅜ in. / 10 mm dowel, 24 in. / 61 cm long (optional)
- Tapestry needle

Continued on page 168

GAUGE

17 sts and 17 rows = 4 in. / 10 cm in patt
Gauge is not critical for this pattern, but the yarn weight and hook size used will affect the finished measurements.

NOTES

- Motifs are worked flat, right side facing, and in tapestry crochet. Each motif is made of 27 rows of 41 sc.
- At the end of every row, fasten off and weave in ends. Start the new row in the first stitch of the previous row.
- Make ten rectangles (two of each motif). Following the diagram provided, sew the ten rectangles together to form the banner.
- Use two colors of yarn together. Carry the nonworking yarn behind your work.
- Start new rows by attaching yarns to first st of previous row, ch 1 (does not count as a st), then follow instruction on chart.
- When changing colors, always finish the last stitch before the color change with the new color.

SPECIAL ABBREVIATIONS

blsc2tog (back loop single crochet 2 together): Insert hook in back loop of 1st sc, draw up a loop, insert hook in back loop of next sc, draw up a loop, yo, pull yarn through all 3 loops on the hook.

blsc3tog (back loop single crochet 3 together): Insert hook in back loop of 1st sc, draw up a loop, insert hook in back loop of next sc, draw up a loop, insert hook in back loop of next sc, yo, pull yarn through all 4 loops on the hook.

MOTIF 1 (MAKE 2)

With A, ch 42.

Row 1: Sc in 2nd ch from hook; with B, sc in next 12 ch; with A, sc in next 12 ch; with B, sc in next 12 ch; with A, sc in next 4 ch, fasten off—41 sc.

Row 2: With A, sc in next 3 sc; with B, sc in next 12 sc; with A, sc in next 12 sc; with B, sc in next 12 sc; with A, sc in last 2 sc, fasten off.

Row 3: With A, sc in next 5 sc; with B, sc in next 12 sc; with A, sc in next 12 sc; with B, sc in last 12 sc, fasten off.

Row 4: With A, sc in next 7 sc; with B, sc in next 12 sc; with A, sc in next 12 sc; with B, sc in last 10 sc, fasten off.

Row 5: With A, sc in next 9 sc; with B, sc in next 12 sc; with A, sc in next 12 sc; with B, sc in last 8 sc, fasten off.

Row 6: With A, sc in next 11 sc; with B, sc in next 12 sc; with A, sc in next 12 sc; with B, sc in last 6 sc, fasten off.

Row 7: With B, sc in first sc; with A, sc in next 12 sc; with B, sc in next 12 sc; with A, sc in next 12 sc; with B, sc in last 4 sc, fasten off.

Row 8: With B, sc in next 3 sc; with A, sc in next 12 sc; with B, sc in next 12 sc; with A, sc in next 12 sc; with B, sc in last 2 sc, fasten off.

Row 9: With B, sc in next 5 sc; with A, sc in next 12 sc; with B, sc in next 12 sc; with A, sc in next 12 sc, fasten off.

Row 10: With B, sc in next 7 sc; with A, sc in next 12 sc; with B, sc in next 12 sc; with A, sc in last 10 sc, fasten off.

Row 11: With B, sc in next 9 sc; with A, sc in next 12 sc; with B, sc in next 12 sc; with A, sc in last 8 sc, fasten off.

Row 12: With B, sc in next 11 sc; with A, sc in next 12 sc; with B, sc in next 12 sc; with A, sc in last 6 sc, fasten off.

Row 13: With A, sc in first sc; with B, sc in next 12 sc; with A, sc in next 12 sc; with B, sc in next 12 sc; with A, sc in last 4 sc, fasten off.

Rows 14–25: Rep Rows 2–13.

Rows 26 & 27: Rep Rows 2 & 3.

MOTIF 2 (MAKE 2)

With A, ch 42.

Row 1: With A, sc in 2nd ch from hook and in each ch to end, fasten off—41 sc.

Row 2: With A, sc in each sc across, fasten off.

Row 3: With B, sc in first sc, *with A, sc in next 9 sc; with B, 1 sc in next sc; rep from * 3 more times, fasten off.

Row 4: With B, sc in first 2 sc, *with A, sc in next 7 sc; with B, sc in next 3 sc; rep from * 2 more times, with A, sc in next 7 sc; with B, sc in last 2 sc, fasten off.

Row 5: With B, sc in first 3 sc, *with A, sc in next 5 sc; with B, sc in next 5 sc; rep from * 2 more times, with A, sc in next 5 sc; with B, sc in last 3 sc, fasten off.

Rows 6–8: With B, sc in first 4 sc, *with A, sc in next 3 sc; with B, sc in next 7 sc; rep from * 2 more times, with A, sc in next 3 sc; with B, sc in last 4 sc, fasten off.

Row 9: With B, sc in first 5 sc, *with A, sc in next sc; with B, sc in next 9 sc; rep from * 2 more times, with A, sc in next sc; with B, sc in last 5 sc, fasten off.

Row 10: With A, sc in each sc across, fasten off.

Row 11: With A, sc in first 5 sc, *with B, sc in next sc; with A, sc in next 9 sc; rep from * 2 more times, with B, sc in next sc; with A, sc in last 5 sc, fasten off.

Row 12: With A, sc in first 4 sc, *with B, sc in next 3 sc; with A, sc in next 7 sc; rep from * 2 more times, with B, sc in next 3 sc; with A, sc in last 4 sc, fasten off.

Row 13: With A, sc in first 3 sc, *with B, sc in next 5 sc; with A, sc in next 5 sc; rep from * 2 more times, with B, sc in next 5 sc; with A, sc in last 3 sc, fasten off.

Rows 14–16: With A, sc in first 2 sc, *with B, sc in next 7 sc; with A, sc in next 3 sc; rep from * 2 more times, with B, sc in next 7 sc; with A, sc in last 2 sc, fasten off.

Row 17: with A, sc in first sc, *with B, sc in next 9 sc; with A, sc in next sc; rep from * 3 more times, fasten off.

Rows 18–25: Rep Rows 2–9.

Rows 26 & 27: Rep Row 2.

MOTIF 3 (MAKE 2)

With B, ch 42.

Row 1: With B, sc in 2nd ch from hook and in each ch to end, fasten off—41 sc.

Row 2: With B, sc in first 12 sc; with A, sc in next sc; with B, sc in next 15 sc; with A, sc in next sc; with B, sc in last 12 sc, fasten off.

Row 3: With B, sc in first 10 sc; with A, sc in next 5 sc; with B, sc in next 11 sc; with A, sc in next 5 sc; with B, sc in last 10 sc, fasten off.

Row 4: With B, sc in first 9 sc, 2 sc in next sc; with A, blsc2tog, sc in next sc, blsc2tog; with B, 2 sc in next sc, sc in next 9 sc, 2 sc in next sc; with A, blsc2tog, sc in next sc, blsc2tog; with B, 2 sc in next sc, sc in last 9 sc, fasten off.

Row 5: With B, sc in first 11 sc; with A, sc in next 3 sc; with B, sc in next 13 sc; with A, sc in next 3 sc; with B, sc in last 11 sc, fasten off.

Row 6: With B, sc in first 10 sc, 2 sc in next st; with A, blsc3tog; with B, 2 sc in next sc, sc in next 11 sc, 2 sc in next st; with A, blsc3tog; with B, 2 sc in next sc, sc in next 10 sc, fasten off.

Row 7: With B, sc in first 12 sc; with A, sc in next sc; with B, sc in next 15 sc; with A, sc in next sc; with B, sc in last 12 sc, fasten off.

Row 8: With B, sc in first 10 sc; with A, sc in next sc; with B, sc in next 3 sc; with A, sc in next sc; with B, sc in next 11 sc; with A, sc in next sc; with B, sc in next 3 sc; with A, sc in next sc; with B, sc in last 10 sc, fasten off.

Row 9: With B, sc in first 12 sc; with A, sc in next st; with B, sc in next 15 sc; with A, sc in next sc; with B, sc in last 12 sc, fasten off.

Row 10: With B, sc in each sc across, fasten off.

Row 11: With B, sc in first 4 sc; *with A, sc in next sc; with B, sc in next 15 sc; rep from * once; with A, sc in next sc; with B, sc in last 4 sc, fasten off.

Row 12: With B, sc in first 2 sc; *with A, sc in next 5 sc; with B, sc in next 11 sc; rep from * once; with A, sc in next 5 sc; with B, sc in last 2 sc, fasten off.

Row 13: With B, sc in first sc, 2 sc in next sc; *with A, blsc2tog, sc in next sc, blsc2tog; with B, 2 sc in next sc, sc in next 9 sc, 2 sc in next st; rep from * once more; with A, blsc2tog, sc in next sc, blsc2tog; with B, 2 sc in next sc, sc in last sc, fasten off.

Row 14: With B, sc in first 3 sc; *with A, sc in next 3 sc; with B, sc in next 13 sc; rep from * once; with A, sc in next 3 sc; with B, sc in last 3 sc, fasten off.

Row 15: With B, sc in first 2 sc, 2 sc in next sc; *with A, blsc3tog; with B, 2 sc in next sc, sc in next 11 sc, 2 sc in next sc; rep from * once; with A, blsc3tog; with B, 2 sc in next sc, sc in last 2 sc, fasten off.

Row 16: With B, sc in first 2 sc, *with A, sc in next sc; with B, sc in next 3 sc; with A, sc in next sc; with B, sc in next 11 sc; rep from * once; with A, sc in next sc; with B, sc in next 3 sc; with A, sc in next sc; with B, sc in last 2 sc, fasten off.

Row 17: With B, sc in first 4 sc, *with A, sc in next sc; with B, sc in next 15 sc; rep from * once; with A, sc in next sc; with B, sc in last 4 sc, fasten off.

Row 18: With B, sc in each sc across, fasten off.

Rows 19–27: Rep Rows 2–10.

MOTIF 4 (MAKE 2)

To maintain the same fabric density as the other motifs, carry the yarn tail behind your work and fasten off at the end of each row.

With B, ch 42.

Row 1: With A, sc in 2nd ch from hook and in each ch to end, fasten off—41 sc.

Row 2: With A, sc in first 21 sc; with B, sc in last 20 sc, fasten off.

Rows 3–14: Rep Row 2.

Row 15: With B, sc in first 21 sc; with A, sc in last 20 sc, fasten off.

Rows 16–27: Rep Row 15.

MOTIF 5 (MAKE 2)

To maintain the same fabric density as the other motifs, carry the yarn tail behind your work and fasten off at the end of each row (working only in one direction).

With A, ch 42.

Row 1: Sc in 2nd ch from hook and in each ch to end, fasten off—41 sc.

Rows 2–27: Sc in each sc across, fasten off.

ASSEMBLY

Weave in all ends.

Starting at the bottom left of the diagram and working up, and working on WS of motifs, join Motif 5 to 4, 4 to 2, 2 to 3, and 3 to 1 with sl sts. Set aside.

Starting at the bottom right of the diagram, rep same joining method for Motif 2 to 1, 1 to 3, 3 to 5, and 5 to 4.

With tapestry needle, sew the two long strips together, matching edges. Weave in ends.

HANGING THE BANNER

The banner can be hung on the wall using push pins, Command strips, or a curtain rod or dowel. If you opt for a dowel or curtain rod, you'll need to crochet a sleeve on top of your banner as follows:

With A, and working across top edge of banner, work 3 rows of sc. Fold over lengthwise and sew the edge to the back of the banner. Insert dowel through the pocket.

CORDS

Make 2 cords to attach at each end of the dowel as follows:

Ch 81.

Row 1: Sl st in 2nd ch from hook and in each ch across, turn, sl st to 6th st to form a loop. Fasten off.

Pass one end of the dowel trough the loop of the first cord, then pass the other end of the dowel through the loop of the second cord. Tie the ends of the two cords together.

MOTIF 1	MOTIF 4
MOTIF 3	MOTIF 5
MOTIF 2	MOTIF 3
MOTIF 4	MOTIF 1
MOTIF 5	MOTIF 2

SEWING DIAGRAM

Behind the Magic

To film the Quidditch scenes, broomsticks were mounted onto electronic rigs several feet in the air. Against a blue-screen backdrop, the actors were rocked around on the rigging to mimic flight. As the movies progressed and the actors aged, the rigging advanced as well, becoming taller and able to hold more weight. "By the last Quidditch match, we're talking about grown men, literally," says production designer Stuart Craig, "which meant different technical needs."

TOP: A concept sketch of students heading to the Quidditch pitch by Adam Brockbank. BOTTOM: A concept sketch of Harry Potter and Draco Malfoy chasing after the Golden Snitch in *Harry Potter and the Chamber of Secrets*, also by Brockbank.

CHARTS

KEY

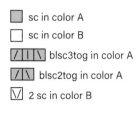

- sc in color A
- sc in color B
- blsc3tog in color A
- blsc2tog in color A
- 2 sc in color B

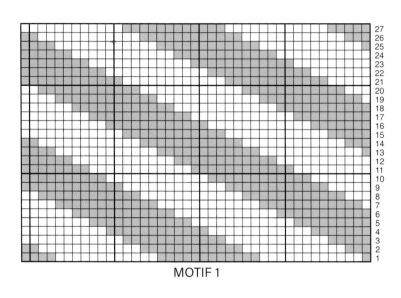

MOTIF 1

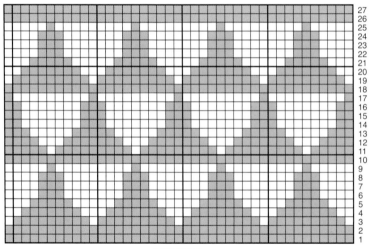

MOTIF 2

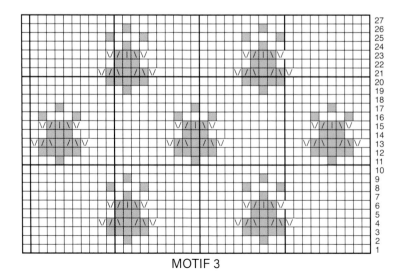

MOTIF 3

"OUR JOB IS TO MAKE SURE THAT YOU DON'T GET BLOODIED UP TOO BAD. CAN'T MAKE ANY PROMISES, OF COURSE. ROUGH GAME, QUIDDITCH." "BRUTAL, BUT NO ONE'S DIED IN YEARS. SOMEONE WILL VANISH OCCASIONALLY, BUT THEY'LL TURN UP IN A MONTH OR TWO!"

Fred and George Weasley, *Harry Potter and the Sorcerer's Stone*

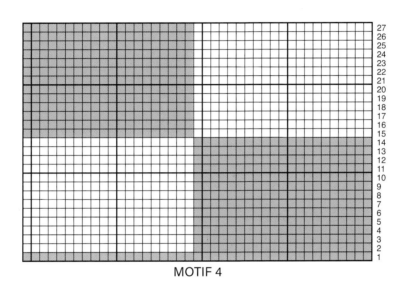

MOTIF 4

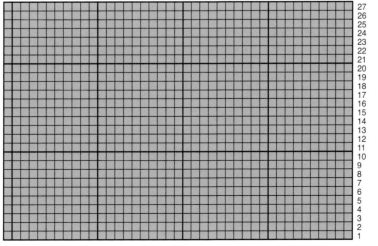

MOTIF 5

Abbreviations

beg:	begin(ning)		pm:	place marker
blo:	back loop only		rem:	remain(ing)(s)
bpdc:	back post double crochet		rep:	repeat
ch:	chain		RS:	right side
dc:	Double Crochet		sc:	single crochet
dc2tog:	double crochet 2 stitches together		sc2tog:	single crochet 2 stitches together
dec:	decrease		sk:	skip
dtr:	double treble crochet		sl st:	slip stitch
flo:	front loop only		sp:	space
fpdc:	front post double crochet		sts:	stitches
fsc:	foundation single crochet		tog:	together
hdc:	half double crochet		tr:	treble crochet
inc:	increase		WS:	wrong side
MC:	magic circle		yo:	yarn over
lp(s):	loop(s)			

Yarn Resource Guide

BERNAT
YARNSPIRATIONS.COM

BERROCO
BERROCO.COM

CASCADE YARNS
CASCADEYARNS.COM

FIBRELYA
FIBRELYA.COM

HAZEL KNITS
HAZELKNITS.COM

HOBIUM YARN
HOBIUMYARNS.COM

LION BRAND YARN
LIONBRAND.COM

MADELINETOSH
MADELINETOSH.COM

PATONS
KNITPATONS.COM

PREMIER YARNS
PREMIERYARNS.COM

SCHEEPJES
SCHEEPJES.COM

SUGAR BUSH YARNS
SUGARBUSHYARNS.COM

WECROCHET
CROCHET.COM

ACKNOWLEDGMENTS

Thank you to Tanis Gray, who saw a little magical light in me and encouraged it to grow. Thank you also to my editor, Hilary VandenBroek. Your ability to see the wizarding world from every direction is unparalleled. I'm so grateful to both of you.

Huge thanks to the designers in this book: Ami, Rohn, Vincent, Julie, Emily, Hailey, Mar, Alysha, Rin, Britt, Emmy, Sara, Kaelyn, Jillian, and Mary. Each one of you is unique, special, and just who I would want to sit with at the Hogwarts house table for some pumpkin juice. Cheers!

And of course I would love to thank my family. My child Emma-Noel, who is a light in themselves. Thank you so much for your support and constant understanding beyond your years. My son, Conan, who was adamant that he wanted every new design I showed him. And to my husband, Sean. I love you around the Forbidden Forest and back again.

Finally, thank you to the wonderful team at Insight Editions for bringing this magic to crocheters like me.

INSIGHT EDITIONS

PO Box 3088
San Rafael, CA 94912
www.insighteditions.com

Find us on Facebook: www.facebook.com/InsightEditions

Follow us on Twitter: @insighteditions

Library of Congress Cataloging-in-Publication Data available.

ISBN: 978-1-64722-260-4

Publisher: Raoul Goff
VP of Licensing and Partnerships: Vanessa Lopez
VP of Creative: Chrissy Kwasnik
VP of Manufacturing: Alix Nicholaeff
Editorial Director: Vicki Jaeger
Senior Designer: Judy Wiatrek Trum
Editor: Hilary VandenBroek
Associate Editor: Anna Wostenberg
Production Editor: Jennifer Bentham
Senior Production Manager, Subsidiary Rights: Lina s Palma
Production Manager: Eden Orlesky

Technical Editor: Ashley Little

Photography by Ted Thomas
Prop Styling by Elena Craig

Thank you to our models: Amanda, Audrey, Bret, Haidyn, Hilary, Max, Megan,
Samara, Sienna, Ted, Violet, and Whitney

A very special thank you to Rusty Hinges Ranch, in Petaluma, California, for
providing a truly magical backdrop for many of the photographs in this book.

Insight Editions, in association with Roots of Peace, will plant two trees for each
tree used in the manufacturing of this book. Roots of Peace is an internationally
renowned humanitarian organization dedicated to eradicating land mines
worldwide and converting war-torn lands into productive farms and wildlife
habitats. Roots of Peace will plant two million fruit and nut trees in Afghanistan and
provide farmers there with the skills and support necessary for sustainable land use.

Manufactured in China by Insight Editions

10 9 8 7 6 5 4 3 2 1